Totally Bound Publishing books by Ellen Mint

Happily Ever Austen

MADELINE'S PARK

ELLEN MINT

Madeline's Park
ISBN # 978-1-83943-797-7
©Copyright Ellen Mint 2022
Cover Art by Erin Dameron-Hill ©Copyright May 2022
Interior text design by Claire Siemaszkiewicz
Totally Bound Publishing

MADELINE'S PARK

Dedication

This book is for all the cute kitties, adorable firemen and the people who love them.

Special thanks to Kristi for being the best alpha reader I could ask for, my editor for helping to whip this book into shape and Jane Austen for inspiring generations of women to not take societal confinement lying down.

Also to my dog, whose constant need for walks lets me create characters and stories from the ether.

Chapter One

"It's safe to come out," Madeline cooed to the fingernail-sized shell in her hand. She'd spotted the little crab trying to crawl over the hot sands when a herd of boys ran past, nearly trampling the poor thing. Rushing away from her parents, she'd scooped the spiral shell into her palm and held it close to her face.

A single auburn curl escaped from her swimming cap, dancing against her cheek as she peered deep into the darkness of the shell. "It's not scary no more," she tried to assure the tiny crab. "I've got you."

For a ten-year-old, the beach should be fun. Waves to paddle in, friends to chase after in the dunes, ice cream to eat on the wooden docks off the bayou. But no. Not even the ladybug swimsuit she'd begged her mom for could erase the dread in her heart.

There were no friends here, there was no bayou, there might not even be any ice cream! Did people here eat ice cream? She'd forgot to ask while packing up her room and staring out the window of the muggy car. All of what she knew in Louisiana was gone forever for this weird place on the coast.

"I don't blame you for staying in there," Madeline whispered to her new friend. "I wish I could."

Absently, she reached up to bat away her single fallen curl, when shadows rose over the shimmering sands. They'd move on, Maddy assured herself. No one had noticed her. They didn't even have a goodbye party at school.

"What'cha got there?" a boy bellowed at her. Tall and lanky, he was the titular beanstalk, while a giant stood beside him. That one didn't speak but he jerked his wide chin at her, sending Madeline spinning away from the pair.

A hand grabbed her shoulder, fingers digging in to turn her back to the increasing circle of boys. She clamped her palms together, hiding away the tiny crab. "Nuttin'," she tried to insist, but the boys sneered.

"You talk stupid. Bet you are stupid. Have to be to not know that any treasure on this beach belongs to me!" He jammed a thumb at his reedy chest as if she should know or care who he was. "Hand it over."

"No!" Madeline closed her eyes tight, whipping her head back and forth in the hope that they'd vanish if she couldn't see them. That cruel boy grabbed her fingers, his dirty nails digging into her flesh. When the pain proved too much, Madeline yelped, and he yanked her hand open.

The tiny crab in its little house was exposed to three, no four, of the pack. In an instant, the leader snatched it up, Madeline crying to give her friend back. "You want this?" he taunted, extending his hand high above her, the shell pinched between thumb and finger.

Swallowing her tears, she nodded as hard as possible. "It's not yours!" Madeline insisted, terrified that the mean boys would crush it or scorch it on the cement or worse. If they'd taken her toys or her five dollars for ice cream, she'd have let them. *But animals is different!*

He waved his hand up high, far out of Madeline's reach. Even still, she kept jumping off the sand, pawing up his arm to try to pull the crab back. On the uneven ground, her balance was off, causing Madeline to splat against his bare chest.

The boy snarled, leaping back. Spitting at her, he said, "Yuck! Don't touch me, you fat fart!"

"Ha, fat fart!" the other circling boys joined in.

Madeline froze in the sand, her arms tucking tight as she tried to make herself as small as possible. Same as when having to share a bus seat to school or at the doctor's. All the while, the cruel, crab-stealing boy stalked around her.

"Not a fart. You're a pimple! A big, red, smelly pimple that needs to be popped!" Lashing his free hand out, he grabbed Madeline's stomach and pinched hard.

She screamed in pain, tears rising in her eyes as she tried to run away. "Stop, stop, please…" Her pleading was barely a whisper, her shoulders pulling inward as she had to dodge a myriad of hands trying to pinch at her hanging gut. They wouldn't stop. They wouldn't listen. And no one would try to stop them. No one cared.

"Hey!"

The fingers and their pinching froze, all the heads pivoting to a boy striding across the beach. Blond hair that glistened like a halo swept down to his cheekbones. He stomped through the sand to reach the lanky one. While not as tall as the leader, he leaned into the boy, causing him to bend lower.

"What do you think you're doing to her?"

"Nothing. I'm not doing nothing, Everett." The leader transformed into a sniveling toad in an instant.

Everett!

Madeline stared in awe at the boy who had come to her rescue. His eyes were as green as Easter grass, his hair brighter than the sun and his face perfect like an angel's.

"Bullplop!" Everett cursed at the boys. Without a thought, he grabbed the ringleader's wrist and twisted it down. "Knock it off, James. And give back whatever you stole!"

With his head bobbing, tears came from the big bully. Once he was freed, James thrust the terrified crab at Madeline's midsection. She barely had a chance to grab at the shell before it fell to the sand. As one, the gang of boys turned tail and ran for the tents on the other side of the beach.

"I don't want to catch you on my sand again," Everett shouted, shaking his fist. He was so tall and…handsome. He had to be two years older. Or? A blush burned up Madeline's cheeks as she entertained the thought of him being a middle schooler.

"You're with the Prixes, right?" he asked, those emerald eyes beaming into hers. Madeline's legs trembled as she nodded.

"They're my folks. I'm, um, Madeline." He didn't ask that, but she wanted him to know her name. To never forget it.

"Right! My uncle rented 'em the beach house." He threw his arms open wide as if her family's arrival was exciting news. "Guess that means we'll be seeing a lot of each other, Maddy."

Giving one last smile that made her stomach shake, he turned on his heel and ran for another group of boys knocking a beach ball around. All the while, Madeline watched him, her eyes doing the squealing instead of her frozen mouth. She didn't want him to hear, to think her weird or uncool.

A prickling sensation broke across her palm, and she opened her hand to find the hermit crab had finally emerged from its shell. Pulling it close to her lips, she whispered to the shy crab, "One day I'm gonna marry him."

Chapter Two

Sixteen years later

"Come here…" Madeline pleaded to the dash of gray. Freezing sleet bounced against her legs, the December New York weather in no mood to help. Her chest slid on a patch of mud, the sequins popping off as she tried to pull herself deeper into the culvert. It was, on the whole, one of the least pleasant experiences of her life.

The construction crew stood in a half-circle, gawping at the woman who'd belly-flopped onto the mud and cooed into the darkness. Madeline frowned, hating that they had to be staring at her flattened backside as she struggled to reach for the tiny ball of fur crying for its life.

"I'm here to help, I promise," she tried to assure the little construction stowaway. Blue eyes darted over her. The muddy kitten was scrunched tight against the wire screen. Madeline tried to tip the borrowed flashlight up, but half of it was submerged in the icy mud. Still, she couldn't see any obvious holes.

With luck, there wouldn't be a way for the kitten to run deeper into danger.

Eyeing up the tight squeeze, she held her breath and reached farther inside. She extended a steady hand to grapple for the ball of fluff. From the darkness, four claws swiped in a deep line across her flesh. The pain stung like a multitude of bee stings, and Madeline screwed her face up to swallow it. But that also meant she was closer.

"Here, little baby." Her voice was soft, the long-swallowed Southern accent flaring up like kudzu. Warmth brushed over her fingers, telling her she had reached the kitten's head. Before it could bite her, Madeline pinched her fingers on the kitten's scruff and began to tug it out.

Oh, goodness! The shrieks of the baby being pulled into the light were ear-splitting. It screamed as if she were murdering it, but Madeline wouldn't stop.

Hooking a hand to the outside, she pulled both herself and the kitten free. As she slid out of the culvert, her sweater lifted up, streaking mud across her vast stomach. The chill walloped her entire body, but she shook it off. She had a more important package in her fingers.

Madeline rose by herself, not that she expected anyone to help, and curled the screaming kitten against her breast. There was warmth, safety and impressive cushioning. While the kitten wasn't too young, four to five weeks, it could almost vanish into her cleavage.

"There you go, little guy," she whispered to the ball of fluff who had ceased its wailing. The kitten turned up to her, warily watching as she tried to pull off the larger clumps of mud.

"You got it, ma'am?" one of the guys in construction orange asked. She glanced around at the burly men who hadn't dressed for the cold, their breath spurting out smoke. All stared at the kitten nuzzled in the crook of her muddy arm. Did they want to pet it?

"Yes," she said while shielding the kitten from more of the drizzle. They had work to do — doubtful anyone wanted to waste their time with her.

"Well, you heard her. Back at it!" the first guy said. With a slow turn, the other men walked away from the tiny dash of excitement. For Madeline, this was normal. She didn't pluck kittens from culverts every day, but finding them in dumpsters, walking down the middle of highways, buried in garbage bags…that kept her busy.

At the sound of jackhammers roaring up, Madeline stared down at the tiny face she had rescued. It peered at the strange world, uncertain of life outside of the culvert. *What am I going to call you?*

"Maddy?"

Her heart stopped dead. *No, it can't be.* New York was known for being crammed full of people. Whoever that was had to mean someone else. Of course.

She focused on the kitten, trying to juggle it safely in her arms when the same sweet-tea voice called her name again. "Maddy?"

No one had called her that. Not in years. Not since high school. No one, but…

A ray of sunshine punctured through the dreary gray world. Hair of spun gold swept back and to the side, a square jawline and strong nose, thin but sculpted lips forever in a wide smile — he was the epitome of gorgeous boy-next-door. The one she had pined for during all of high school. The boy she had dreamed of taking her to prom, of giving her a ride in his truck, of asking her to be his girlfriend.

Everett Berry, a man so jaw-dropping it was a wonder bluebirds didn't perch upon his shoulders, was talking to her. Asking about her. Staring at her in concern because she had fallen stupid.

"He...hey! Everett? What are you...?" Madeline whipped her head around, fearing this might be some prank reality show. Or worse, one where people got together to try to make over a dumpy friend.

"It is you!" His smile somehow brightened to new heights, piercing the pressing clouds around them. "You haven't changed a lick since high school," he said, his eyes darting from her rounded face to her rounded body.

Madeline tasted the scorn he was too tactful to phrase. *Look at you, just as fat as ever.* Sure, he never said it. He was far too kind to point out the obvious. But he didn't have to. She heard it every day, from every person around her, from the world pointing out that she was wrong for being cushioned.

"I've, um, gotten older," she muttered, her cheeks burning as she glared down at her lazy sweatshirt coated in mud. She hadn't even bothered with jeans, had only thrown on a pair of sweatpants and run out to save the kitten. This was how he had to find her, not dolled up in a fancy dress...

Madeline, when do you ever put on makeup or wear cocktail dresses? Where would you find one that fits? No, it was while she looked like she had taken a swim in the mud on laundry day. Great.

"But you." She pointed at Everett as if he didn't know who he was. "You look..." *Perfect.* "The same, I mean, younger. Um, you look good."

He laughed at her stumbling, raking a hand through his golden locks. How she wanted to run her fingers through them. They had to be as soft as silk and smell of sunshine on a summer day. Everett opened his mouth, no doubt about to say his goodbyes, when the kitten hidden in her arms mewled.

Madeline raised it up, checking to make certain it was okay, and Everett leaned closer. "Still running out into the rain saving baby animals?"

Her cheeks burned even hotter while she watched the glorious man scratch a nail over the kitten's tiny head. All Madeline could do was nod along. Yep, rescuing animals. Mostly kittens, as she couldn't keep dogs in her place. Though, if she did find a lost puppy, she knew who to give it to.

"Weren't you gonna be a vet?"

"That was the plan," she said with a shrug. "Then I took a chemistry course and whew, never mind." *God, stop bringing up your past failures!* "What about you? You went to college to study some, um, business thing?" *A business degree with an emphasis on multinational finance.*

Everett's smile dimmed a touch, his striking green eyes searching around the construction zone. "Yeah, that...didn't work out the way I hoped. Got into a construction program later and volunteered for the firefighters. Much more my speed, and I don't have to wear a tie every damn day either."

She genuinely laughed at his sweet joke, but there was no denying that Everett was built for a suit. The last time she'd seen him in one was graduation when he and his friends had sneaked under the bleachers with a case of beer. They'd had no idea she was even there.

Silence fell between them, just the grinding sound of the city being chunked up and repurposed breaking the air. Should she say something? Ask him how he was doing? If he was with anyone? Visiting the city or staying? If he was single?

"I do website SEO stuff!" Madeline blurted out, panicking as she realized how sad that sounded. "Ads, more or less. Though I keep hoping to finally, er, do rescue animal stuff full-time…" Her entire vocabulary leapt into a cement mixer and solidified into nothing but slack-jawed staring. "What, uh, what brings you to New York?"

Last she knew, he was living back in North Carolina along with a good chunk of their graduating class. If they hadn't paired up in high school, they did in college at UNC. Madeline felt like she had been the single one to run screaming away as fast as she could with her hot diploma in hand.

"Got a job here working for the city," Everett said.

"That's fantastic!" Madeline squealed before pulling it back. "I mean, New York is…I don't really have to tell you what it is. Big City. People kinda everywhere."

Everett nodded along with her babbling as if she were coming close to making a lick of sense. From the top of the scaffolding, a voice shouted, "Hey, cat girl! If you're done, you need to leave!"

"Sorry." Madeline waved at the man, wincing deeper into her stained sweater. "Sorry," she repeated to Everett. "I need to get this little one to the vet. You've got some deworming in store for you." The last part she said to the kitten. She doubted Everett had anything but the cleanest of bowels.

Christ, why did you think that?

Waving once more to the construction crew who were far too busy to worry about her, Madeline dashed to the plastic fencing put up to keep the rabble out.

Everett walked behind her, watching as she tried to fish out her phone while juggling the kitten.

"How are you planning on moving this little guy?" he asked, getting in one last chance to pet the tiny head. "Because I could take you. Still have my truck. Haven't gone full city yet." He laughed while scratching the back of his neck.

"Oh, usually I call this guy. He runs an Uber and lets me bring in cats I find that…" Her lips kept going because internally she was shrieking. Everett Berry wanted to drive her somewhere. Like she was with him. Well, not with him with him—that was impossible. But an honest offer.

Glancing down at the kitten who seemed resigned to its fate, Madeline smiled wide. "Yes. That sounds…perfect."

A smile that could launch a thousand ships beamed upon her while he gestured down the street. "Then follow me."

Always.

Chapter Three

After a deworming, a full checkup and a mostly clean bill of health for the kitten Everett had named Sparky, Everett volunteered to take them all to Madeline's apartment in his truck. It looked out of place next to all the BMWs and Priuses, but as she buckled the old lap belt across her stomach, a strange magic yanked fifteen years from Madeline.

She was all of sixteen again when young Ev Berry had spotted her trying to walk home on a broken flipflop. He'd pulled over and offered her a ride. It was her one time in his truck, her filthy feet brushing against old bags and receipts while the summer sun had glinted through his golden hair.

Now, older and wearing sensible footwear, Madeline cupped Sparky safe in her lap. Same as before, Everett kept one hand on the wheel and the other stretched across the top of both headrests. In her foolish teenage days, she had thought it was a move. Hoped and prayed that it was.

But when he'd arrived at her parents' door and let her out, all she'd gotten was a tip of his head and a suggestion she wash her feet off.

That was how Everett was. Open with everybody, relaxed, calm, considerate and a gorgeous firefighter.

It didn't take long for them to get to her place. The brownstone had seen better days, but at least the roaches were only the size of her pinkie and not her fist. And the garbage pile sitting on the curb could house at most ten rat colonies as opposed to the usual rat kingdom.

"This is it," Madeline announced. "Monte's going to be so angry I took this long."

Everett's easy smile snapped away. "Are you okay?"

She handwaved his worry. "A little cuddle time will soothe the savage beast."

Madeline prepared to dash for the door, so he needn't bother parking, but Everett pulled to the side, trapping a delivery truck in. A nervous fear rose up her, and she kept glancing around for any cops. "Thanks for the ride," she said, hoping he'd get the hint that he had to keep moving. Things weren't like back home here. Not even Everett Berry could smile his way out of a ticket.

Okay, if he uses all his perfect teeth he can.

"So, I was thinking, why don't we…catch up?"

Madeline paused with a foot out the door as Ev picked at the fuzz poking out of the passenger headrest. "Catch up?" she asked.

"Dinner, or lunch. Nah, dinner's better given my schedule. We could meet at a restaurant you like, or…"

"Or?" *Yes. Why are you arguing with him?*

"Give me your phone," Everett ordered. With nary a second thought, Madeline passed it over. After hitting the last key, his full smile beamed at her, and she didn't care if he had bricked her phone.

"Dinner at my place, seven-thirty Thursday sound good?"

"Perfect." She all but drooled on his upholstery. "Yes." Madeline grinned brighter. "Yes, it sounds...I can do that."

"Great."

Clutching the phone with his address tight to her chest, tighter than the angry kitten, Madeline slipped to the sidewalk. Just before he pulled away, he called through the open windows, "Bring your appetite."

At the door to her apartment, she managed the three locks while juggling both the kitten and her expectations. It was kind of him to make the offer, but she should refuse. Send him an email.

"Here you go," she said to Sparky, placing the kitten in the padded box she'd cleaned after her last rescue. The kitten dashed to a bleach-stained towel, burrowing into the darkness until it felt safe to come out. That wouldn't happen until it got hungry.

A jangling of a bell down the hall told her the other important resident was aware of the hour and required sustenance before he collapsed into a ball of despair. Madeline turned to her stocked cupboards for an acceptable can of wet turkey.

Everett Berry, firefighter, had not asked her to join him for *dinner* dinner. It was...it was this. She finished popping off the lid and scooped the food into the wide glass bowl as it was the only thing Monte'd eat out of. Food in exchange for services. Nothing more to it. Nothing but...

Beth, her best friend, was off on a writing holiday. A *not to be disturbed, very serious* holiday. But maybe a quick text would be okay? Hauling up her phone, she read over his address one last time as if memorizing it were life or death, then told Beth everything that had happened.

It was doubtful she'd get a response. Beth wasn't alone in a cabin furiously writing — she had taken her musician boyfriend with her. And they hadn't seen each other in a month, so…

A ring from her phone interrupted Madeline stirring formula supplement into the beefy cat food. Placing it to her ear, she heard Beth scream, "Mads, that's a date!"

Chapter Four

"It's not a date!" Madeline shouted into the phone wedged between her shoulder and ear. Her hands were busy yanking every single piece of clothing out of her closet in despair.

It was D-Day. More like not-D-Day, as she had to keep reminding Beth for the week. Ev was always a friend, had never glanced twice at the way she had stared in adoration at him. He needed help finding his way around the city. Nothing more.

"Mads…" her closest friend in the whole world said patronizingly.

A bright pink and white tunic fell into Madeline's hands. She sniffed it, getting a whiff of age and…oh, obvious pit stains worked into the synthetic fabric. Shifting the phone to her other ear, Madeline asked, "Don't you have a book to write?"

She knew the answer and the reason why Beth was calling her instead of texting. No doubt going stir-crazy waiting for a car to arrive, she'd been offering date suggestions for the past hour. Madeline ignored all of them, especially the 'just wear tight jeans and a low-cut blouse'. That'd work for Beth who was tiny in every sense of the word. If Madeline wore a single shirt cut as low as Beth did, priests would leap from the streets to bludgeon her with Bibles. The joy of carrying around two orbiting moons on her chest.

"I'm taking a break," Beth complained. She'd been at this book thing for a year. It was into the triple revising stage now. "And it is so a date. Men don't ask you to their place for dinner out of the blue."

"Maybe in the city," she responded while weighing a long teal shirt in her hands. The color was striking against her hair, but the fit made her look like a refrigerator box. Still, probably her best option.

Madeline tugged down her phone and scrolled to find her success dress. Peacock blue with a keyhole neckline that'd leave her feeling daring but not scandalous. It nipped into the waist while flaring out to accommodate the at-most size twelve model's hips. Still, it'd work on her double-that-size body. This was the dress for when she made it. When she cut the ribbon on the animal shelter she'd been dreaming about building for years. When she had an engagement party to attend in her honor. If her life ever fell into place, it was the first thing she'd buy.

Which was why it sat in her online cart growing dust. Her life was a mass of cat fur tumbleweeds and piles of ugly and useless clothing. Madeline bounced her foot through the mountain of synthetic fibers coated in rhinestones and other garish bric-a-brac. She didn't like the seventies fresh out of Reno look, but she didn't have a choice. There weren't a lot of options for girls of her size that didn't make one think shut-in grandma that knit sweaters for cats and owned three Bedazzlers.

Laying the two dark navy options across her arm, Madeline dug for pants. Wasn't there an adorable pair with embroidered hearts on the back pockets? Most advice columns warned people of her shape away from wearing anything that'd draw attention to her 'problematic areas,' but she loved them. Slipping them on made her feel slightly more flirtatious than usual.

Hm, maybe they were in...

Madeline turned, and her stomach dropped as she stared at the black trash bag beside her bed. Her always-thin sister had asked Madeline to loan her some pants for her pregnancy. Happy to help, Madeline had gone through her old stash and found the least worn and most likely to accommodate a growing belly. She gave her those special heart butt ones to make her sister feel special during her trying time.

A week later her sister had returned them, laughing about how at nine months pregnant those jeans were too big for her.

Madeline hadn't worn a single pair since. Hadn't even gone through the black trash bag her sister had returned them in. She'd just left it where it fell, her stomach tying into a knot whenever she caught sight of them.

"Oh!" Beth's voice rattled over the phone, shaking Madeline from her dour turn. "I heard a car pull up!" The excitement burst down the phone line, nearly bringing a smile to Madeline's cheeks.

Chuckling at her friend's glee, Madeline said, "I'll let you go then. Say hi to Tristan for me."

"I will…eventually," Beth added. At least one of them was going to get laid. Before she could hang up, Beth said, "And it is so a date!"

Shaking her head at Beth's insistence, Madeline yanked out a calf-length skirt. It was supposed to hit at the knee, but her legs kept that from happening. Last time she'd worn it was to a funeral. Running her fingers over the crinoline inlay, she said aloud, "Now I'll wear it to the wake for my sex life?"

Be happy. Smile. Be nice. People have it far worse than you.

An angry meowing diverted her dour turn to the ball of orange and black fluff crawling out from under her tossed clothes. "Is that where you got to?" she called to her cat, Monte the Count. Sparky was sleeping in his special nest. The kitten kept true to his name during the wee hours of the night. The rest of the day he slept as sound as a board, Madeline having to wake him for his feedings.

Her cat, the first one she had found upon moving to New York, slicked a paw down the orange side of his face. The other was brown striped to match his body, her little chimera baby. Well, little in the abstract sense. The Count looked like he could swallow a kitten whole. Despite growing surly with age, he worked wonders with the kittens. Kept them warm when they were cold, snuggled them if they were weak and played with them when they were strong. She couldn't ask for a better partner.

"I hope you can hold down the fort while I'm gone," she said to her cat. His yellow stare burned through her, Madeline blushing as if it were her duty to remain and funnel tuna into his gaping maw. "It's a friendly visit is all."

With a man whose name I once covered notebooks in. It was a long time ago, Madeline. And he's probably got a beautiful girlfriend who's cooking for both of you because she's that sweet and unconcerned about you.

A brown paw swept over her hands, Madeline turning to look at her only baby in this world. The Count meowed once, concern evident in his face. No doubt he was wondering why she was taking so long to feed him, but Madeline patted her comforting kitty.

"It's not a date."

* * * *

"I need it for tonight." Everett trailed behind Will, one of the old hats at the station, not that he let that fact get in the way of his adverse phobia of advancing. If Ev stayed on for a full two years, he'd wind up outranking Will.

Will flipped on the tiny kitchen switch and a thousand roaches scurried. "Damn things," he cursed, stomping his heel where nothing remained before turning to the sink crusted over with a mountain of dishes. It was doubtful the metal sculpture could even be pulled apart. The station relied upon the kindness of strangers donating new pots and pans to the people who had kept their apartments from burning down. Cleaning them was a bridge too far.

Ev hunkered down to look in the bottom cupboard while Will loomed overhead. "Whatcha need that for anyway?"

"I can't find my pots anywhere." He suspected they had either wound up being sold with his house back in North Carolina, or in the bottom of Soggy Sand Lake.

Will sniffled. "Since when does a bachelor need pans anyway? That's why you get a wife."

Ev jumped, banging his hand against a set of Bundt pans shaped like castles. "Tried that," he muttered. And he was still looking over his shoulder every time he smelled lemon and lavender. *Ah, there it is.* Everett hauled out the stock pot and placed it on the counter above. As he closed the cupboard door, he moved to stand up and caught Will inspecting the pot used exclusively for firefighter chili cook-offs.

Will muttered, "What happened? No, wait, let me guess, she got fat and you got out of there?"

Will cracked up at his own joke, braying over Ev whispering, "No." The whole reason he'd run as far as possible from his old job to New York was to escape those questions. *"What went wrong? Why didn't you try harder? This is what's broken with the young, they won't try when things get hard."* He'd heard it all in the pews behind him during church. When it had started up around the Thanksgiving table, Ev had to get out or else.

"Look, I'll get this back tomorrow. Clean and everything, I swear."

The grizzled fireman scratched his chin in thought. "A'ight. Not as if I'm lord keeper of the pots. If you walk off with a hose, however, we're gonna have a problem."

"Great." Ev banged his palm against the bottom, then tucked the pot under his arm. At this rate, he should be able to pick up the last of the ingredients before Maddy arrived. With a courtesy nod to his elder, Ev turned on his heel to make a hasty retreat...only for the station to shake from the bleep of a siren.

Will didn't rush for his gear but crossed his arms and sighed. "They must be back, right quick too. He's gunning hard for chief."

Easing his way out to the second-story landing, Ev glanced down from the banister at the main firetruck rolling into the station. The stench of smoke took a second to reach him. He turned to politely cough into his shoulder, when Will slapped him and pointed. At that second, the rider's side door opened, and Ev's gut clenched.

Hayden Crawford stood on the runner and whipped his hand around like a debutante at the Fourth of July parade. "Excellent job, everyone. Chris, you handled that hose magnificently." Hayden beamed at the youngest firefighter who had come to the program straight from high school. Ev could see the blush rising on Chris' cheeks even under the soot.

"You don't think he'd oust Chief Parsons?" Everett asked from the side of his mouth. All Will did was shrug.

The rest of the firefighters stiffly piled out. Their joints must have been struggling to loosen after facing the fire's heat. They took their time, checking the truck, stripping off their gear. Only Hayden kept his jacket and even helmet on as he dashed for the stairs.

Ah, crumbs. Ev jerked as if he could get down the stairs before Hayden reached them, but no luck. The man with a smile that'd sell sand to camels took the steps three at a time without missing a single breath. He gripped tight to the railings, his body blocking the single exit, while staring at Ev.

"Ah, Berry. Isn't this your day off?"

"Yeah."

Hayden cricked his head to the side. "Trying to get in good with the chief early by putting in hours off the clock?"

His ears told him he was imagining the edge of a threat. Hayden's voice was genuine, a friend concerned about another. But the goosebumps wouldn't stop pricking all of Ev's blond body hair straight up whenever Crawford spoke.

"Nah, he's just here for the stock pot," Will butted in. Wonderful.

"Yeah, taking company property...but I'll bring it back tomorrow. Need it for a girl I got coming over." *Shit, why did he say that?*

Hayden's interest increased tenfold, his eyes softening even as his lips pulled back in a hard smile. "You've got a date, Berry? Already?" He sounded shocked, like Ev had the face of a fishing net snagged in barnacles at the bottom of the ocean. "Good for you." Hayden smacked him on the arm, at the last second putting in more force than necessary, but Ev fought off the wince.

"Well, I'm not...she's a girl I knew back home. I mean, I ain't even sure it is a *date* date. She kept mentioning this Monte fella and I..." Why was he telling him this? Ev smacked his palm harder against the pot while Hayden looked him over.

"That so? Well, you know what they say, all's fair in love and war."

He'd had enough of war in love to last a lifetime. Hayden didn't move on, just kept staring, super polite. It set off another round of roiling inside of Ev. "So they do," he said, wanting to bullrush down the stairs.

Laughing once more, Crawford smacked him on the back, then strode for the Chief's office. "Sir," he shouted before tossing open the door without knocking, "wonderful news from the crew."

The glass rattling in its frame as the door slammed shut mercifully cut off Hayden's hubris. Ev didn't realize he was banging his fingers against the pot until he felt Will staring at him.

"You and the captain have some bad blood we don't know about?"

Nope. Ev had never seen the man before he got here. And far as he knew, Hayden was nothing but polite and inviting. There was just something about him...

"Not at all," he muttered under his breath.

"That's good, 'cause Parsons's been floating the idea of his retiring again and..."

And if he stayed, Everett would have to report to a man that people saw as a golden boy, but every instinct warned him was a copperhead lurking in the water. The sound of a hose fight breaking out down below shook him from the job's politics. He didn't have time to think about that. He had a maybe date to get ready for.

When he got to the stairs, Will called out, "That girl of yours. Is she cute?"

Maddy his? That sounded ludicrous, but Ev smiled softly. "Yeah," he said and dashed down the stairs.

Chapter Five

This place has seen better days.

Everett's house sat nestled between what looked like an old bodega converted to studio apartments and a warehouse. Skinny like a brownstone, the front was at most a single room wide, though that illusion could be due to how the front-step railing split from the concrete and swung out. Shutters dangled helplessly from the windows, one of which was papered over in old magazine ads. A sapling twisted out of the roof, providing shade to whatever small animals were nesting inside.

Sympathy washed through her with one look. He must have been in a bind to accept a home this unseen. Then again, if the rent wasn't astronomical, maybe he came out the better.

She'd settled on the funeral skirt, the stretchy navy tunic with billowy sleeves and a small pair of heels. Madeline never wore anything above three inches out of fear of slipping and breaking an ankle. Taking one last glance to make certain she had the address right, Madeline walked up the crumbling stairs. The top one bowed like someone had taken a massive bite straight out the middle.

"It's not a date. It's friends," she repeated while bouncing the former curls she'd straight-ironed down to waves. Madeline pressed a finger into the bell and the button sunk deep inside.

Oh no! The ringing continued through the house despite her taking her finger out of the hole she'd created. Scrambling, she tried to yank the fallen plastic out, her nails scraping down the tiny hole. "Come on, please! Stop making that…"

The door flew open, her heart stopping dead as she turned to face a no-doubt enraged Everett. When his eyes shifted to Madeline hunched over the broken doorbell, a smile fit for an angel slid across his lips. He'd brushed his hair to the side and slipped on a tan turtleneck that hugged his chest. A flour towel dangled from his waist, hiding away most of the front of his dark jeans. Ev looked dressed for rehearsal day in heaven's choir, and it was she who wanted to sing.

You broke his doorbell, idiot.

"Sorry," Madeline cried, shooting to her feet. Confusion crossed his brow, and she pointed to the now trapped doorbell.

After checking it out, Everett laughed. "Don't worry." He made a fist and banged once above the bell. In an instant, the button popped out and the unending ringing ceased. "Happens all the time. Please, come in."

He stepped back, allowing Madeline to gaze around the construction zone. A tarp acted as a runner down the main staircase, ending at a pile of cement blocks piled up where the stairs had rotted away. Old wallpaper peeled in dangling strips from the edge of wainscoting that'd be beautiful if half of it wasn't bowing from water damage. Dust coated almost every surface. Madeline prayed her asthma wouldn't act up as she turned to the man showing it off.

"Your place is…lovely."

Everett snickered. "Madeline Prix always says the nicest things. It's a dump."

A gasp of relief at the truth escaped from her before her brain played back the first half of his comment. Her cheeks lit up at the thought of him even noticing.

"Got this from my uncle. He used to buy decrepit real estate and fix it up to sell for a profit."

"And he wants you to rebuild this place while working as a firefighter?" That sounded like an unending amount of work.

Ev smiled wider and brushed down the towel clinging to his thigh. "Nah. He moved upstate to some small farm with his husband. Couldn't sell this so he said I could have it for a song. Just have to make it livable."

"You can do it," Madeline cheered. She'd never seen him swing a hammer, but she had full faith that Everett could do anything he set his mind to.

His gaze slid down her, ramping up her blush. Madeline twirled a finger through her hair, her eyes drifting to the hole in the drywall which revealed what had to be the parlor. When the twirl turned into a curl, she slapped her hand away from all that hard work she'd ruined in an instant.

"Guessing you're hungry. Hoping, at least." Everett chuckled, waving her further inward.

"I could eat," Madeline said, trying to not appear too desperate. She kept her eyes peeled for signs of a lady's presence, but the only specters haunting this house were cobwebs.

Everett took the lead, allowing Madeline to take a sweeping glance at his backside. The jeans were tighter than a cowboy's, a thrill ramping through her as she realized she could look without anyone calling her out.

"Is there anyone that'll miss you?"

"Hm?" She struggled to yank her gaze from his bubbly booty, her cottony brain playing back what he'd asked. "Oh no, I turned the heating pad on for Sparky and left lots of food. He's already gained three ounces."

His sunshine smile blasted Madeline into glittery pieces. "Your doing, I bet."

"Cats are good at eating," she whispered to herself, well aware of her kitties' food bill.

"What about Monte?" Everett asked out of nowhere. He twisted on his hips, staring Madeline down as if the question was life or death.

She shrugged. "He should be fine."

"He won't wonder where you are?"

"He'll sniff my shoes later, and if he's not happy, probably puke in them," Madeline said without a thought, but a rictus of horror snapped away Everett's smile. "It's not a big deal. Cats vomit all the time. I swear he does it for fun."

"Cat? Monte is...?" Ev swayed as if something had run him over. She was about to ask when the smile burned even hotter, and he shoved open a swinging door. That at least worked and didn't squeak like death on a tricycle.

To Madeline's shock, it wasn't an open pit filled with lit charcoal but an actual kitchen. The counters were granite, though only a half-section was uncovered from a protective tarp. A stainless-steel refrigerator hummed beside what looked like a brand-new gas stove. An ethereal blue light glowed from both the digital clock and around the dials as if it had traveled from the future.

"Wow," she gasped, staring around the section of the house that looked like someone had stolen a modern kitchen from a hardware store and dropped it in place. Her gaze landed on Everett whose soft green eyes were lingering over her. "This is beautiful." She finished with scratching at her shoulder in a nervous habit.

"Thank you. Been shaping it up for a month," he said while picking the lid off the stockpot on the stove.

All perfect kitchens were forgotten as the smell of seafood boil, creole springs and bacon-smothered okra enveloped her. "Is that...? Lord almighty." Madeline's long-smothered accent flared hard and swerved west.

Everett chuckled in his more gentlemanly North Carolinian while hers was pure bayou. "I thought you might like it."

She grabbed a spoon, filled it with the inviting dish and ran it under her nose. Madeline didn't taste it—she wanted to live inside it. "Mother of pearl, I haven't seen real gumbo in..." Dumping the spoon back in, she swirled through the bobbing vegetables to spot the shrimp rising to the surface. "Shame it's not crawdaddy season. Only way to get through spring was with a whole bucket of 'em and..."

Everett's hand found its way to the small of her back. His face rested so close, she could stare into his pores — which were perfect, of course. A dash of brown hair mixed in with the sandy scuff along his jaw and cheeks. Madeline wanted to run her thumb along the lines and smooth it all down for him.

It's not a date.

Wrinkling her nose, she banged the spoon on the edge of the pot to clean it off and took a step back. His hand glanced off her. "How in the world do you know how to make proper gumbo?"

"Back home I worked with a guy from New Orleans. Best way to fill up ten men famished from working in the sun was a fat pot of gumbo. Sweetened up my boss too, so super plus."

Madeline clapped her hands together, her body radiating with excitement. She hadn't had it in years. *Does he remember how much I've missed Louisiana? No, don't be silly.* He knew how to make gumbo, so that was what he did. Nothing to it.

"Bowls?" she asked.

Everett handled the dish capturing, ladling the hearty gumbo up to the rim of a pair of teenaged amphibian fighting squad cereal bowls. *Still a bachelor.* The thought dampened Madeline's joy as she stared around the kitchen. *What man puts all his focus on fixing up the kitchen first? The kind with a lady at his side.*

"Where should I...?" She twisted around the small room hemmed in by counters, careful to keep her gumbo steady.

"The dining room is —" Everett began, his hand once again glancing to the small of her back to help guide her. They passed through a gap in hanging plastic sheeting. Madeline's breath caught at the dining room table propped up on cement blocks. "It will be the dining room, one day. God willing."

"I'm sure you'll make it look beautiful," she crowed, truly believing it, given the kitchen.

Everett bowed his head, peering up through those lashes thicker than a paintbrush. Half of their class had squealed about his eyelashes in junior high. It was high school when they'd moved on to his biceps, pecs and glutes courtesy of a swimmer's workout. But Madeline had never given up on those lashes and what they'd feel like stroking her cheek.

"Oh." Ev pointed at the solitary desk chair pulled up beside the table. "I forgot to...okay, you sit here." Dropping his gumbo on the other side, he tugged the wheelie chair out. The plastic was cracked along one armrest and the middle piston leaned to the side.

Madeline eased her way to the chair, worried that, like the rest of the house, it could go at any second. If that happened, she would have no choice but to walk into the sea and never return. To her relief, it was a sturdy but teetering chair that supported her.

Grabbing up a toolbox, Everett carried it across from her and sat on it. It was an obvious challenge for the six-foot and climbing man, his legs twisted to try and accommodate the small seat. In fact, his head barely reached above the table, letting Madeline look down on him for the first time in their lives.

Everett coughed, his voice lowering as he raised his spoon. "Bone appetite," he declared with a goofy grin to emphasize the joke.

The gumbo was good, very old-church picnic, stick-to-your-bones-for-a-month food. Madeline devoured the first five spoonfuls and declared, "This is exquisite. Best I've ever had."

"Glad you think so. I was worried you'd sniff me out as a fake."

Madeline smiled at him, but her stomach churned at the fake comment. "Will there be...is anyone...? Do you have anyone helping you with this place? It's so big and rickety. A lot to bite off. Not that I don't think you can handle it."

It was a while before Everett reacted to her bombardment. "Gonna take a few years, no two ways about it. But if I keep to the schedule, I can get it done."

He sounded proud of accepting such a gargantuan challenge. Madeline couldn't imagine such a thing. But there he was, setting out to reinvigorate a dilapidated and maybe haunted house with his bare hands.

"Can I tell you something, Maddy?"

"Always," she said fast.

Everett stirred his spoon through his bowl, almost none of the gumbo left. A slow scraping sound echoed amongst the dust and rotted beams. "I left home, Williamston, because…" He curled his thumb under his ring finger as if rolling something that wasn't there. Which was when Madeline noticed the tan line.

Scoffing, Ev held up his naked hand. "Kept telling her I couldn't wear it at work, it was dangerous, but she insisted. Now, stupid as it is, I miss fiddling with the darn thing."

He was married. He was still married? It was a separation or…? "Kathy," Madeline whispered. His high school girlfriend, his perfect high school girlfriend. They had looked made for each other. Captain of the swim team — golden hair and emerald eyes — with the dance squad leader with her white-blonde hair and deep brown eyes.

Kathy was the perfect Southern belle, the sorority sister in nothing but Kate Spade sundresses. Madeline had wanted to fit in so bad, she'd gone into their store once. The saleswoman had looked her up and down and suggested she buy a scarf. No tablecloth from a Jimmy Buffet concert dress for her.

"Who?" Everett asked, before shaking his head as he figured out the answer. "Oh, Kathy Clark. No, we broke up freshman year of college. I married junior year, which was the biggest mistake of my life." He glanced at Madeline, his lips moving but no words coming free.

After staring at his ringless hand, he flung it back through his hair and shrugged. "No kids at least. I wanted to wait. She didn't. Maybe I always knew in the pit of my stomach that it wouldn't work."

Williamston was a tiny town in the scheme of things. They said that if you shared a piece of gossip at one end of town, it'd reach the other before you finished your sentence. A divorce would be news for quite a while, especially from a Berry. It didn't happen, not without a police report involved.

"That can't have been easy." Madeline reached over, brushing her fingers over his in comfort.

Ev watched her, his gaze gliding back and forth before he cupped his hand to the back of hers. She was sandwiched between him, which sounded like a very dirty dream she might have had once. Gulping from the embarrassing thoughts in her brain, Madeline couldn't look at him.

"You were always so sweet, Maddy, sweeter than sugarcane. Dip her finger into your glass and you've got sweet tea."

"That... No. I'm just...I try to be nice. It doesn't always work. Sometimes I'd..." *Bite my tongue so hard it'd bleed to keep the mean thoughts at bay.* Ev was different. She didn't have to put up the wall for him. She wanted him to be happy and would do anything to make it so.

He rose off his seat. A loud, metallic clank echoed from the toolbox tipping over, but Everett didn't pause. His hand cupped to Madeline's cheek, and her heart stopped dead.

This isn't real. It's not happening. It's a dream, and you're going to wake up in three…

That ring-less finger twirled around her curls, tickling them against her neck.

Two…

Everett's perfect pout pursed, Madeline's brain circling in alliteration to try to find sense in this. When the tip of his long nose glanced against her round one, she slipped her eyes closed.

One…

An alarm erupted behind Madeline. She reached back to try to slap it off, dead certain she was in bed. But Ev was still there, poised above her, his lips glistening as if he were going to press them to hers. The ear-grating alarm wouldn't cease. Madeline winced as she slunk back from his grip and fished out the cause — her phone.

"Sorry, sorry, I… It's an alarm in my apartment. Goes off if anyone's in there who shouldn't be when I'm out. I got it for my cats. My foster ones, though sometimes Monte can get up to… Never mind."

"Is something wrong?" Everett asked, both hands planted to the table as he leaned back.

So much for that one moment, Madeline Prix. You ruined it.

She frowned at the app. It was a catch-all designed to go off should anyone break into her apartment. Usually, it meant that Monte slapped the sensors for fun, but it could be a sign of the kitten in trouble, or worse. "I'm not sure. I'm sorry, I hate to say it, but I should go check on Sparky and…"

"Not a problem. I'll drive you," he said, smoothly rising and reaching for a hoodie laying in a pile of tarps.

"Really?" Madeline gasped, shocked that he'd offer.

"Of course." Everett extended her his arm as if they were at some cotillion ball, and she took it.

Don't get too close, leave some room in case of…

Madeline glanced back to the table where he'd cupped her cheek and sure seemed about to do the impossible from her dreams. Burying that ever-watchful guardian inside, she snuggled her hip against his and the side of her breast glanced against him as well.

If Everett cared, he gave no sign. Fishing out his keys, he graced her with his soft emerald gaze and said, "I don't want you to worry. Ever."

Chapter Six

It was probably nothing. Madeline kept repeating that while Everett patiently chauffeured her back to her apartment. He'd gone to so much trouble with dinner, and she'd messed it all up. At least he kept a patient smile.

Images of burly men in ski-masks flashed through her mind as she moved to unlock her door. By the second deadbolt, her hands shook so much, her keys splattered to the floor. Ev scooped them up and gave her a calming wink.

When the door rattled open, Madeline dashed inside. "Monte? Little Bub? Are you...?" Flipping on the light revealed the two culprits. They weren't in masks, but their guilt was clear with evidence all over the kitchen. A mess of cereal and cracker boxes were scattered across the table, each chewed open on the bottom until a handful of fine crumbs had rained down. Sitting primly in the middle of a circle of stolen food was her live-in bandit.

"Monte Cristopher!" Madeline scolded her twelve-year-old for being a terrible influence on the young. Sparky mewled, his head caught inside one of the boxes that his fellow ornery cat had stolen.

For his part, Monte raised his tail and strutted off the table to the counter. "Don't give me that look, mister. You are in big trouble! Huge!" Madeline chastised her unconcerned cat as she tugged Sparky out.

Bright pink and purple dust coated those fiber-optic whiskers, the kitten's entire muzzle covered in cereal marshmallows. "Look at you, poor baby." Madeline licked her thumb to try to smear the mess off. She got an attempt at a hiss for her work, but the kitten was too small to have any power behind it.

"I should have never left you alone with the Count. He's an awful influence."

"Aw," Everett said, scratching a single finger along Sparky's black fur. Madeline's heart skipped at the reminder that she wasn't alone, and he had watched her talk to her cats as if they were people. Very naughty people.

For his part, Monte slunk into the kitchen sink, yellow eyes glaring from just above the countertop. Oh, he knew he was in trouble, but he didn't much care either.

"Is everything good?" the man she had let into her messy apartment asked.

"Yep." With a wary eye, Madeline darted her gaze around the reminder that her place was on the fast track to Spinsterville. All she needed were a few balls of yarn and some more cats. Backing up to try to gather her pile of sweaters hung over the two kitchen chairs, she pointed toward the top of her cupboards.

"That's where the sensor is so, in theory, the cats won't set it off. The Count must have knocked it when he took to tossing boxes around. Yes, I know it was you. And no, you don't get a treat for forcing me to come home early."

Ev stared from the meowing cat that had caused all this back to Madeline as she tossed her sweats into the closet. "Count? Is there a third cat?"

"No, that's Monte. My one and only. Only one I can't get rid of. When he's being his usual prima donna self, I call him the Count." He was her fickle gentry feline, whom she wouldn't abandon no matter how much utter destruction he caused.

When the scratching wasn't enough, Everett brushed Sparky up against his cheek. The kitten realized how much fun stubble could be and rubbed his glittery purple muzzle all over Ev's face. Before this moment was lost, Madeline fished out her phone and recorded a tiny black kitten smearing cereal dust all over a hot fireman.

After finishing his good scratching, Sparky paused, his still blue eyes staring deep into Everett's. With a quick lean forward, Ev booped the kitten on the nose with his own. And Madeline got it all on video.

"Are you...?" he asked.

"Sorry." She gulped, her fingers turning to butter as she tried to pause the recording. "Sorry, I was...I just thought that a handsome man nuzzling an adorable kitten video would help with donations."

Everett smiled so picture-perfect that Madeline regretted hiding her phone away. He should have photographers following him every second of the day. Everyone needed to see his beautiful sunshine face. "So..." He placed the kitten in the middle of the table and ran a single finger up and down Sparky's spine. "You think I'm handsome?"

Every person who has ever met you thinks that, Madeline thought. Right? She did not say that aloud.

The blush climbing up his cheeks said otherwise. She raced to hide away her slip with nonchalance. "It's hardly news. All of the girls in high school were…"

Hopelessly, endlessly in love with you.

He snorted, switching from the kitten to scratch the back of his neck. "High school was a long time ago."

"Not long enough," Madeline whispered to herself. She'd been ecstatic to get accepted out of state, to pack her things, say goodbye to her 'sort-of' friends and start a new life in New York. All except for Everett. Leaving him had been the one thorn in what was to be her rosy future.

But here he was without the boys' football team hurling balloons of their own pee at anyone too slow to run away. Without the girls dissecting every female body part down to its mathematical acceptableness in the bathroom. And without her sister scoffing so hard she choked the time Madeline had mentioned her unending crush aloud. She wasn't yet twelve at the time, but she'd known that someone like her didn't belong with someone like Everett Berry.

"How's your family doing?" he asked, causing Madeline to tremble as if he'd read her mind.

"My sister's on her third pregnancy."

"Congratulations," Ev cheered.

"How about you?" Madeline bounced back at him before remembering the whole divorce, town gossip, crushing dread issue. She winced, mentally flicking herself before pivoting. "Your uncle? Uncles? I had no idea there was another in New York."

"Uncle Damian was not invited to many barbecues, which is a shame because his potato salad would beat my momma's. And don't you dare tell her I said that."

As Madeline laughed at his request, Ev's darkened smile rose from behind the clouds. That was what drew everyone to him. He was just so happy all the time. Rain or shine, nothing got him down. And he treated people good, even those he didn't have to.

"Sorry," she whispered, her head hanging down. At Everett's confused chin turn, she added, "For ruining your dinner by worrying about my evil cats."

They both glanced at the cruel Count who licked himself with one leg extended like a ballerina on the barre. Monte didn't look up once as he got down to business.

"You can see how in mortal danger they are." Madeline sighed, bustling back through her mess of a kitchen. She swept the ripped-open boxes into the trashcan, all while shooting laser eyes at the unimpressed cat of mischief. "If you want to head home, save your gumbo—"

"The gumbo can keep. Unless some rats are swimming in it. I've heard stories." Ev leaned closer, his hand gliding up the back of her forearm until he cupped her elbow.

"Highly exaggerated. But if you said cockroaches the size of rats…"

He beamed even brighter, his lips pressing nearer to Madeline just as he'd almost done at the other kitchen table.

Ditzy Maddy off in her daydreams again. He probably spotted a piece of food on your face and was about to wipe it off. What else could it be?

Madeline slunk back, Everett's hand releasing as she fished out her phone. "Mind if I share the video?"

"Please." He resumed scratching the kitten who had found a new best friend. "If it'll help feed these starving babies. Oh, I know you are, little one."

She couldn't deny her toes curling in her shoes and the euphoric blush on her cheeks at his baby talk with the kitten. Cutting the video and adding a glittery banner for good measure, Madeline lost all sense of the outside world. Silence invaded the once easy air, bringing her question back from the dead. Why doesn't he go? He had his somewhat dilapidated house to get to. It must be better than this. Madeline finished placing Sparky back in the box he shouldn't be able to get out of and turned to make the suggestion again.

"Wanna sit?" Everett said so fast she glanced to the kitchen chair…which had binders for clients and a pharmacy bag filled with tampons on it. The cringe took on a whole new level, Madeline trying to yank the bag off without him noticing, when Ev added, "On a couch?"

"Oh, I have that. I mean…yeah, sounds good. There will be cat hair."

He laughed hard. "I wouldn't expect anything less."

More than a couch—Madeline had an entire living room set. The low coffee table was covered in her laptop, old mail she kept meaning to recycle and dozens upon dozens of receipts. Tax time was a hellish nightmare in her world. A single sunk-in armchair sat turned to face out the filthy window at the creaking fire exit instead of the TV.

Bustling in past Everett, Madeline shoved anything incriminating under the couch. "Here it is, a room to live in. Not that you can't live in the others. I don't have a death room because that would be mean."

And there was why she didn't talk to anyone until college. It wasn't that Madeline had gotten better at this—she'd just met more people who were willing to put up with her nonsense.

Everett's staring at you.

Dropping to her ass fast, she almost submerged into the couch, its cushions greedy to swallow her whole. She expected Ev to dust off the chair and take it. But he glided past the coffee table, bumping an old magazine in the process, and sat down beside her. His added weight shifted the balance of the couch, so Madeline started to roll toward him. She hooked an arm around the outside, digging in so she didn't wind up on his lap.

It was a nice lap. Long and lean, probably warm. *No. Don't be an idiot. Smile and wonder why he wants to hang out. Do people even do that anymore?*

"I was thinking," Everett said, slapping his hands against his knees, "of that time Tom made us bottle like a thousand fireflies in old pickle jars."

He snickered at his memory, staring through the distance. "The plan was to release 'em all in school on the last day. Senior prank. Course, he failed to take into account that the bugs could fit through a gap in the lid. He was cleaning 'em out of his trunk until graduation. I suppose there aren't any fireflies to catch in the city."

"'Fraid not. There might be a restaurant, or club or sex shop named Firefly. Though it doesn't have the same innocent intent."

"Might at the sex shop, if you paid extra." Everett winked, melting Madeline into a deeper puddle. Was this the first time she'd ever sat so close to him she could feel his body heat wafting from his shoulder or reach over and cup his knee?

No. There was the museum.

"Something on your mind?"

"It's…silly." She flinched, her heart spinning in a loading circle. "Not important—"

Ev leaned closer, his sandy hair bouncing in the move. "Come on, not as if there's an itinerary to follow."

"I was thinking about…" Madeline twisted her fingers into interconnecting rings, rolling both together along with her words. "That school trip to the maritime museum."

"The one with the whale skeleton? I swear it wasn't me who dared Big Dog to ride it."

"You could talk a lemon into turning sweet," Madeline threw out without a thought. "I mean, you…everyone knew that you were good at…at sweet-talking and…" *Fucking hell, Mads. Grow a pair!*

She was always hazy on what growing a pair meant for girls, and God knew she didn't want even bigger breasts. Her bras were expensive enough.

Madeline was too deep into berating herself to notice when a hand cupped her knee. As soft green eyes burned into hers, her bones melted. Her voice shook as she said, "You sat beside me." Ev glanced at the armchair in clear confusion. "…on the bus, to the museum. When no one else would."

"I did?" He shrugged, because to him it had been a Tuesday, while she would never forget it to her dying day. Or how he was rolling his hand back and forth over her knee right now. "Well," Everett drawled, "I'm sitting by you again, so what does that mean?"

That you're the sweetest man in the world.

Madeline tried to say it, but her voice lodged in her throat and refused to come out. The chances of her speaking coherently while under his emerald gaze were nonexistent. Ev scooted closer, gliding his thigh along hers and scooping his hand around her cheek. Twirling her fallen curl in his fingers, he asked, "Maddy? What do you want?"

She lost her mind. There was no other explanation for her, Madeline Prix, tipping her face to Everett Berry and kissing him. It wasn't like she didn't have experience, fumbling not-worth-bragging-about experience, but in that moment she became a teenager again. Lips pursed, she brushed her mouth over his. Barely more than a glance, but a tingle reverberated through her at the dry kiss. Gulping, she leaned back as her brain lit up with what she had done.

"Oh God," Madeline gasped, wiggling further back into the couch. She slapped a hand to her rebellious lips as if afraid they might leap free to assault him a second time. "I am…I'm so sorry."

Everett chuckled while brushing his thumb over his bottom lip. *Let me die here. Strike me dead with a heart attack, or have the couch eat me. Anything to end this awkwardness.*

"Well." Ev twisted on the couch to stare deeper at Madeline. One fist pounded into the cushions for leverage as he leaned closer. Madeline had nowhere to go, her heart leaping about like a cricket on mowing day.

The thumb that'd brushed his lips clean swiped over hers, smearing the lipstick she put on. A smile tugged on his mouth, and he whispered, "Let's try it again." Everett Berry plunged his lips to hers. *Repeat, Everett Berry is kissing me, Madeline. Yes,* that *Madeline.*

Heat burst against her cheeks, her hands rising to hold him so he'd never stop. She didn't get far, cupping his elbows, but Ev took control. One hand caressed her cheek, guiding her to the right as he licked his tongue across her bottom lip.

Merciful heavens, he tasted so good. Chewing on sweet grass while sipping lemonade good. Smelling the hot dock baking in the summer sun good. He was home, he was safety, he was Everett Berry, the only man she'd ever wanted.

And he was kissing her.

Madeline's tongue met his, overpowering his tender sweeps across her lip, and she rolled her tongue with his. Ev shifted on the couch, his leg straddling wider as if it had to accommodate his crotch. Oh shit, was he getting hard while kissing her? That…that was impossible but amazing.

Take it further.

She grabbed the hand on her cheek, his thumb still caressing down her smile line. Everett's kisses paused, his hazy gaze trying to take her in until she placed his hand at the top of her breast. He had amazing hands, the palms capable of cupping a basketball, but even they couldn't circumvent her buoys.

At first, Ev slipped his palm up and down across her left tit while sucking on her lips. As he traced his hand under her breast, he whispered, "You don't waste no time. I like it."

He wrapped both of his hands around her back and pulled Madeline with him until they were reclining on the couch. She gasped, scrabbling to keep up while his lips traversed up and down her cheeks and neck. Once she was positioned above him, he trailed his fingers under her shirt. Starting at the back, his nails swerved in little figure eights, Madeline's forehead butting against his as she tried to mentally urge him higher.

When he hit her bra band, he paused. She was in her serious tackle, the kind that'd require thirty stout men to undo. Still, Ev wasn't about to back down on tugging the bra apart while his lips swept around her face and missed their mark.

"I swear, this never gets easier," he said, a laugh sputtering free. Should she let him keep trying? He wasn't close to managing, but it might not be kind to...

All those years of changing in the gym without taking her shirt off worked to Madeline's advantage. Snaking a hand under her the sleeve of her shirt, she tugged one bra strap down and freed her arm. After that, it was simple to unlock the mighty hooks and pull the whole thing out. With a jolly wave, she banished the bra to the floor. Everett's sight shifted from the lost underwire trap to Madeline.

"I'll never understand how girls can do that."

Madeline was about to explain when he swept his palms over her free-to-roam breasts. A thin, stretchy sheet of rayon came between them as Ev rolled his hands back and forth from the sides down into her treacherous cleavage. Losing herself in his tender swirl of her shirt over her nipples, Madeline brushed her forehead against his for a kiss. When Ev pinched both her nipples in synch, Madeline gasped in shock. She opened her eyes to find an entertained smile rising upon his lips.

"The shirt's fun and all, Maddy," Ev whispered, his calf beginning to glide up and down the edge of her dour skirt. "Feel like I'm a kid giddy about stealing second. But..."

He swept his finger down her stomach, Madeline sucking it in on instinct. At first, he played with the straight hem of her shirt, but his palm began to curl further back to her ass. Ev ground his hand deeper in, tugging the elastic of her panties back and forth over her skin through her skirt.

Two thoughts ran through Madeline's head. First, she hadn't let anyone see her naked in the light for going on five years now. If Everett Berry took one look at her and ran for the door, she'd die on the spot. And second, her panties were soaked through at the idea of him rounding to home.

Madeline snatched at the hem of her shirt, prepared to yank it off like a bandage, when she paused. Giving a little shimmy with her shoulder as if doing a pole dance, she inched her shirt higher. A sliver, then a full moon of her so-pale-it-radiated belly emerged. Ev's wandering hand rested against her skin, the heat from his body pooling down hers. Same as her ass, he started to knead into the giving flesh, and Madeline panicked.

Without a second's pause, she flung her shirt where the bra had landed, scattering the unused coasters in the process.

"Now that's what I'm talking about," Everett cheered. Wrapping his hands around her back, he tugged Madeline closer while sitting up himself. Hot lips traced along her right breast, his face vanishing into their mighty silhouette. She ran her hand through his hair, savoring the soft, fine strands when Ev pursed his mouth around her nipple and pressed.

"Holy hell!" Madeline cried, her legs buckling from the shock pounding through her. The hands at her back pulled her closer, Everett working harder. He circled her nipple with his tongue in an intoxicating dance,

Madeline lost in wonder at the small tremors he produced until he pursed hard and kicked off an earthquake.

"Thought you might like a little pressure," he cooed, switching to her other breast. While that received the same spine-tingling sucking, he slipped his hand under her skirt. Climbing fast beyond her thighs, when Ev bit on her nipple, he swiped a finger straight down the center of her panties.

Heat broiled across her body, sweat beading on those very tits he wouldn't stop sucking. Madeline felt herself falling forward. The only thing stopping her was Ev's face buried in her cleavage. She knew she was wet, but the press of her soaked panties deeper against her was the bayou at the height of monsoon season wet.

"What about here?" Everett asked, his voice strong and clear. His finger worked in through the edge of her underwear, circling first along the strip of pubic hair she had missed when shaving, then playing with her inner lips. A groan rose up from Madeline's sucked chest, her hips tipping to encourage him to explore deeper.

Third is yours for the taking.

"Ah," Ev gasped out of nowhere, his hand retreating. The fear of him fleeing knocked into her brain, but it was to his own crotch he reached. "Getting backed up here," he said, unbuttoning his jeans.

Sweet merciful heaven. Everett Berry's, well, twig and berries. Tree and berries. Stones. Humongous stones.

"Still with me, darlin'?" He cupped her cheek, pausing in his reveal.

Madeline nodded hard, trying to will away the squeal she felt running through every vein in her body. Scooting back along the sofa, Everett slid his pants down in the process. A sigh of relief escaped him as he guided his cock to the forefront. Those lush lashes fluttered when he ran his hand once up and down the hidden shaft.

It was some other hand that reached for it, someone else's fingers that drew down that hard cock nestled beneath his boxers. No way was it Madeline's. No chance in hell was she brushing her palm to pump his underwear over it. Nor sneaking her pinkie in through the fly to glance a touch of her flesh over his.

Everett squirmed on the couch, his head tipping back as he jerked his hips in time with her hand. Without a second's hesitation, Madeline snatched at the band of his underwear and tugged them down.

God, it was even better than she could have imagined. Well-proportioned, neither too big nor too small, it was a penis that didn't intimidate. And his carpet totally matched the drapes. It answered every question a horny teenage Madeline had dreamed up.

Well, there was one more.

"Mmm." Everett staggered up to his elbows on the couch cushion. Madeline's attention was on his cock falling flush against his round of abs. When he scratched his nails over her straddling thighs, she focused on him. He wound his fingers around the high band of her underwear, tugging them lower.

"How's about you lose these?" he asked, doing most of the pulling for her.

Madeline nodded, half-way to obliging, when she asked, "And then?"

Everett smirked. "We'll think of something to do. Checkers, maybe?"

Laughing at his calming distraction, Madeline wiggled back and forth on the couch to try and free her panties. It wasn't until they were almost off that she shook her head and realized she should have lost the skirt as well. When she was about to undo the zipper, Ev grabbed her hand.

"Nah, nah." He shook his head, drawing her concern. Tugging on the middle of her skirt, he lifted her hemline while saying, "I like it on."

"But not the shirt?" she asked even as her thighs clenched to pulse a thrill of pleasure through her pussy.

Everett drew a hand along her breast, his fingers barely touching as he leaned back. "Tits like yours need to be free."

The internal squeeing hit level ten at that. Madeline planned to swoon later at him complimenting her breasts. There wasn't time, as Ev dug into his pocket to fish out a gas station condom. "Good to be careful," he explained, rubbering himself up.

Holy shit, Madeline. You're going to…to sleep with, no, you're going to fuck Everett Berry on the same couch you watch courtroom dramas on. This was the best day of her life.

Everett finished by checking the seal against his cock then gave a quick slap on her ass. Blushing bright, Madeline climbed to him. She wanted to remember every second of this, the scratch of the wearing couch on her knees, the catch of her skirt between them. The way he rubbed his leg over the inside of hers. The fire in his eyes that burned only for her.

The entire length of his shaft nestled between her. Madeline tipped her hips down, brushing her clit against him and starting a new tremble of pleasure through her. *Dear God in heaven, let me wow him.*

"Ah Maddy," Everett groaned. He grabbed himself, putting his cock in place, the head circling right against the kiss of her inner lips. "So fucking sweet!" he cried out while thrusting in.

Ev began to buck his hips, but he couldn't move far. Madeline swayed with him, attempting to corkscrew herself around his cock as she lifted off. It must have worked. Everett leaned his head back into the cushion as he gurgled. Another moan rattled through him, Madeline increasing the pressure as she put those Kegels to good work.

"Shit, shit…" Everett gasped. She stared up into his emerald eyes as he opened them wide. "Darlin'…" His panting slowed, bringing Madeline's bouncing to a standstill, but he grabbed both of her breasts. "I want to hear you screaming too. Use me, ride me harder than anyone else."

Use him. Fuck him.

Can I…?

Her pussy cried at her to do as he'd asked already.

No more coy swirling—Madeline pounded hard against him. She tipped back, her breasts pooling across her chest, as she inclined to the perfect spot. Ev's cock knocked against all of her, igniting the rising tide. And when she slammed down and that perfect head found her G-spot, Madeline screamed.

"Yes!" Everett cried in response, his fingers pinching her nipples while she rode him. "More. Come on, baby."

Everett Berry had called her baby.

You're fucking him! Who cares what he calls you?

Without a second's pause, he slipped his finger down between where she joined him and began to rub against her clit. His other hand kept tugging on her nipples, switching fast from one to the other. God, it was all Madeline could do to keep from exploding.

Heat pooled everywhere. A raging volcano arced through her breasts, hot springs piped through her thighs, and the devil's own fire raced from that single touch of his finger.

Everett's cool voice cut through her rabid panting. "Scream for me."

And Madeline did. Her orgasm erupted across the entirety of her body. Her tongue grew numb, her eyes blurred, her legs shook and her pussy clamped tight to the perfect cock inside. Her nose also started itching like mad out of nowhere.

But rather than scratch it, Madeline ignored the itch while staring at a grinning Everett. She bit down on her lip, her breath struggling as she admitted, "You are…some kind of demon!"

"Been called worse in my day, but I choose to take it as a compliment."

"You…" Madeline gasped, her body still riding every thumb-biting tremor reverberating through her. "You should."

"Now, how about I watch you bounce?" he asked, clenching his abs to sit up higher. Madeline joined him, the pair kissing hard. Ev thrust himself into her, causing her to gasp into his mouth. "Bring me home."

"I've always wanted to," Madeline admitted to herself.

Watching him lie back and trust her, she started to jackhammer herself around him. On cue, her freed breasts began to bob and bounce like airships in a tornado. But the rising joy on Everett's face made the strain worth it. "Yes, yes," he cried, stretching his legs out as he rose up to meet her. Madeline followed his rhythm, sweat dripping down her flying tits as Everett gave one more, "Yes!"

His bucking froze, his hips locked in tight and he grabbed at her thighs. Madeline watched in awe as Ev tipped his head back deep into the couch. His sandy hair fanned out over the cushions while his Adam's apple rose higher and higher up his throat. All the while, his bottom lip quivered as if he were holding back a thousand screams of pleasure.

That was what Madeline wanted to believe, anyway.

"Fuck," Everett gasped, rising to meet the woman still on him. "That was...I mean. God, you're..." Picking up her fingers, Everett pulled the tip of one into his mouth. After dragging it across his lips, he rolled his tongue around her forefinger and declared, "As sweet as I expected."

Madeline closed her eyes tight, her palms swooping over Ev's chest. Everett Berry. The hottest, kindest, sweetest guy she'd known her whole life. It had to be a dream, a hallucination brought on by bad shrimp. There was no chance that he...

A crash snapped her gaze to the coffee table. Monte skidded in his aborted landing, slick magazines sliding with him. "You are still in big trouble," Madeline chastised her cat who flopped down and tempted her with his fluffy belly. "Bribery will get you nowhere," she said even while running her fingers through the soft fur.

She knew she'd get two swipes before her little Count moved to nibble her fingers off for daring to touch him. All her senses crashed around on her at once. She was still straddling Everett, her knee balanced on the hard edge of the couch. Cool air seeped in through the awful windows—a December night in NYC was not one to be ignored. And warm hands were rubbing up and down her thighs, a floppy smile across his sunny face.

"I should…" Madeline moved to get off him when Everett wrapped a hand around her shoulders. He pulled her down against his chest, her hip digging in between his legs. She could feel him trying to single-handedly yank off and tie the condom while his cock snuggled against her belly. A cozy smell of worn leather and old books wafted off his hoodie as she nuzzled against the man inside.

"So," Ev whispered, swaying his palm along her back. His blinding green eyes burned into hers, the twinkle increasing, as he said, "in case you're wondering…"

Was he going to admit he was still married? Dating someone else? Just looking for sex and wanted her off him?

His hot breath twirled down her ear as he said, "I've got more than one condom."

Chapter Seven

He knew he wasn't in his bed by the lack of stains overhead and that obstinate drip. No matter how hard he looked, how many pipes he tightened, nothing would stop it. Everett's second clue was the mass of red curls trying to invade his mouth. They were a wily horde, evading his attempts to push them down with his chin or even the nuclear option of his whole hand.

There was little choice but for him to lay back and accept his new life in the hair.

"Mmm," the woman in his half-hug murmured, her cheek plastered to his naked chest. Did she have some work thing to get to? What time was it?

Everett was about to shake her awake when fifteen pounds of orange and brown fur leaped from the edge of the room straight onto both of them. While he wanted to spring out of bed, Madeline lashed an arm out and picked her cat up without a second thought.

"Good morning, my lord. Shall it be kippers in the solarium for you?"

Monte meowed like he'd been starving for a hundred years, earning a knowing snicker from Maddy. "Of course the plate will be golden. Can't allow you to suffer…" Her voice faded as she turned to catch Everett watching her little joke with the cat.

"Get off." She twisted, pushing the cat to the cold and food-less floor. As she sat up, the tiny strap along her lacy nightgown slid off her shoulder. Before she'd even noticed, Everett ran his hand along her arm and returned it to where it belonged.

"Thanks." Maddy blushed, her body turning like she intended to flee the bed. The thought stuck a pin in Everett's brain, his hand lashing out to cup her stomach. He buried his face against the side of her neck, digging his chin in as if to rub away a knot.

"Done so soon?" he asked, his fingers winding their way under the short, translucent nightgown to curl along her skin. Placing a trio of kisses against her neck, he worked up to her ear. The first hot breath was answered by a giggle which shook her buoyant tits. Or maybe it was his hand rolling under one.

Maddy let him get in a few more copped feels before she asked, "What about your fireman-ing? Don't you have to get to that? It's already…?" A tiny clock with a gear-based couple on the perch sat upon the nightstand beside her. "Eight-ten. That's… Probably late?"

Her concern was, as always, adorable. "I'm not on this week. Next week will be fourteen-to-sixteen-hour days, so for now I try to get in all that construction work and sleeping I won't be doing next."

"And all that fucking," she said with a shrug before gasping, her soft Southern hands piling over her mouth in shock.

Everett laughed, tugging each down. "I've heard worse," he whispered, his lips pursing against her smooth jawline. "Done worse too."

Spinning on the bed, Maddy wrapped her arms around him. Everett was already reaching to tug that frilly negligee off when a most unpleasant ringing filled the room. She yanked up her phone, quickly putting in the passcode while Everett leaned back on the bed.

"Scammers?" he asked. "I swear if I could, I'd delete the phone bit off my phone."

"No." Madeline shook her head, a hint of concern rising. "It's my friend, Beth. She's on a vacation and wouldn't call unless…" Biting on her lip, she placed the phone to her ear and said, "Hi?"

Everett began to rub a hand along her back, not trying to eavesdrop though he couldn't hear much anyway. All those years of being too close to machinery had done in his ears.

"No?" Maddy suddenly shouted and leaped to her feet. He rolled from the unexpected change in the cheap coils. Everett sat up to try and comfort her, but she wasn't crying. She was tearing up, but also smiling.

"What is it? What's wrong?"

"Beth is engaged!" Madeline shouted as if it were the best news in the world. "To Tristan. He's a…you don't know him, or her. You might have heard of him. Sorry. Do you mind if I…?" She jerked her head to the door, her body already shuffling away.

"Go ahead," Everett said, well aware that he couldn't impede the wedding plan squees no matter how hard he tried.

Maddy made it a step out the door before she paused and said, "Tell me everything!"

No doubt it was all some super romantic tale involving big screens at ballparks and diamond rings that cost the same as a used car. Hopefully, that guy got it all to her exact specifications or he was gonna be in hell for the next ten or so years. Elise had been all tears and smiles over the picnic, less so the tiny ring he had bought off a cousin. His mood turned sour at her name ringing in his thoughts, almost as if he could summon her by mistake.

"Oh my God." Madeline gasped, jumpstarting his panic. "You have to let me design your wedding website. Yes, you need a wedding website. Just…trust me. I have so many templates that would…"

Her squeeing faded as she must have walked out to her living room. Was that where he'd left his pants? The shirt was in that vicinity and the underwear wound up in the bathroom?

Boy, they'd been about everywhere the night before. Couch lovin' was nice and all, but it was hard to beat a bed. Lots of room to maneuver, edges to grip for her or him, pillows at the ready to help keep her in position. Everett smiled like a greedy bastard who had made off with a whole ATM. At the pathetic meowing, he glanced down at the supposed Count. "Here I thought you were the man in her life."

That earned a yellow glare from Monte, whose tail bounced back and forth at the thought. Okay, maybe he was Maddy's man and didn't like the new interloper. "How about I get you some breakfast? And if you still hate me, pistols at dawn."

Easing down the hall, Everett spotted his pants resting under a framed photo of a colorful cast on stage covered in signatures. He wanted to inspect it closer, but the cat wouldn't take no for an answer. Sounded like his last boss.

Maddy stood on one leg, the phone pressed tight to her ear as she listened to her friend. She kept aimlessly kicking her other foot through the air like a nervous tic. It'd be hilarious if she weren't also in next to nothing with the harsh kitchen light turning her little nightie transparent. Ev must have made a noise as she turned from her flamingo dance, and a blush rose clear up to her forehead.

Giving a tiny wave, he worked his way into the kitchen, discovering his boxers in the process. It wasn't proper for a gentleman to eat dry cereal in a lady's home without his half-chub tucked away. If Maddy did that little foot swaying again that lifted her ass higher into view, he'd be having to hide away more than the half-er.

"Okay, cat. Hope you don't mind me calling you cat since we are fighting for the same woman." Everett talked to the unimpressed Monte while digging through the cupboards. He'd hoped for cereal or bread but struck a dozen tins of Heavenly Banquet's cat food.

"Creamy Gravy Lovers," Ev read, then watched the massive fluff ball lick a brown paw down the orange side of his face. "Sounds like you."

Fishing a small metal bowl out of the dish rack, he twisted the can and gave it a single shake. Most of the regurgitated meat byproduct fell in. When he passed it to Monte, however, the cat tipped his head back and meowed like Everett had cursed his mother. "What? Not enough?"

Aware he was being held hostage by a cat, he dug the spoon around the sides, scraping them as clean as possible. Certain that was all he wanted, Ev dropped the bowl on the floor and moved to wash the spoon off. All he got for his troubles was more wailing, the cat squat on his haunches and crying as if the world had ended.

"What's the problem now? Do you need a little touch of watercress? Should it be in a crystal goblet?" Not about to be outmaneuvered by the feline, Ev picked the food up and left it on the counter. He'd always done that with his dogs growing up when they were in the mood to play the 'I can wait you out for something better' game.

But Monte the Count leaped straight off his four paws and sauntered over the counter. He gnawed upon the chunks of gravy chicken while keeping a yellow eye on the interloper in his kitchen. Everett was drawn in by the fluff, his hand raising to pet the feasting kitty, but a low growl warned him off it.

"Now that you're happy, what about…?" Peeking in on the little one revealed the kitten fast asleep in a nest of blankets, the paws visible. "Guess it's just me to take care of." His quick check of the cupboards revealed little more than cooking ingredients. Sure, he could pretend to be some fancy chef…and set her apartment on fire in the process. He had gumbo, mac and cheese, collard greens and grilled cheese with a tomato in his repertoire.

An idea struck him, and Ev tipped out the trashcan. Four boxes sat in the more or less clean bag. And the cats had only taken little nibbles out of the ends. He'd eaten worse.

By the time Madeline finished her call, he sat at the table, spoon dipping into a mix of bran flakes and multi-colored marshmallows. She glanced at Ev being able to handle himself, then her fluff ball finishing his breakfast. "Sorry that took so long."

"People get excited about that stuff," Everett said as diplomatically as he could. He'd been paying off his wedding right up until the divorce.

"Still, it's not good manners to…" Maddy paused, leaning closer to inspect the meaty chunks in the bowl. "Someone's eating special this morning." The cat lord allowed her to run her hands over his back, the tail dipping and rising with every pet.

"Sorry, I didn't know if… He was crying and —"

She cut him off. "It's good. He is such a drama queen about breakfast, lunch, dinner, afternoon tea, elevenses. Monte's probably glad you're here."

Everett shrugged. "Guess I'm an easy man to manipulate. Do you want a bowl?"

"I should check on the kitten first. Can't believe he's still sleeping. Must be a growing day." Maddy scooped the palm-sized baby up from his nap. As he rose into the air as if being abducted by aliens, teeny mewls escaped. "Well, good morning to you too. We have a guest for breakfast." She turned the kitten to Everett so that both tiny milky-blue eyes and wide aqua ones stared at him. The latter focused on his spoon while the former smiled.

Maddy busied herself feeding the kitten, who stomped into the bowl and chowed down. Everett's gaze bounced around the room, noticing her stash of frames covering every wall. He'd guess the tiny Asian woman was this engaged Beth by how many pictures she was in. But the real draw was a corkboard covered in pictures and pictures of kittens.

"You sure have saved a lot of cats," he said, jabbing the spoon filled with sugared milk towards the board.

Maddy glanced to see what he meant and blushed. "I try. Didn't take too long for me to be known as the crazy cat lady around here. I mean to help…um. Saving kittens. Then I adopt them out."

"You get help with that?" Sounded like a ton of work to him and the most baby animals he'd dealt with was when a squirrel gave birth in his old grill.

Maddy shrugged. "Some. The shelter here will work with me on occasion, though we butt heads over some topics that aren't worth mentioning."

"That can't be good if it's got Ms. Prix fuming."

"I ain't fuming." Her pretty cheeks lit up pink at that. "A'ight, I fume a touch. They only ever want the kittens. The elder cats I got to find homes for myself."

Her eyes turned misty, and she gazed at her wall festooned with rescued cats. "Sometimes I think what I'd do if I had my own shelter. How it'd be part park so the cats could lay in the sunshine. That's my win the lottery dream. What about you?"

Getting his feet back under him seemed damn near impossible, never mind this mythical 'what would you do with a million dollars burning a hole in your pocket'. Everett wiped his mouth to stall for thought before blurting out, "Travel?" When she didn't press for more information, he supplied it. "See Europe. The Louvre or Versailles."

The pretty girl sitting across from him nodded. "There's also the Gran' Prix."

"Sure, but those dinky Formula One racers ain't got a thing on…" Ev began before trailing off.

But Maddy placed a hand on her hip, her bright gaze burning into him. "You think I don't know horse hockey about Nascar? Where are we from?"

Everett laughed hard at her putting him back in his place. He'd spent too much time tap-dancing around the women here. They'd coo over his accent but turn cold and rail about him being a hick if he let on to knowing anything about the south. Seemed they wanted the wrapping paper and not the package inside.

Being with Maddy was a reminder that the world wasn't completely broken. She was all sweetness and sunshine, her cheeks turning as red as her hair from laughter. Scooting forward on his ass, Everett picked up her hand. She stared down, her lips slack as he rubbed back and forth over the knuckles.

"I should say —"

It was his turn for the phone to blare, this time from the hallway. Leaping up, he raced to his lost pants. Could be an emergency that needed all hands on deck, and here he was wasting time by... As he woke his phone, he realized half of New York wasn't burning down. It was his alarm.

Oh shit!

Cramming one leg down his jeans, he hobbled around to try to remember where his shirt wound up. "Crap, Maddy, I fully forgot I've got the pipe guy coming today. And if I'm not there he'll turn around and refuse to come back for three more months."

There! Everett scurried into his old shirt. He paused, trying to smooth over his hair while his brain ran through more ways to rescue his ass.

Madeline eased up to her feet while he jammed on his shoes, the socks wadded up in his back pocket. Funny, she looked so small in her bare feet, like he could scoop her up and carry her home.

"I wouldn't want that to happen," she exclaimed as if he weren't being the worst cad running out on her like this. Why did he schedule the pipe guy for today?

The fact you thought you'd be home last night may have been an underlying factor. Funny, he'd even put the good sheets on his bed before she came over.

"You're not upset at me turning tail?" Everett paused in his rambunctious twist through the apartment, hands patting his pockets to make certain his keys or wallet didn't fall out.

"Why would I be?" she asked so earnestly it made his heart pop. Wrapping a hand around the small of her back, he pulled her up on her tiptoes to plant a hot kiss to her lips.

"I'll call you," Everett whispered beside her cheek before placing another more tender kiss there. "Later, I will," he promised, dashing headfirst for the door. "Bye."

Running for his truck, Everett wasted no time pulling onto the road. Hands wringing over his steering wheel, he prayed he'd get through the damn rush-hour traffic of parents dropping off kids then turning around for work. Dozens of dreary-eyed students marched through the drizzle that had bitten into his T-shirt.

"Dumbass, you forgot your hoodie." He snickered at the foolish move before shrugging. It wasn't as if he didn't intend to see Maddy again. Though it was going to make for some cold nights until then. *Probably time to buy that winter coat everyone goes on about up here.*

The good news was that he pulled up to the house to find no one parked outside or an angry letter taped to his door. At least he'd beaten the pipe guy. While backing into the parking space that cost as much as an apartment back home, Everett felt his phone buzz in his pocket. He thumbed it awake to find a message from Maddy.

Did you forget something?

Ev put his best double thumb-typing to work.

I hope the cats like it.

It's their new nest and toy in one.

That caused him to laugh, leaning back as he thought of Madeline's thighs clenched around him. They were so much fun to nibble on, her laughter warping the very air around them. With a deep smile etching into his heart, he typed.

Had a great time.

Nervous energy rumbled through him. Everett slipped out of his truck then walked to his door. What if she hadn't liked it? What if she was being typical Madeline Prix, always nice to everyone? He made it up the first cement step when his phone revealed her text.

Me 2.

She'd had a great time! His smile straining to the brink, Everett worked his key into the lock. An urge overcame him to break out into one of those unexplainable songs Maddy loved and dance about his broken-down house singing about love. For once it felt like everything in his life was going right.

"Well, well, Everett Berry…"

He knew that voice deep in his brain. Like the way one couldn't escape a rotten tooth, it was impossible for him to forget it. Turning around, the keys dropped from his hand as she finished speaking.

"You are a hard man to find."

Chapter Eight

Play it cool, Madeline.

No reason to get excited because you spent the night with the hottest guy in the world. The man you've been crushing on since you figured out what a crush was. The only man you can ever love.

"Eee!" A tiny squeal escaped while shaking her phone back and forth as if confetti would fly out. In doing so, she bounced her elbow against the mouse, sending her CSS script flying. It didn't matter. The website to sell marked-up baking soda toothpaste didn't matter. She had slept with Everett, and if the treacherous parts of her brain tried to question its occurrence, she'd glance down at his text.

He'd said it first, that he had a good time. He had liked it. He liked her.

Okay, one more squeal, then back to work.

Spinning in her desk chair, she stretched her hands high to the ceiling. Madeline's heart surged with so much happiness she wanted to run around all of

Central Park giving out cotton candy. It was the dream she'd never dare think possible and it had happened. Her yipping and dancing must have disturbed the balance as Monte rolled in from his necessary twenty-three-hour nap to glare at her.

"Sorry," she apologized to her cat as if he were a withered landlord coming for the rent. Out in the living room, she heard a crash of boxes which told her Sparky was awake as well.

Take care of the zooming kitten, get that damn website's ordering system up, then… She fiddled with the phone, scrolling to Ev's name. Hovering her finger over the button to text him, she froze. *It's too early and you know it. You'll freak him out.*

Accepting that patience was called for, Madeline scooped up her angry cat and left Everett to wait. Two days was the minimum, but she doubted she could last that long. What she needed was a distraction. "I wish Beth was here."

Madeline managed twenty-four hours to the minute he left before she texted Everett a cheery good morning. His response was simple.

Hi.
Wish I could talk, but house stuff to deal with.

She knocked against her forehead for probably waking him up after a long, hard day at construction. *Bet he worked up a sweat so bad he had to lift the edge of his tank top to wipe his brow.* With the image of his abs in her head, Madeline typed back.

Hope you have a good day.

Back at you, Maddy.

The next time she waited another two whole days. Her joy bubble wouldn't burst, no matter how hard the question of why he wasn't texting her tried to jam a needle into it. Maybe he wasn't the type to talk over text. Maybe he needed a suggestion on what they should do together? It was December, so most anything fun had to be done inside. Nearing Christmas meant the stores were a mess.

Wait. An idea struck her, and Madeline typed fast.

I was thinking for your first Christmas in the city you might want to walk the park. We could get a bag of roast chestnuts to share.

There. A reasonable date idea that to the naked eye could even look like friends hanging out. Not that friends did things like *that* on the couch. He didn't want to be friends again, did he?

Her phone shook, alerting Madeline to his text fifteen minutes after her question.

Would love to. But still busy.

Joy and sorrow in one fragmented sentence. She tried to force on a smile, well aware that repairing a house was a lot of work. And he'd be staying at the firehouse soon which would mean she'd have even less of a chance to see him.

Trying to not place so much of a burden on him, Madeline texted.

I understand.

He replied whip fast to her this time.

Maybe after next week, before Christmas. Could get Chinese food?

Foolish doubt. See, he's swamped with work. He's not trying to avoid me or pulled the one and done of other terrible men. This is Everett Berry. He would never.

Can't wait, was the last text Madeline sent to him. Her heart hardened to assure her that the next round should be on him. It was Everett's turn to contact her. Plus, Beth was finally back from her vacation and engagement celebration. Madeline hadn't been able to tell her much about Everett with him right in her apartment at the time.

It didn't seem wise to talk about how a man had the thighs of a god and left her quivering for hours in front of him. There was losing the high ground, then there was digging a trench and hopping in. *Visit Beth, check out her ring, swing by the vet's for some more vitamins.* She wasn't freaking out about Sparky's slow growth, but it made her nervous. He ate more than Monte and had some powerful bowel movements, but he was staying so tiny.

Madeline glanced to her couch where her Count snuggled on the far cushion and Sparky lay with his tiny booty against Monte's. Both were sleeping atop Everett's hoodie. She'd tried to keep it away from the cat hair, but those two would tug it off the coat hook to snuggle on. Then Madeline would have to yank it out from under them and carry it around breathing in the scent of his body, all fresh sawdust and worked leather.

It *was* getting cold out. They hadn't seen snow yet, but the rains could freeze into slush in the streets overnight. Keeping it for another week would be unnecessarily cruel. The image of Ev with a tattered blanket around his shoulders, shivering in his drafty house tugged on Madeline's heartstrings.

Visit Beth, go to the vet's, drop off his hoodie…

While she grabbed her keys and tried to brush off as much of Monte's cat fur as possible, she stared at the clock. His fire station was close to the vet. It was nearing noon. Why not take him out to lunch for a treat?

The perfect plan for a perfect man.

* * * *

After standing by the front desk for ten minutes in the hope someone might stop by, Madeline wandered around the side of the fire station. The garage door was up, revealing a peek into another world. A man with what looked like a plastic kid's helmet on his head sat on the cement ground surrounded by a pack of wild fire extinguishers. He kept reaching over, plucking one into his lap, testing the handle, then returning it to the circle. Another man watched on, half of his hoagie's lettuce scattering to the floor as he explained the intricacies of the work.

Beside the firetruck itself stood another two men and a woman, the latter of which was rolling up the hose. None of them were Everett, leaving Madeline uncertain of who to talk to. Maybe the sandwich man could point her in his direction? She took a step inside, then another. Still, no one looked up or toward her.

That damn invisibility cloak must be cranked to high.

On the side were a series of lockers. Most of the contents were spilling out of the cubbies and baskets. Madeline was careful to step over them. She stared down the line of names. E. Berry sat right beside an H. Crawford. The heavy fireman coat hung on the hook. Did that mean he wasn't working or he wasn't out fighting a fire?

"Hey!"

She was so used to being forgotten, Madeline didn't even turn around until the voice added, "You can't be here."

Oh dear. She clung tighter to the hoodie and turned to face origin of the booming voice. It was the tone and temperance of a man who'd brook no challenges to his orders, exactly the kind to turn her knees wobbly.

"I…I'm sorry. I-I waited in the lobby, b-b-but…"

Her head fell out of habit, and she could only see his shoes. They weren't just nice—they shone like he polished them every night.

"What are you doing here?" The tone became clipped and instructive, and Madeline risked a glance up.

Dark eyes struck her first, blacker than Beth's coffee, and short hair with a fade on the sides richer than midnight's toll. His cheeks were gaunt, his face long and chin prominent. It gave him the look of a debonair man who welcomed people to his castle of the damned. The thought caused Maddy to shiver.

"I'm looking for Ev. Everett."

"Berry?" He snorted once, and his tone flipped instantly. "You must be the girl he kept talking about."

Oh gosh. Her cheeks lit bright red. He'd been talking about her? "I don't know anything about…I'm, um, Madeline."

"Hayden," he said, extending his hand to her. As she took it, he cinched his fingers around hers. She expected a hard shake to show his dominance, but Hayden gave a gentle bounce. Before letting go, he brushed his thumb over the back of her hand. "Any friend of Berry is of course welcome to stop by. Right, guys?"

The others gave noncommittal grunts before returning to their jobs. "One big happy family here. Though I'm afraid to tell you he's not in today."

"Oh." *Don't feel bad. It was only supposed to be a chance encounter anyway. Not like they'd planned anything.*

"If you don't mind my being a little nosy, what did you want to see him about?"

"Nothing important," Madeline said feeling more and more foolish for her actions. Who even went to a guy's work unannounced like that? Stalkers, that was who. "I just…he left his sweater at my place, and I wanted to return it to him." She held up the hoodie for proof, and Hayden ran a finger over the sleeve.

He snickered and shook his head. "Leaving his things at a random woman's house. Sounds like Berry."

The hairs on the nape of Madeline's neck stood on end. Random woman? "What does?" she pried.

Hayden smiled bright, his lips framing teeth like tiny kernels of white corn. "Being unable to keep track of his stuff. You wouldn't believe how often I find his coffee mug on my desk. Well, you might since he did the same to you."

A laugh of relief came over Madeline, and she smiled at the man. There she went leaping straight to the worst conclusion, and about Everett Berry no less. Maybe, for once a guy liked her without any malfeasance. "Thank you for telling me. I'm sorry to bother you…" She started to back up, growing red hot at her foolish move, when she remembered the hoodie in her hands. "Could I leave this here for him?"

"I'd be happy to store it for Berry." Hayden reached over to take the sweater, when he paused. "Actually, why don't you take it to him? I believe he's home, been home the past few days. Lots of important work to be done there, I'm guessing."

Of course, his construction. No wonder he'd been so caught up and didn't have time to respond to her. He obviously had to get as much done as he could before returning back to work. With a kick in her step, Madeline took off for Ev's house. "Thank you," she said to the kind man. Why'd she even have a dark thought about him? *It ain't nice to judge people like that, Madeline.* "I think I will try that."

She dashed to escape the garage, when Hayden raised a hand up to wave to her. "I heard talk that he's got someone special visiting him."

Special? Maybe his uncle had returned to help out. *Already meeting the extended estranged family, Maddy Prix? How very forward of you.* She giggled at the thought, then returned the wave once more with a loud, "Thanks ever so much."

* * * *

A giant pile of long, plastic tubes — most the circumference of her fist — rested on the muddy lawn. Seemed the pipe guy had arrived, thrown them from his truck then peeled out. No wonder Everett was in such a state. He had to have been working fast, carrying them all by his lonesome and still unable to get everything inside.

Pity swelled through her, Madeline promising that she'd help. Her couch-carrying skills were legendary. Why would a ten-foot-long pipe be any different?

Skipping up the steps, she pulled back the screen door prepared to knock, only to have the main one blow back. Blonde hair hanging pin-straight from a sweetheart face, cheeks rouged to perfection with a single dimple on the side. Tiny body hugged in a wrap dress of crimson, her short frame hoisted up on stilettos with red soles.

"Kathy," Madeline's stricken brain blurted. It was high school all over again. Kathy Clark, primped and perfect even after gym class, paused to stare at the meat sack stumbling before her.

"Do I...?" she began, when another voice spoke behind her.

"What's the matter?"

For a blisteringly stupid second, Madeline wanted to believe that she'd got the wrong house. By some amazing coincidence, Kathy Clark was living in a place the exact duplicate of her ex-boyfriend's one street over. But as Everett wandered closer, a hand sifting through his matted hair, Madeline caught one look at his bare chest, and everything went dark.

Shame burned up her shins, across her belly, down her chest, and embedded two hot circles on her cheeks. She tried to run away, but her feet were frozen. All she could do was lean back as Kathy's false eyelashes batted in confusion at her.

"Oh, one of the workers," Kathy declared in her sing-song voice. Leaning closer to Everett, she placed a peach coral kiss to his cheek. "See you later, babe," she called, gliding past Madeline as if she weren't even there.

It had to be a nightmare. A cruel one that forced her to watch Kathy, as pretty and thin as when they were eighteen, pause at the sidewalk and turn to wave at Everett. Exactly how she used to down the school hallway while bored teenagers shuffled between them.

Deep inside, Madeline could feel a spark of rage trying to catch. The cruel memories burned hot of how she'd been forced to stand on the sidelines watching the best couple in school display their affection. But from the bottom of her heart sheets of ice crackled. Despair swarmed over the flame, smothering away the anger until all that remained was a broken woman whose eyes pleaded with Everett to make everything not look as it did. He too appeared spooked, like a raccoon caught digging in a trashcan. Both hands raised up, his lips asking, "Maddy?"

"I brought you this," her dead voice announced, and she shoved the hoodie at him.

Everett slapped the sweater to his naked chest, but his eyes wouldn't leave her. "Maddy, I can… This isn't what…"

"No." She skittered away, leaping down a step until Everett loomed above her. *Don't lie to me. Don't add lying to me on top of…everything else.*

"She's…" Madeline scrambled around the dying shrubbery. The words clawed at her throat, leaving it ragged from the truth. "I mean, she's Kathy Clark and I'm…I'm not. You don't need to explain anything. I understand just fine."

It was a miracle she could form anything coherent at all. One half of Madeline's brain was screaming in an eternal rage while the other sobbed in the corner. She had no idea what would come out if she opened her mouth again. Spinning on her foot, Madeline ran from the house.

Everett didn't chase after her, didn't try to calm her down. All he did was stand there and call her name one last time. "Maddy."

Chapter Nine

Please open up!

Madeline raised her fist to knock again, when the door parted a sliver. "Mads?" Beth gasped, hurling the door fully open and wrapping a hand around Madeline's shoulder. Tiny in that adorable and svelte way, Beth had to stretch to reach. She was dressed in one of those robes people stole from spas, her hair drenched.

"I came at a bad time." Madeline winced, realizing she had interrupted Beth's shower.

But Beth, intrepid reporter that she was, ignored Madeline's apology and dove right to business. "What's wrong? You look...well, you look like that time we got food poisoning from Yoshi's Chicken."

A smile at the memory of the horrible week they had spent bonding and puking tried to take, but Madeline's heart was too damaged. Slamming both her arms around Beth's patient shoulders, Madeline burst into tears.

Warm hands patted against her back as Beth closed off the hug Madeline begged for. It was a small reminder she wasn't some hideous creature to be chased by villagers with pitchforks. "Mads, please. I've never…"

Seen me this bad.

"Here, sit. I'll get you something to drink. Eat?" Beth grabbed at the cabinets still sporting a fresh coat of paint. She'd barely moved into her solo place before the sudden book vacation, which meant it was still cleaner than a hotel.

"No food," Madeline gasped, her stomach full to bursting with every memory of Everett. The entire mess roiled.

"Here." Beth picked a simple glass of water, leaving Madeline to attempt to literally drown her sorrows. "What happened?"

"It…it was Ev."

Beth snapped cold in an instant. "What did he do?" Her hands crushed around the plastic cup as if it were glass, and she needed to shatter it for a quick weapon.

"I'm so stupid," Madeline sputtered, her tongue letting free the curse squatting on her brain. *Everett Berry, be with you? Use you, sure.* He'd hit a low and gone dumpster diving. *But to honestly want to date you, be seen in public with you?*

"You are not and you know it. You're amazing." Beth's pep talk had the opposite reaction, Madeline sinking deeper into despair. If she was so amazing, why had he run back to his ex?

"I'm not. I can't be. I can't ever be if…" The truth was laid out in the tea leaves of her past. Men didn't stick around. Not in that 'true love, I can't be without you for the rest of my life' way. Not even in the 'I like you and you help pay rent' way. They'd mess around with her for a few weeks, then move on. Every damn time.

Just like Everett.

He was supposed to be different.

He was different.

"Madeline," Beth chastised her, but like a kindergarten teacher who wants their pupil to succeed way. She drew back a fallen curl and placed it behind Maddy's ear before continuing. "I know you're in a bad place now, but you are the kindest and sweetest person I've ever known."

God save her, she wanted to believe that. To ignore all evidence to the contrary, all fifteen plus years of it, and laugh. *It's not my fault that no man wants me, it's theirs.* That was the most pathetic thing in the world.

But Beth was pouting, and Madeline could never let her down. She moved to pat her friend's hand as if to tell her everything would be okay, when a shadow passed through the hall.

"What is your Wi-Fi password again? I swear this new phone never saves it."

Tristan Harty stepped into the kitchen with nothing on but a pair of low-slung boxers. He was too focused on his phone to notice Madeline trapped in this increasingly awkward situation. The musician glanced up and, at spotting her, leaned back like that would hide his nudity.

"Madeline! I...I didn't realize you had company. Hello."

Her scalp prickled at the tension as her brain pieced together what she had burst in on without a second thought. "Sorry," she muttered, rising so fast the chair tumbled to the floor. "I should have, I mean, you'd be together. Of course." Beth in a robe, Tristan in his underwear, and her stuck in the middle. "And I'm interfering."

Like how you walked in on Everett and Kathy.

The tears started in an instant, Madeline cramming a fist to her eye to hide them.

"Mads…" Beth tried to reach for her, but Madeline was fast to spin and reach for the exit.

"Sorry for bothering you. I'll, I'll leave you alone." She dashed for the door and slammed it shut behind her. Pulling in a breath that felt like broken bottles of acid, Madeline's lips trembled while salty tears dripped down her cheeks. Before any of Beth's neighbors would come to see what broken garbage was wailing outside their door, Madeline ran for it.

* * * *

Huddled in her armchair, Madeline clutched a throw pillow to her chest. She hunched her legs up tighter, her gaze boring through nothing. Exhaustion swarmed, all the pain draining to a dull, unending ache. Napping sounded preferable to being awake. At least in dreams, she could keep pretending none of it had happened.

But as she glanced to the couch, a soul-withering shudder climbed up her spine. God, she was going to have to get rid of it. Or burn it. Or ignore it and wait for the ache to go away. Same as always.

Sparky kept pouncing on her sock, trying to outwit it, but Monte sat perched on the table staring at her. His yellow eyes had homed in on the miserable Madeline when she had stumbled through the door and he wouldn't let up. Nearly an hour on and he monitored her digging her arm tighter into the pillow and sobbing harder.

With a single meow, Monte leaped from the table onto her lap. To her shock, the aristocratic cat began to rub against her arms and purr. He rumbled so hard Madeline reached out to keep her hand from going numb.

Her little Count meowed again and climbed up her chest. Rubbing harder, he itched his face against hers, the whiskers tickling her nose. She wanted to laugh at the sensation, to play with her cat who was now worrying about her, but exhaustion deadened her.

A knock at her door startled Monte. He abandoned his sudden show of affection, acting as if nothing had happened. Wiping off her cheeks and feeling only salt, Madeline rose to her feet. Sparky dug his claws into her sock, and she dragged him across the floor.

Before opening the door, a thought struck her hard. *What if it's him? What if he's here to apologize? To explain?*

What if he was here to tell her off? To explain that she read something else into it and all he wanted was sex?

In her beaten state, Madeline would take the punishment. She opened the lock and tugged back the chain. Five different bags with multiple scents were thrust in her face.

"What the...?" She staggered back before looking up into the forced smile of her best friend.

"I got dinner," Beth said, revealing she was carrying food from their favorite sushi, pizza, Indian, sandwich and Italian places.

"You got a week's worth." Madeline snorted, sliding back to let her in. She made certain to keep the kitten inside the apartment as Beth busied herself with laying out a feast Roman emperors couldn't have finished.

When the first two plates hit the table, Madeline flinched from deep in her fog. "What are you doing here? What about Tristan?"

Beth placed a hand on her hip. "He's an adult. He can handle himself."

Wincing at the innuendo, Madeline continued on, "But you two don't get to see each other very often, and…"

"Mads." She grabbed Madeline's shoulders, pausing the apologizing inquisition. "You are in pain. Don't try and deny it. I know you too well. No way will I let my best friend suffer without me just for some…boy." Beth let go and pulled out the mass of egg rolls she always insisted on. With one in her hand, she said, "Boys are stupid," and took a massive bite.

Beyond stupid. Break your heart into a million pieces and leave you on the curb stupid. Answer your wildest dreams, then turn around to be with the pretty girl stupid. Incapable of caring while acting like they did stupid.

"Let's see," Beth announced, "I got a medium pizza because that's all you ever want. Some Po'Boys, which are not easy to come by right now. A pile of chicken parm, and a basket of—"

Madeline launched forward, enveloping Beth in her arms. Her friend dropped the banquet and turned to hug her. "Thank you," Madeline gasped, "thank you for…" *Caring about me.*

"Any time, sickness or health."

Chapter Ten

What in the nine hells was he doing? He let her walk away without any explanation. Stood stupid on the porch, thicker than the bricks left piling up under the foundation, just staring in the distance as she ran. *Everett Berry, what is wrong with you?*

That counselor would have said he was 'repeating the same old patterns.' He hadn't even wanted to go, the whole thing nothing more than being told to read the Bible, pray on it and somehow the marriage would be fixed. Was God gonna repair the missing chunk she took out of his scalp, too?

Numb fingers brushed over the hole where no hair would grow. He'd been trying to hide it under longer hair, to forget it, but every trip to the barber brought it all right back. *Can you cover that bald spot with a part? Yeah, wife got mad and burned it with her curling iron. You know how it goes.*

He heard the clutch popping before seeing his truck creep over the horizon. Everett's legs started moving before his brain did. He leaped off the rotting porch and jogged around the pipes after the woman who'd taken his truck without even asking. She'd snatched the keys off the table while he was washing his face. Again.

"I got coffee," Kathy called with her full Carolina lilt. Before she could turn the keys, Ev reached in through the window and yanked them out himself.

"Why did you say that? Why did you do that?"

"Do what? Get you coffee?" She hopped to the grass in her heels, the pink and yellow dress far too thin for winter in New York weather. "Yes, how dare I be so kind and considerate." Kathy thrust the cup at him, forcing Ev to accept it or face boiling coffee splatting on his jeans.

"You weren't considerate to Maddy."

"Who?" Kathy blinked her eyes rapidly as if her brain couldn't run without a kick from them.

"Maddy, Madeline Prix. The girl you…" He stared back at the porch where his old hoodie had fallen.

"That was Ol' MacDonald herself? Whew, she ain't changed much, huh?"

"Don't go calling her…" Ev argued at her, but Kathy gave him the full sorority sister glare. It had been known to wither ten men's spines to jelly in under five seconds. Every past misdeed roiled in Ev's mind, his head hanging as if he felt a need to confess.

The door knocking against the hinges drew him back to the porch where the good thing he'd chased after had been smashed to pieces. And Kathy knew what she was doing. With a snarl, he swiped at his cheek, finding a smear of her lipstick on his hand. "Why'd you goddamn kiss me? You're here as a favor to your ma'am."

"Oh God, Evie, stop getting so bent out of shape. It's what they do in France."

"We ain't in France!" He wanted to tear his own hair out and finish what the burn mark had started. But as his voice carried across the rundown but quiet street, heads poked out of windows. Blistering with the knowledge that he had a foot and a hundred pounds on Kathy, Ev dropped his open hand to his thigh.

She gave her 'I won' smirk, sashayed to the porch and went right into his house as if she owned the place. Ev pulled in a deep breath. *Visualize the words. Think about the tone. Be forceful*. He strode for the door she had left open and called in from the threshold. "Weren't you gonna be gone in a couple days? That was a couple days back already."

Kathy didn't go near the power tools, nor the mess of sheetrock he needed to put up. No, she skipped past it like a fairy that could only sleep in the petals of a rare orchid. "I told you, I have another audition."

"When?"

That paused her from scampering up to the half-finished bedroom she had claimed, leaving him with a sleeping bag in the kitchen in his own house. "Why? Why're you so quick to get rid of me, Everett Berry? You think there's something better out there?"

Yes. There was sweeter. He opened his mouth, prepared to get her out of his house, when she turned her venom on him.

This weren't no fast-acting neurotoxin. No, Kathy'd had decades to perfect the slow pan down his body with her eyes, the rising tick of a sneer on her lips, and the cross of her arms as she steadied herself for a war. "What makes you think you'd deserve better?"

"Well…"

"Failed at college, failed at your construction job. Failed at marriage. You're nothing but a big, fat failure. Anyone with a lick of sense in her brain will see right through that. If she won't at first 'cause you smile pretty, she sure will when you ruin her life."

Damn it. Ev tried to find calm, but every breath out shot from his nose like a rampaging bull. He never should have answered the door when he'd seen who it was. Kathy could ruin heaven itself if she thought the clouds weren't fluffy enough. But…deep in his heart, he knew she was right.

Maddy… What was he thinking? It'd never work.

"Oh, don't pout so much." Kathy swept around him, sliding under his arm the same way she had in high school. Almost like she'd never even left. "I'm here. Who knows you better than me? Good and bad. I'll help you clean this pigsty up, give it a lady's touch."

"Then you'll find your own place?"

Her lipstick barely twitched, and she nodded. "Of course. Now, if you'll excuse me, I have to take a call with my agent."

Like that, Kathy vanished to her important call, leaving Ev standing alone in the cold. He reached back to close the front door, when he caught sight of his hoodie still left on the ground. Picking it up, he was about to wad it up under his arms, when he spotted two hairs. One was black as night and very short, the other red as fire. As he picked the red off, it twirled around his finger.

"Were you raised in a barn? Shut the front door!"

"Sorry," Everett mumbled, pushing his last means of escape closed.

* * * *

A week and a half on and nothing had changed. She hadn't even gotten through half of the food Beth had left behind. Madeline was unable to summon the energy to bother microwaving it. If her stomach had growled in hunger, she'd rolled over and ignored it.

She'd driven herself hard to forget Everett, to forget his face, his scent, his smile. Taking on three website side projects on top of her main one, Madeline was up all hours of the night and day coding and formatting as fast as her system could keep up. Until the fateful day she dared to check her phone to find tons of private messages from people concerned about her lack of new kitten pics.

They all referenced the video of Everett nuzzling Sparky against his cheek.

Her in-control farce had imploded. Madeline had slunk off to bed and refused to get out until her heart stopped aching. It'd worked for about an hour until her gluttonous cat bounced four paws onto her face. Monte was forever concerned where his next meal came from. "The only reason you don't eat me is because I feed you," Madeline muttered to her occasional companion but altogether thorn. Her cat took it all with a shrug, well aware of his limitations and not caring how others viewed him.

"I wish I had that kind of confidence. Or the energy to wash my hair." She feared there were small colonies of undiscovered civilizations nesting in her matted curls. If she put it off any longer, the whole thing wouldn't be salvageable and she might get to learn if she could work bald.

She shuffled for the kitchen, her feet never leaving the floor, until she caught Sparky leaping at something. At least he could still find joy in the world. With deadened limbs, Madeline rustled for the cat food tin. She grabbed the first one in the cupboard without caring what it was. She used to change them up so her Count didn't get bored. Now it was too much work to bother.

"Here you go, your highness," she muttered, dropping the dish on the counter. Monte gave her a long slow glare as if sizing her up before leaping to eat. With him busy, Madeline reached for the kitten food, when a knock bounced off her door.

"It's open." She muttered the same line she'd told any delivery guy and the one Jehovah's Witness who'd probably regretted his missionary work.

Instead of them, it was Beth who stuck her head in. She glanced to the living room and the chair where Madeline whiled away most of her life before whipping over to find all three of them by the counter. "That's dangerous, Mads. You should lock it."

Madeline shrugged. Way she saw it, either burglars would realize she was in here and leave, or…it wouldn't be her problem anymore. Turning back to Sparky, she made dead certain he was the one to eat his food and not the full-grown cat eyeing up the tasty, extra-meaty kitten chow.

"When did you last leave your apartment?" Beth asked, digging a finger into the stale takeout box piled up beside the chair. "Mads?"

"I don't remember. I think I had to get milk for…" She waved to Sparky whose entire muzzle was covered in 'filet mignon'.

"And then…?" Beth prompted as if that weren't a good enough reason.

"What and then? Why would there be an and then? What could possibly be outside that I'd need?" She crossed her arms over the Care Bear-themed sweatshirt, the brown one with his heart crumpling in half. It wasn't an outfit one wore in public, or even alone on laundry day. Had she put a bra on? Or panties?

Beth, the stubborn fixer of things, stomped closer. She eyed up Madeline's knotted mane, the dropped noodles that had found a home on the top of her cleavage and the kitty litter stains along her fingers. "You need a change of scenery," Beth announced after taking in the mess.

"I don't want to go anywhere," Madeline whined. "Everyone's in their Christmas gear, singing carols, drinking cocoa, talking about visiting Rockefeller Center without doing it because oh my God the traffic." Happy.

She couldn't stand the happy people. Every smile sent her deeper into her cocoon. It wasn't fair to them. They all had loved ones to be jolly with. Madeline had her cats who'd at least wait a few hours before eating her if she died. Monte was a gentleman like that.

"Trust me, Mads." Beth grabbed her hand and tugged on her like Madeline was an exhausted toddler. "Where I'm taking you, there will be no Christmas cheer."

Madeline tried to muster up an excuse, but she couldn't find the energy to be bothered. Instead, she let Beth pull her from her apartment regardless of how unready she was to see the world.

* * * *

Beth was going to kill her.

The thought was ludicrous. Beth was a good friend who had absolutely nothing to gain from Madeline's murder, but it was all she could think as they pulled up next to an abandoned pit of despair. A single, sad chunk of sidewalk lingered beside the curb, the rest obliterated to dust.

Instead of an ice cream shop or a new gym, it was the beginning of a concrete graveyard with the bones of the city prodding from the ground. Brown weeds prodded between the abandoned steel beams left rusting into the topsoil, most of them with jagged saw leaves that'd puncture gloves. Madeline clung to the seatbelt as she stared in horror at the mess it had taken them almost a half hour to reach.

Beth, seeming to be unaware of the terrors, leapt from the borrowed car with Minnesota license plates and dashed for the crumpled steel sign. Whatever it once was had been long bleached away by time. "Well, what do you think?"

Retracting the seatbelt, Madeline eased to the edge of the car. She tested the ground, fearing it too would somehow crumble under her weight and send her careening straight to the devil's hot tub. "Is this one of those visualizing things?" she asked carefully. "See how much worse your life could be? At least you have a house that isn't this?"

"What? No. Mads, look." Beth pointed past the obliterated chunks of concrete to a torn up chain-link fence in the distance. "See all the way to that line, that's where this property ends."

Uh-huh. Her friend could find some strange paths when she was researching articles. One year Beth had gotten into pickling, leaving Madeline with a bathtub full of jarred vegetables no one in their right mind would eat. But a passion for property lines of condemned lots seemed out there even for her.

The longer Madeline stared at her without speaking, the more Beth kept waving as if she'd get it. To finish, Beth pointed both hands to the single twisted tree and shouted, "It's a park."

A needle park, maybe.

"There's a grass area, there's already some fencing, though you can add more, of course."

"What do you mean *I* can add?" All she could see were the destroyed remains of what had once been, but her friend pranced around like it was a diamond.

Beth paused before she dashed over the rotted guts of a wall and returned to Madeline's side. "You keep saying you want to have your own rescue center."

"Oh, come on." Madeline turned away, almost rolling her eyes at the thought. "That's just…talk. Dreams."

"Maybe it's time to stop talking and start doing."

"You have got to stop doing puff pieces on influencers. It's rotting your brain."

Beth sighed but did snicker a moment before she took both of Madeline's hands and turned her around to face the mess. "Long as I've known you, all you've gone on about is wanting one thing."

To marry Everett Berry. She wasn't so foolish as to think one night together meant he'd do right by her honor, and they'd run off to the chapel. But that had been her dream once. She'd nearly forgotten about that silly girl who'd rescued crabs and dreamed of marrying her beach prince.

"I don't," Madeline began, tears rising in her eyes. She shook them off and focused on the new mess Beth wanted her to bring into her life. Though this would be one for her, for the kittens and cats left forgotten in the rain. *Don't be silly, Madeline Prix.* "I don't even know how to swing a hammer."

"It's not that difficult." Beth jammed a hand to her hip and stared her up and down. "I can teach you how."

My own rescue center? The whole idea was ludicrous. Madeline Prix running a place with those little bubble windows so the kittens could look in at the visitors. A huge cat tree in the middle of the adoption area where they'd be allowed to climb to their heart's content. And a porch... she'd dreamed of a big porch where the fattest, laziest cats could sleep in the rocking chairs under the summer sun.

No, she couldn't. She didn't have the time, the talent. How was she going to rebuild this place from nothing? "I can't," Madeline said, causing Beth to sigh and shake her head. "I get it, you're trying to give me a project so I won't think about..."

"Fuck him. This has nothing to do with men who I won't wish hookworms would swim up the urethra of because you think it's mean. Mads." Beth dodged to get in Madeline's waning view. "You don't need him to make your life worthwhile. You don't need the ring to chase after your dream."

Says the woman already sporting hers. Madeline flinched at the cruel thought that invaded her mind. "How...? There's no way I could afford even this land."

At that moment, an eardrum-rattling bass dropped from a car turning down the road. Madeline didn't know much about cars, but that one was fancy. She expected it to roar on past, but as the wheels came to a slow then a stop, she swiveled to Beth.

"Funny you should ask," her friend said before adjusting her business casual clothes.

In horror, Madeline stared down at her stained and warped sweatshirt and even sadder sweatpants. *Who the heck is in that car? Beth!*

"You've heard of Chantelle?"

"Some music person, I think." Madeline tried to remember back to the growing Rolodex of Beth's contacts. Since she had started dating Tristan, it had gotten a lot more terrifyingly A-list.

"Writer, actor, singer, that sort of thing. Well, they're in the musical with Tristan, and we got to talking…"

Madeline's focus twisted from the mystery guest to her friend revealing vital information out of nowhere. "Musical?"

"The one he's subbing for after the last guy was caught, well, you know. I told you all about it."

Did she? Shame bubbled up inside her, each surge telling Madeline she was an awful friend. *How did I forget that Tristan's in a musical?* Sure, he could sing, and sort of shuffle around dancing. But…

"Can he act?" Madeline asked.

Beth's genuine smile flattened to a grimace, and she wafted her hand back and forth. "Eh. He's got four months to figure it out. Chantelle!"

A flurry of Skittles flounced from the back of the car. It took Madeline a moment to see past the berry-hued skirts covered in giant beads to find a body below. A hula-hoop-sized necklace hung off their neck, rolling around as they dashed first to Beth's side. The two traded air kisses, then Chantelle turned to the site. "It's amazing, isn't it?"

"Chantelle, this is who I was telling you all about. Madeline Prix."

"Ah, the cat lady." Chantelle extended a hand gloved in purple mesh like an old-fashioned lady would to a gentleman. Madeline took it, uncertain what to do with it. She settled for a weak shake before forcing on a smile.

"Sorry about how I'm dressed. I…"

"Oh, don't be silly. Couch chic is very popular right now in Milan. Love the bit of nostalgia too." They pointed to the Care Bear warped by Madeline's bosom. "I take it our little Beth here has told you all about my plans."

"Your plans?" Madeline whispered. She thought she'd be the one in charge of the center from layout to day-to-day affairs.

Chantelle fluffed the ruffles on their shoulders and shimmied back and forth. "This whole area is such a dour mess. I can't stand it. I've been working with various local artists, free-thinkers and dreamers to turn this neighborhood into something spectacular."

Gentrification was hardly anything new, but what did that have to do with Madeline? Or an outrageous singer who was in a musical with Tristan?

"And what better to suit my kitschy Americana meets technicolor dream than a kitty cat rescue center right beside the future bookstore?"

Um. Madeline swiveled to find that a rundown factory that proclaimed to make pencil erasers sat in the lot one over. Chantelle waved a hand at it. "We're still working on that lot. Don't worry, in two years it'll be a beautiful bookstore shaped like a pile of novels in a basket. Eduardo has the plans."

Chantelle snapped their fingers for whoever this Eduardo was, or maybe the plans themselves, but Madeline kept shaking her head. "This all sounds very…exciting. But I don't have the kind of money to rent a lot."

"Oh, don't worry." Chantelle smiled and winked. "I own it."

"You do?" Madeline sputtered.

Leaning to her ear, Beth whispered, "Oil money. Very old oil money."

Madeline's eyes bugged. The person dressed like a parrot shaking its feathers off under a waterfall could be a secret Vanderbilt or Rockefeller. Unaware of Madeline's brain clogging, Chantelle handed over a hand-drawn image of an idyllic street where children played soccer, ice cream was sold in carts and a kitty cat adoption center sat in the center. "That's where you'd be. See, isn't that bookstore the cutest thing you've ever seen? I want to spend an entire afternoon there already."

"You…" Madeline stared at the plans, then looked into the sharp gray eyes hidden behind blue sunglasses. "You're serious?"

"As a heart attack. Beth couldn't cease extolling your skills as a kitty whisperer. I did have a little looky-loo through your socials. Adorable, and a built-in audience base will help greatly in the first few months. Now, my charity should be able to finance the first year of operations, but I hope to have it running independent in eighteen months—"

"Wait, charity? How…what exactly do you want me to do?" Madeline had her own business. It involved her sitting in front of a computer shouting at code, but it paid the bills. This sounded like a wish ready to go full monkey's paw at a moment's notice.

Chantelle placed their cheek next to Madeline's and swiveled her head to face the lot. Waving a hand, they said, "You do your magic."

"Uh…"

Beth stepped in. "You'll have complete creative and operational control as long as the project does not run more than ten percent over budget and can become self-sufficient in two years."

"Yes, all of those legal things." Chantelle puffed at the necessary details that left Madeline's jaw dangling. They wanted her to run the place? "My team will be by later with the forms for you to sign, background checks, all that boring stuff. Oh, and we should get someone to stop by and clean all that up. There's wonder to create."

"Uh-huh." Madeline nodded dumbly as Chantelle hugged her, then skipped for the car.

"I'm afraid I must dash. They have new lines for Lydia. Talk to you later, cat lady. Beth, give your sourpuss a hug from me."

"He'll hate that," Beth called out with a laugh.

Chantelle shoved their head through the window and smiled diabolically. "I know."

As fast as the typhoon had entered her life, Chantelle vanished, leaving Madeline gawping at the site. "What just happened?"

She hadn't felt a surge of emotion in weeks. It wasn't pity or despair, not exhaustion or anger. No, staring at the death trap on a rundown street, Madeline finally felt hope.

Beth hugged her tight and said, "The start of something amazing. Now let's get out of here before we freeze to death."

Her own rescue center. There was so much to do, to get ready. Madeline had to read up on construction, on the city's laws. She'd have to dust off her old business class notes. Call the other shelters. Her life had gotten much too busy for some silly old Everett Berry to fit into it.

Still, even as she ran to Beth's car, her mouth chattering with a thousand long dormant ideas, her heart wondered what Ev would think of her little park.

Chapter Eleven

Three months later

"Why isn't this working?!"

He did not need that squeal this early in the morning. Everett stumbled down the rickety stairs he should have replaced the supports on two months ago. There'd been plans to finish at least the main hall during his time off, but it was all wasted in a blink of an eye. Dressed in his blacks proclaiming him to be a proud member of the NYC firefighters, he darted around a tall tool chest that had become a permanent fixture in the house.

She stood over the sink trying to push on the knob. With her blonde hair swept up into a skin-tightening ponytail, Kathy snapped it around like a whip to turn her accusations on him.

"I told you." Everett groaned. "You have to use the wrench." Yanking up the requisite tool, he hooked it to the shut-off valve he had installed to make the kitchen sink usable. A stream of piss-yellow water dribbled from the faucet, then the clear stuff followed. "There."

Tossing the wrench to the counter, he turned to fish out his cereal box. Kathy wasn't finished yet, her lip in a full-on pout. Or maybe that was the lipstick she painted outside her natural thin line.

"Why haven't you fixed it yet? I've asked you to put a sink in time and time again, but all you do is sit around on your ass. You're so damn worthless!"

Hm, his cereal box felt a lot lighter. Hefting it out of the cupboard, he poured three O's and a pile of dust into his plastic bowl. Great. No breakfast, which was probably also his fault.

"Ya know, if you don't like it, there's the door." Everett waved in the direction of the new stained-glass door she'd insisted on. It had cut deep into his budget, but she'd said it was vital for curb appeal. The curb with weeds splitting up from the cracks.

Kathy's hackles smoothed as she curled a hand to his arm. Everett flinched at her touch, but as she smiled, he tried to relax the knot in his spine. "Babe," Kathy cooed in his ear. "Don't think that. I'm here for you, no matter what."

Ha. Sure. For better or for worse.

"Okay," he answered in resignation. "I should get to work." Shrugging her off, he fished for the new coat the city winter required. It made him feel like he was being eaten by marshmallows, but at least it was warm. Unlike when the heat in his place broke for a week, and Kathy had insisted they stay at a hotel. He knew better than to argue money with her. Ever.

"My poor baby," she kept cooing and tugging back the hair that stuck to his forehead. "They run you so ragged."

Someone has to pay the bills.

"I like it," Everett said, a pained smile on his lips. Kathy leaned closer to peck a kiss to them. Before it dawned on him to return the affection, she was already busying herself with whatever she needed the sink for. Midway out the kitchen door, Everett said, "And make sure to turn that off when you're done." There were no more shifts he could pick up to pay for a massive water bill.

"I know, I know." Kathy waved him on. Did she listen? He wouldn't know until he got a warning from the utilities company.

Stumbling into the gray March morning, clouds rumbling across the horizon for yet another cold rain, Everett sighed. He thought his life was going to jump to a new track when he moved here. Why did this feel like he was stuck in place?

* * * *

Don't panic.

Madeline stared across the cleaned and prepped grounds ready for a fence, the poured foundation ready for walls, a noticeable lack of either, and the panic attempted to burst from her chest and spew all over the contractor. He'd appeared one day, as had the handful of dumpsters and workers chucking bits of the old building inside. The first meeting had been him barking orders at Madeline and ignoring her every time she tried to show him the plans.

"Why is there a gap?" she asked sweetly, her lips pursed into a smile so tight her jaw ached.

Mr. Jensen shifted the wad of gum in his cheeks to the other side and hitched up his belt. "'Cause we ain't got the fourth wall."

She'd been on pins and needles this week. All the hours and months digging in the mud, laying out the foundation, putting in permits and begging for approval had finally led to this. But instead of raising the pre-built walls shipped in from elsewhere and nailing them to the support beams, all they could do was stand around and stare.

When Madeline had arrived, they'd been nailing up the first two sides. But as she got out of the car, the nail guns came down and all the men stared around like they were waiting for a bus. "I don't understand," she whispered. "Why isn't there another wall?"

"Says it's caught on a dock somewhere."

"But you have the others."

Jenson's solitary response was to shrug and gnash on his gum wad.

The animal center had been her life since accepting the project. The plans would even dance about in her dreams, taunting her with paint swatches. Now, she glared at the half-skeleton house with a handful of walls circling the outside while a brave squirrel dashed into the middle and nicked someone's sandwich.

This was a disaster.

Her phone rang. Madeline answered without looking because if she glared at the gaps long enough maybe the missing walls would appear. "Hello?" *Please be the shipping company promising they'll drop off the next load in fifteen minutes.*

"Darling!"

Shit. Madeline mouthed it, but Jensen caught her and smirked. "Hey, Chantelle. What's...up?"

"Wonderful news. That frozen yogurt stand will be both vegan and organic."

And what does that have to do with me? "Great," Madeline said, fighting to put any enthusiasm in her voice.

"Things are coming along swimmingly... What? I think Tristan has the book."

Madeline blinked at the sudden shift in topic. "Are you...at rehearsal?"

"Of course, love. Don't worry, it's a mess on stage and they have very little need of me. You know how it goes — the director has a minor heart attack, screams he'll fire everyone, trounces off, then returns with cupcakes. Typical jitters."

As long as Madeline lived, she would never get used to working for Chantelle.

"So, got any cute kittens yet?"

"We're..." Madeline gulped and stared at the pile of chain-link gates left lying in the mud. They were supposed to be put up next week beside those walls that didn't exist. "We're a few weeks out from being able to add any cats."

"Oh, don't fret over the details."

That is literally my job.

"What matters is the vision. And we're all excited to see what you've come up with. In fact, I might be able to pull off a little *coup de grâce* of my own."

Madeline hugged tight to her phone, her heart racing. "What is it?"

Chantelle's voice turned light as whipped cream. "It's a surprise, darling."

"Well, if that's all...I should let you get back to rehearsing." The big musical was going to open in less than a month. She hadn't seen much of Beth since then, and when she did, her friend looked ready to claw apart anyone that so much as hummed. Life with a famous singer maybe wasn't all sunshine and roses.

"And you return to making magic!"

Yeah. Wave my fingers and make walls appear from nowhere. Madeline said a few more goodbyes— Chantelle always needed at least four before hanging up. She said them on autopilot while scrolling back through emails to find anyone to contact about missing walls.

As she was about to end the call, Chantelle's strong voice suddenly called out, "Oh, and a building inspector will be by later today."

What?

"An inspector?"

"Yes, from the city. Have to make certain it doesn't all fall over or burn down. Boring stuff."

Not fall over? Madeline swiveled to the walls bouncing in the spring wind against their pathetic tether. Mother's sweet tea, they were gonna condemn this whole site. Then what? She was supposed to receive ten adorable kittens in a month for the soft opening. Where would they go? Could she keep that many in her apartment?

In such a panic, she barely heard Chantelle say, "He's some fireman so watch for a big red truck. Bye!"

Fireman? No.

No, it couldn't be.

She didn't have time to ask Jenson what to do. She didn't have time to even think to call whoever worked for the city and cancel. Her brain barely had a chance to churn over the idea that it could be Everett Berry walking into her life to destroy it just as a car with a fire station emblem on the door rolled up to the site.

She was doomed.

* * * *

Everett strolled into the station. Willy and Christopher were hard at work arguing over who had to clean the truck. Ev thought he could sneak past both, when Will shouted, "Hey, new meat!"

Five months on, and he was still the newbie who had to smile and take all their shit. It was preferable to the other nickname.

"Phew, you're nearly late there, you lucky sonnofa."

There it was. It began the first time Kathy had stopped by the station and all the guys got to ogle her in a skirt far too short for winter. In an instant, they took to calling him the lucky sonnofabitch who didn't deserve someone so fine at home. Everett had shaken it off with an "I know, I know" back then, but now he was tempted to tell one of them to take her.

Will was in his late forties, divorced and balding, but Chris might be able to swing a chance if he didn't always smell like mustard and garlic. The former smacked Christopher in the arm with the sponge. "You know how he gets when you mention his lady."

"Only if I do it around him," Christopher admitted before blanching and whipping his head over. "Nothing too bad. But damn, man. She is fine. Even for New York fine and there's models all over the place."

"It's…" Everett reached a hand out, watching Chris' body shrink. When he patted the man on the shoulder, he said, "…cool. Talk don't mean anything."

"Exactly right. Though if your lady ever wanted to get into a three-way with two firefighters…"

"She'd ask for me," Jill Reed said. "Ain't none of you boys know how to work a hose, never mind man one."

That left Chris and Will groaning, but they had to swallow their curses as Jill was a captain to their meager lieutenant status. "Hey, newb." She slapped Everett on the back and walked him away from the two who had yet to get to work.

"You okay there, Berry? You look a little peaked around...everything."

"Just..." He rubbed at his jaw and winced at the razor burn. "The curse of sleeping in a house under construction."

"Well, if it gets bad you should bunk here. No one wants a drowsy firefighter on call. Understand?"

"Got it." He shook off the lingering sleep in his eyes. That had to be all it was. "Was there anything else or..."

"You're on inspection duty," Jill announced, bringing an instant groan to Everett. "Gonna start giving me the same amount of lip as those two?" She passed him the sheets required of every inspector. They were long, tedious and amounted to a backache with very little of the romantic aspects of the job. No one was going to swoon over a fireman in his black T-shirt and pants filling out paperwork.

"Who will be training me?" Everett asked, annoyance thundering in his voice.

"You're gonna be tailing Crawford on this one." She read his disgust at the idea in an instant. "What beef do you two have?"

"None. None at all." There wasn't a single cross word Ev could point to, nor any cruel action to justify his feelings. But he flat out didn't like the man. Every time he was near him he waited for a reason, but five months on he had nothing. And everyone else seemed to love him.

"I'm not here to be your therapist, so get over it and get to work." Captain Reed turned to walk to the break room before pausing. "And the chief wants to see you. Now, Lieutenant!" She clapped her hands, causing Everett's body to twitch and dash for the stairs. In an instant, the entire firehouse broke into laughter, everyone enjoying the joke at the newbie's expense.

Everett joined in because he knew how this worked. Lifting his legs, he gave a stupid dance as if he had any tap skills. With that, Ev climbed the stairs three at a time. Down one hall was the bunk house for those on call, down the other the chief's domain.

"Get in here," came the low rumble of Chief Parsons before Ev could knock. Chief Parsons sat perched behind his desk, hunting and pecking at a keyboard attached to a computer that ran Windows 7. With bulldog features and a smooth head, Chief Parsons looked like the kind of man who'd rip out your jugular.

"Sit down, Berry. Cookie?" the chief asked while foisting over a massive pile of oatmeal raisin cookies on a platter.

"Ah, just one," Ev said despite his hatred of raisins. *Never refuse a boss's offer of cookies.* "Uh, sir?" He pointed to a black smear spread across the back of the chief's brown hand. "You have a...a mark?"

"From the grandkids. Don't worry about it. It's permanent." Parsons crammed a cookie in his mouth. Chewing thoughtfully, the chief sized up Everett who was trying to not fidget. "You're young, ain't ya, Berry?"

"Um…I'm twenty-nine, sir." Was this a test to see if he was mature enough for more work? Or to see if he was spry enough to take the harder work?

"Excellent." Parsons slapped his desk. "You must be in touch with the youths and their phones and apps and whatnot."

Did he think twenty-nine equaled high school? Regardless, Everett kept his mouth shut.

The chief pulled a file out of a drawer in his desk. "Every year we have a little dance. Raise money for the force, show we're out there in the community. You know the drill. Old Moses used to run it, but his eyes have been going and, between you and me, he ain't got it anymore."

"I under…of course." Everett nodded along as if he knew what they were talking about. He'd seen Moses once, the man shuffling back to the break room at the announcement of donuts.

"So, here." The chief dropped his file on Everett's lap, then returned to his ancient computer.

"Here what?" Everett thought aloud, turning the folder around to see it was marked 'Firemen Balls'. They hadn't missed the opportunity to draw a dick and scrote on the cover either.

Parsons picked up another cookie. "You run the ball. It's this May. We always do it in May. Lovely time of year, May."

"I don't know anything about how to…"

The friendly, happy-go-lucky man vanished, and the pit bull emerged. Punching a fist to the desk, the chief rose to his full height over the sitting man. "What part do you think you have a choice in? I give the orders, you do 'em. And that's how it works until you become chief. Get it?"

"Ye…yes, sir." Everett nodded, his stomach sinking. Plan a fancy New York ball, dance, whatever? Last time he was at a party, the refreshments were a keg, the music a radio in a truck and the entertainment was drunkenly chasing pigs. "This party…?"

"Ball."

Everett nodded as if he knew what the difference was. "Is it important?"

"If you want to keep your job, it is. Money raised helps us to afford the new recruits."

Shit. "Then I'll get right on it," Everett shouted.

Parsons launched to his feet, the tray back in his hands. "Take one more for the road. I shouldn't eat 'em. Doctor says they're bad for my blood." The chief chowed down on his third.

After taking one more cookie, Everett tramped down the stairs. He tried to read through the file, but his brain couldn't decipher the words. Plan a party. Host a ball so important if they didn't raise enough money he was out on the streets? Then what? He was barely hanging in already. To lose this job would…

It'd send him right back to the little town that spread gossip like venereal wildfire. All those snickers behind hands and orders for him to man up already.

"Hey, Berry."

Oh God, not now.

Hayden Crawford leaned against the company car with a wide smile. "I was about to head out to start inspections."

And he'd been ordered to spend the entire day beside Hayden while not fussing over the massive albatross the chief had hung off his neck. Hayden probably knew about this, maybe even suggested him for it.

He loomed over Ev. "You ready to come with?"

Ev swallowed and took in a breath. How much worse could his day get?

Chapter Twelve

The car door cracked open as the clouds overhead opened up, blanketing whoever came to inspect Madeline's pile of rubble in golden light. She threw a hand above her eyes and fought against the tears to try to squint. Was that blond hair?

Her heart stilled, her breath collapsed and her legs tried to run in every direction.

The heavenly gold faded to reveal a man with dark hair, and Madeline could breathe. It wasn't him. But when she looked again, his face sang to the back of her brain.

"Good morning, Miss, I'm —"

"The building inspector," she called over top of him. Madeline's cheeks burned, and she danced back and forth as he clipped closer. He looked like a man typecast as the rake with a heart of gold. The sharpest of his features were the eyes, black as ebony and deep-set below a prominent brow.

"Do I know you from somewhere?" Madeline asked.

His tight lips slipped upward into a smile. "You keep stealing the words from my mouth. Hayden." He extended his hand, and she took it. "Hayden Crawford."

"Madeline Prix." She shook his hand with care, the jelly feeling dropping from her stomach to her legs. *Bet if you fell, he'd catch you.*

Quiet, brain.

"I believe you booked me for the hour." He said it so innocuously Madeline choked at her brain leaping to impure thoughts. Mr. Crawford's gaze drifted to the construction site reminding her there were bigger problems afoot. "That doesn't look good."

"I know. The walls, they're…" She tried to wave in the construction manager, but he'd hunkered down over his phone and refused to look up. "On the dock? I'm so sorry about this, about wasting your time. I had no idea you were even coming, and the walls being…or the fences. Should we at least put the fences up?"

"Wait, wait." Hayden caught her frantic hands that'd been swinging between panicking and praying. He ensnared the back of her hands and wrapped his fingers around. "It's all right, no need to fret. We'll get it all sorted. Let me call my assistant."

He turned back to the car and whistled. Whoever was in there was hidden by shadows, but Madeline's concern was all about her pile of dirt. "What is this project?"

A disaster. Without any walls or fences no one could see what she was trying to create, and it was all Madeline's fault. She should have been diligently tracking the supplies, messaged Jensen to make certain everything had arrived and kept Chantelle in the loop so they wouldn't do anything unexpected. Three months in and all she had to show for her work was a dirt lot and the skeletal frame of her dreams.

"An animal shelter," Madeline whispered.

Hayden snorted, unimpressed by her unimpressive building. "Ah, you got the clipboard?" he said to his assistant, beckoning Madeline to turn around.

Shuck an oyster!

"Hi, Maddy."

Her mouth opened.

You have some nerve showing your face around here, Everett Berry!

Her mouth closed. Damn, he looked like an angel strolling off the beach. The sun cast a golden halo around the crown of his hair.

A breath slipped from her that held a single, squeaky, "You…"

Hayden glanced up from the clipboard, his eyebrow raising as he turned from Madeline to Ev. "You know her, Berry?"

Tell him how you slept with me, then ran back to your perfect ex. Laugh at how stupid I was for thinking for a second that you'd ever like me.

Though, as cruel as that sounded, it'd be preferable to him denying he'd ever met her. Did Ev even think about that night, or had he erased it from his memory?

"Yeah, we went to school together," he whispered and lowered his gaze right to Madeline's. She expected a sneer, a smirk, anything but the stricken shock on his face.

"Small world. Let's see here." Hayden flipped up the pages that Madeline recognized had her handwriting. *Did she fill that out? When?* "Your site is owned by…Rock and Stone Oil?"

"Um, yes? Is that a problem?" She'd had to visit the big fancy office in Manhattan once. Madeline, dressed like a kindergarten teacher, had been hemmed in by a dozen faceless men in gray suits while Chantelle presented like a flamingo dipped in gold. It had been the most awkward day of her life…until Everett Berry strolled back into it.

Hayden glanced to the pile of rubble, and he rubbed his chin. "No, reputable company. I'm surprised they'd be treating this so…lackadaisically."

"It's more of a passion project," she admitted.

"You're getting your kitten center?" Ev asked and, for a brief window, all that had happened between them vanished. With glee, Madeline turned to him and bobbed her head up and down.

"There's gonna be a park area, and a porch, and I've found a swing where the kitties can sleep, and…" *He walked out on you. Left you crying into buckets of oatmeal until your cat comforted you.* "Assuming it gets off the ground." She turned away and stared at the old factory that had yet to be even torn down for Chantelle's bookstore.

"That all sounds…it should be nice. When it happens."

"If," she whispered.

Look at me, Everett Berry, I'm still the same worthless lump you found in that ditch chasing after kittens. It was no wonder he'd run back to Kathy.

"Well, that won't do." Hayden strode for the mess of half-finished walls. He gripped the frame and gave it a little shake. The whole thing tipped to the side, Madeline almost dashing to catch it.

"What the…?" Ev ran to the far beams and did the same. "Why aren't these reinforced? This thing would fall down in a light rain. Who's in charge of construction?"

"That'd be Mr. Jensen." Pointing to the man who'd been trying to inch farther out of the conversation, Madeline found herself standing beside Everett.

"You, Mr. Jensen!"

Madeline shrank at the snake eyes Jensen turned their way, but not Ev. No, he strode over the fallen boards and lost nails to look Jensen in the eye. "What are you pulling? Those walls need to be anchored to the foundation. The wind would rip a wall clean off."

Jensen snickered. "They're fine the way they are."

"I'd be shocked if you used more than ten nails apiece on them."

The construction manager snorted and rolled his eyes. He jerked his thumb at Ev and the other guys on his payroll laughed along. "Can you believe this fucker, white knighting 'cause he watched a few how-to videos?"

Ev jerked upright, putting him at his full height above Jensen. "Your shoddy construction is going to get someone hurt or worse."

"What are you gonna do about it?"

Madeline took off, shoving herself between both men. Jensen pushed her hand away before it got near him, while Ev kept bumping his chest against her palm. His hands remained unclenched, but in her mind she could already see them flying. How in the almighty lord could she explain to Chantelle that she let the construction manager get beaten up by the fire inspector?

"Can we calm down? Take a breath before we say or do something we regret?"

The fire in Everett's eyes burned hotter. He jerked closer to Jensen, pushing on Madeline's hand. "Please," she whispered. The coiled muscles unclenched, Ev falling back on the heels of his feet. But he didn't step back either. "Okay. We're all good. There's just the matter of the walls…"

"No." Jensen spat at the ground near Madeline's foot.

"What do you mean no? You're contracted to —"

"This here is what we call a 'toxic environment' and I ain't required to work in one. You want to have brain-dead pretty boys running around shouting threats at me, you won't be getting any more work. Let's go, boys." He whipped his hand around in a circle, sending the handful of construction crew to gather up their gear.

What were they doing? Madeline ran through the mud after them, barely noticing as her cute shoes sunk deep into the nail-infest ground. "Wait, stop. You can't…"

"I can do whatever the hell I want. It's a fucking free country." Jensen tossed Madeline away. Bit by bit, all the tools vanished along with the men. She stood in the mess of unfinished walls and spools of wire, her dreams a wreck at her feet. The porch was gonna go there, and the cute cat tree over by the window. There was even gonna be an espresso machine.

How was she going to explain this to Chantelle?

"Maddy," Ev whispered, "I didn't think…"

"Do you ever, Everett Berry?" she snarled. Her anger was justified, she knew that in her heart, but as his face crumbled, so too went her resolve.

In a soft voice, she mumbled. "I'm…I'm sorry. I just, I have to get this done by May. How's that gonna happen? It took me two months to find that crew."

She'd agreed to this to get Ev off her mind. It had worked, until he had marched back into her life and ruined her new dream. She wanted to laugh and scream at the same time.

A warm arm wrapped around her shoulders. Even though she hated him in the pit of her stomach, Madeline leaned against Everett. Her heart craved his comfort while her mind recoiled from it. But, as she found the strength to look, she stared not into green eyes, but black.

"I'll help," Hayden declared.

"What?" Madeline forgot about scurrying out from under his arm and froze.

"I've got construction experience, maybe not as illustrious as Mr. Jensen's, but I've never stomped off a site in a tizzy. All this needs is, what, the walls and then the roof before you can bring in an electrician? No problem."

"Really?" Madeline sniffed in the least pretty way possible. Hayden turned her to face him and wiped at her eyes.

"Happy to. I've got some leave I can use to get this place right as rain, Miss Prix."

"Please, please call me Madeline." She caught his hand and shook it hard, a giggle catching in her throat.

Hayden smiled. "A sweet name for a sweet girl."

Gosh. Her entire face burned, and Madeline had to turn away. "I can pay, same as what they were getting."

"Well, that's the cherry on top of getting to spend more time with you."

Madeline's mind shattered. All she could do was take Hayden's hand and shake it over and over. He couldn't mean...?

"I'll help too."

What?

Her head bobbed to the second voice of its own accord because her mind refused to acknowledge it had heard that. Everett Berry, the man who had made her gumbo, slept with her then run off into the night stood proud with a two-by-four in hand. The same man who had threatened and chased away the construction crew working on her dream raised a hammer. She should refuse. Spending more time around him would rip open the wounds she'd barely begun to heal from.

Madeline, admit it. You haven't even gotten over the way he fed Monte, never mind how soft his lips are. This was a disaster she had to stop now. Madeline opened her mouth, but Hayden beat her to it.

"It only seems fair, Berry. This was all your fault."

Her refusal twisted into a panicked grin. "Sure," she said. "The more the merrier."

Ev nodded as if this were the best idea in the world, while he and Hayden pored over the blueprints. A week doing hot, sweaty construction with Everett Berry. Beth was going to kill her.

Chapter Thirteen

He didn't see Madeline for another three days. Not that he was counting them down. Not like she'd have any reason to want to see him after the mess he'd made of her life. Ev slipped out of the back of his house, praying Kathy was too busy practicing her modeling to hear him.

Dawn had almost cracked over the horizon. It used to be his favorite time back home, when the bullfrogs were starting up with their twangy song of love and the herons flew overhead looking for their breakfast. He would wake up early before class just to sit in that golden hour when God tore off the wrapping on a new day.

Here, it felt like more of the same. People rushing along the sidewalk to get to where they needed. Cars idling with horns wailing around the city. Even the light barely changed, most of it cut off from reaching him by the tall buildings looming above. It went from a blue gray to a yellow gray as the clock ticked on.

"It's on you if you freeze," Everett threw out to cover over the sound of Maddy drooling at him. She had to be. Hayden was the type to cause that in girls. "Now, can we get to work on these walls?"

"In a moment, first…" Hayden scooped up the white box and pulled back the lid. "A little breakfast treat." Tucked inside were three coral-pink donuts and a pale pink eclair with a ridged cookie on top.

"I spotted them in a little shop in Philadelphia. Everyone was raving about Brandy's Sweets."

"What the heck were you doing in Philly?" Everett asked. His principles told him to refuse a donut, but the longer the box stayed open, the louder the siren song called to him.

Hayden jerked a thumb back to a flatbed. "Picking up the walls."

"You got them?" Madeline leaped up on her tippy toes to see past Hayden. "How? I couldn't even get anyone to talk to me there. They said they'd only work with Jensen."

He leaned closer, almost placing his lips to her ear. "I have my ways. Now, please. When I saw the madeleine éclair, I had to get it for you."

Oh, come on.

Maddy swept her sweet fingers over the dessert, and she plucked it up. "That's so kind of you."

His smile damn near oozed, causing Everett to clench his fists. Then Hayden cocked an eyebrow and swerved the box to him. "Go on, you can have one too."

"No thanks. I'm full." Ev turned his back on him and hauled up a beam. Lining it up with the frame, he pulled out the hammer and nail.

"Did Kathy make you breakfast?"

Everett's swing missed the beam, his hammer flying through the gap and smacking against the construction sign. He wanted to tell Hayden to mind his own business, but a soft gasp from Maddy stitched up his mouth. She glared at the dirt where their feet were and wouldn't look up.

"We should get to work. Lots to do," Madeline muttered. She placed her single-nibble eclair on the pile of sheetrock and slipped off for the walls on the flatbed. Hayden took no time chasing after her, leaving Ev staring at the small bite where her lips had caressed the frosting.

This is all your fault, Everett Berry.

* * * *

Stepping back, Madeline struggled to pull in a breath as she stared up at the start of her dream. Her whole body tingled like she'd rubbed her socks on the carpet. Four walls, and another two inside, were already up. She'd been so focused on nailing a board that it was a shock when she looked up and found two men on the roof.

Hayden's tight shirt was vacuum-packed to his abs, the sweat turning it into a second skin. He wore a pair of work gloves that obscured his forearms but left those biceps in full glory. All the picking things up and swinging hammers had drawn out the veins. He glanced over his shoulder and, when he caught Maddy staring, flexed his arm until his biceps popped like a pair of bowling balls.

Why is it so hot out here? Madeline waved a hand at her burning cheeks, when she caught the flapping of Ev's flannel shirt. He'd knotted it around his waist and left his skin ready to be kissed by the sun. Unaware she was staring, Everett climbed the ladder with one hand hooked around a board. It set off the swerving line of his shoulders and the muscles clinging to his back. They were so developed the channel straight down the middle drew her eyes to the top of his pants and the hint of dewy ass cheeks trying to poke out from below.

As Everett reached the top, Hayden reached over for the board. For a second, Ev clung tight to the wood he brought up and both men glared. It was a full-on buffet of men's tight thighs, squeezable bottoms, bracing glowers, delectable shoulders and tempting biceps.

You should not be staring, Madeline. It's not polite.

It's a little look. That won't hurt anyone.

What about Kathy?

Why was she cursed with such a cruel conscience? Why couldn't she get the one that whispered, 'Eat the entire can of whipped cream. Who will know?' Stepping back, she faced the mud pit that'd need sod and landscaping, and spotted a man on a bike with a red saddlebag.

"Boys!" Madeline shouted up the ladder. Whatever little fight had broken out was settled with Hayden whipping the board away when Ev turned to her. She accepted the bags from the delivery man and held them up. "Lunch is here!"

The three sat together on the cement block where the porch would go. Madeline had her legs turned to the side, her sandwich's cardboard case resting on the floor. The men flanked her, Hayden's legs wide as he fought to keep his sandwich balanced on one thigh while the other brushed against her. Everett had turned to face the street, so Madeline caught the back of his jaw.

Odd, there seemed to be a dark spot behind it.

She placed her tuna salad down and picked up a napkin. As she almost touched him, Everett whipped his head around, his eyes wide as a gator's. "I think you got some mud or something behind your ear," she said, holding out the napkin.

Ev's hand flew to the area. He didn't respond, just sat there breathing ragged and staring. Did he think she was going to wipe it off herself? Wasn't that Kathy's job?

When he didn't take the napkin, she returned it to her teetering lap and shrunk deeper into her food. She'd wanted to help. Maybe she wasn't supposed to touch him. Maybe he found her that disgusting. God knew the rest of the boys back home had She was an idiot to even think...

"I dare say we make a great team," Hayden announced and slapped a hand to his thigh. Craning his head, he stared up at the nameless building still missing a door and windows. Madeline turned to follow, spinning away from Ev. As she did, struggling to keep her legs tucked tight to herself, Hayden glanced his hand over her knee. She jerked in shock, but he brushed a finger across her thigh then placed his hand on the ground.

"Is it living up to your expectations?" he asked.

Staring up at the gray, blank building, Madeline struggled to see anything. Drab and sad in equal measures, the squat thing could be some mid-tier bank or a satellite battery store on a strip mall. Nothing about it screamed 'this is a place for adorable kittens', much less Madeline's dream.

"I guess so," she said, then winced at her answer. "Yes. It's going great. When can we start painting?"

Everett scoffed. "Not for some time. No point until the electricians wire the place. For the...the sake of matching."

"You are a ray of sunshine, Berry." Hayden jumped to his feet and stretched his arms wide. "May I?" Even at his full height, he bent so his face almost touched Madeline's and held a hand out for her trash. The wind blew her curls across his eyes, obscuring the dark focus in a mess of wild red.

"Thank you," she said, handing him her sandwich wrapper and cardboard before suddenly reaching inside. "Sorry, sorry. Forgot the pickle."

Hayden smiled at that before he turned to find the dumpsters the old crew hadn't had removed. She watched him until he vanished behind the building. "Here," Everett said, handing her the sandwich baggie with his pickle spear.

"You don't want it?" Madeline pressed, the back of her neck burning.

"Don't much like 'em, and I'd rather it go to someone who does than the flying rats or the running ones."

Rather than unroll it, Madeline clasped the second pickle between both hands and held it. Her stomach twisted up until the idea of eating another bite made her feel queasy.

"It's funny, my buddy, he had this theory about pickles."

"If it's Tom, I don't need to know what he thought about where to stick his pickle."

"Nah, nah." Ev laughed. "It's someone else. He says a relationship can only work if there's two types of people in it—one who eats the pickle with a sandwich, and the other who doesn't." After the words left his mouth, he stopped staring past Madeline and swiveled his head until his green eyes struck her.

Stabbing on a smile, Madeline raised the pickle he'd given her. "Kathy must love these."

"Uh…not really." He sprang back around, giving Madeline the full view of his back. Ev's head hung even lower as he picked at the edge of the cardboard box. "We should…I should talk. Tell you about Kathy."

What did he want to tell her? How perfect she was? How songbirds perched on her vanity mirror each morning? How happy he was waking beside her instead of rolling off of Madeline?

"You don't," she forced out, her lips aching from how hard she pressed her smile against her skull. "We're adults. We…didn't make any promises."

"It wasn't what it, what it looked like. She was just staying at my place and kept staying. Then you showed up and I…I froze."

How stupid did he think she was? Silly enough to hold out hope that the handsome prince would choose the ugly stepsister instead? Madeline tried to conjure up a rage storm inside, but the longer she stared at Ev, the harder it took to catch.

"But you're with her now?" She tried to state it as an accusation, but Madeline's wobbly hope twisted it into a question. Biting her lip, she watched Everett twist his head back and forth before dropping it in a sullen nod. Of course he was with her. Maybe he wasn't lying, maybe she had overreacted to an innocent guest situation. Either way, in the end, he had picked Kathy and not her.

She couldn't cry. She was wearing a tool belt. There were rules against anyone crying while carrying a hammer. Pushing to her feet, Madeline said, "Then I'm very happy for the both of you. Excuse me." As she turned from Ev, the toe of her shoe drew a hard line between them.

In a full fluster, Madeline dashed about the site, her hips knocking boards askew until she struck a box of nails. The sound of them tumbling to the floor like sharp rain sent her reeling. She struggled to the ground, fighting to gather them up before anyone noticed.

"Careful there." A hand swept over the back of hers, holding it from the mess of nails. "Don't want you to prick your finger."

She lifted her head to find Hayden crouched down, a hearty smile in place. "You might fall into a deep sleep for a hundred years."

Madeline's entire face burned hot at his comparing her to Sleeping Beauty. Hayden pulled out a long metal wand and waved it over the fallen nails. They all leaped onto the magnet, keeping any fingers from the sharp ends.

"That's pretty smart," Madeline said. When Hayden finished, he held a hand out to her and helped her rise. As she popped up onto her feet, he didn't lean away. Hayden stood stock still, Madeline forced to try to catch her breath deep in her personal bubble. This was uncharted territory, where the air thickened with the dark scent of man and his shadow eclipsed the sun. She fidgeted, trying to find a way to slip away while also staying.

Hayden slipped a hand up to the side of her cheek, and Madeline froze. His impenetrable gaze flitted back and forth across her eyes and warmth spread from the back of her ear down to her neck. What was he doing? Hayden rolled the tip of his tongue across his lip, and Madeline's life flashed before her eyes. She knew what

Red Riding Hood felt like staring down the teeth of the wolf.

And, in the flap of a butterfly's wing, the sun returned. Hayden smiled brightly and pulled his hand forward to reveal a splinter of wood between his fingers.

"I didn't want you to hurt yourself."

"Th…thank you," she muttered while pawing back through her curls.

Hayden placed the splinter in her palm, then cupped both his hands over it. "It would break my heart if anything happened to you."

Uh, okay. She couldn't pick him out of a lineup, but that sentiment was the most bracing thing a man had ever said to her. Madeline smiled wide in response and nodded. She had no idea what the answer was, but Hayden seemed to accept it. With a little whistle, he hoisted up the hammer and turned to the wall.

"Back at it. Eh, Berry?"

"What?" Ev called. He was scrolling like a madman through his phone, and Madeline frowned. Instead of working to fix the problem he'd caused, he was too busy texting with Kathy. At least Hayden seemed to care, and none of it had been his fault to begin with.

She dashed past him, not caring that her elbow bumped his arm. While Madeline scooped up another plank and held it up for the interior bathroom wall, Hayden ribbed Ev over whatever he was staring at. Not caring what cute thing Kathy said or did, Madeline tuned it out. She was probably sitting on the granite counters in Everett's kitchen stirring a pitcher of lemonade while photographers snapped her picture for Perfect Woman Monthly. Or maybe she was making a collage of all the wonderful memories she'd had with him, everyone cooing over how they looked like the couple on a wedding cake.

"Afternoon, lovely."

"Holy hell!" Madeline was mid-hammer swing when her nerves jumped the track. She couldn't stop the trajectory of the smash into the middle of the board instead of the nail. After checking there was no large crack down the plank, she glanced over her shoulder.

Chantelle looked like a Pollack painting had walked out of the museum and into a construction yard. It hurt to stare at their suitcoat for too long thanks to the multi-colored splatters. "Things are looking wonderful, just marvelous."

"Maddy? Who's this?"

She'd never thought of Everett as imposing. Sure, he might have the build to throw down with a grizzly, but he had the heart of a teddy bear. Or so she'd assumed until he turned around at the shock of Madeline cursing and found a stranger there.

"This is Chantelle, they're…" She'd drawn the attention of Hayden as well, who shut off his bandsaw. "They're working with Tristan on the musical." That wasn't going to make any sense to them. "Tristan's —"

"Your friend's fiancé, right? Beth?" Ev said, catching Madeline off guard. He remembered?

"Yes, exactly."

"I didn't know he was in a musical." Everett's wide stance softened.

"*Pride and Prejudice.* Perhaps you've heard of it?" Chantelle glided closer to the men, then chuckled. "Or perhaps not. Madeline, my dear, who are these robust gentlemen?"

"They're the ones I told you about, the firemen who offered to help put up the walls."

Chantelle clapped their hands and tugged the end of their skirt up. Looking Everett in the eye, they said, "I see, rather yin and yang situation with them, huh? Which is which?"

Madeline glanced from the blond, bonhomie Everett to the black-haired, debonair Hayden. She'd trusted Ev with her heart and quickly learned what a mistake that was. Never again. And Hayden...? Why did her breath catch, and insides churn every time she looked at him?

"Well, firemen, pleased to meet you. I must speak with the animal center director for a moment. You can return to your banging."

Hayden chuckled at Chantelle's orders but didn't start the bandsaw back up. It was Everett who Madeline watched, his eyes trailing past the unmistakable Chantelle to...her. She bit her lip and looked away when an arm wrapped over hers. "Timeline, dear. What is this looking like?"

"We, um..." She glanced to the boys. Everett shrugged and waved his nail gun about. It was Hayden who slipped into the conversation as if he were invited.

"I'd say, given enough encouragement, we can have this place walled and roofed off in another day or two at most. Right, Berry?"

Everett crinkled his nose and stared at the interior's mess and the holes in the roof. Before he could answer, Hayden said, "Oh, I forgot, you're busy with that other project of yours."

"Another project?" Chantelle inquired. "Details, please."

Keeping Kathy Clark happier than a pig in shit.

Madeline bit her tongue. "He's got his own house to work on. I'm sure that's more important to him than—"

"That ain't it. I've…" Everett fell quiet, his head dropping lower. "I got put in charge of organizing the firefighters' ball. It's the main source of funding for the station. Without it, I'm out on the streets."

He didn't say that to Chantelle, but Madeline. Everett cupped his hands together. "I wish I could help finish here. There's a lot of work left if you want to hit…when's your opening date?"

"Early May," the chipper chanteuse said without a pause.

"May, as in this year's May?" Everett whistled in shock. "Well, ah, that's the ball, too." He caught Madeline's eye to whisper, "Sorry."

She wanted to tell him it was okay. That it wasn't his fault she was trapped in a time crunch. Even if he hadn't chased off Jensen, it seemed unlikely they'd have gotten this done. What little he'd done was kind enough. If anything, she should apologize to him.

God, could she ever stop feeling for Everett Berry?

"Splendid." Chantelle clapped their hands hard. *Did they miss how impossible this was?* "We must pool our resources together, you proud fireman and your balls of delight."

Madeline snickered at the full-on blush dashing across Ev's cheeks.

"And you daring kitten collector. Think of the opportunity. What goes together better than a brave firefighter and the cute kitten stuck in a tree? Nothing, that's what. It'll be a match made in heaven." Chantelle bowled over them before anyone could even respond. They grabbed Madeline's hand and put it in Everett's.

Both glanced down at the same time, Madeline shocked that he gripped her hand and that she held back.

"Wonderful. I'm glad that's decided," Chantelle declared.

Madeline dropped Everett's hand and tried to chase after her benefactor and sort-of boss. "What is? What just happened?"

"You two will work on a collaboration with the firemen's ball and our still nameless kitten center. We can help to provide funding for the venue, canapés and whatnot. And the gathering of the elite in the sprawling neighborhood will garner attention for the new kitten center. Delightful. I'm so glad I stopped by."

"Um." Madeline tried to give chase to the force of nature that had wrecked her life, but she kept turning back to find Everett shocked. "I don't know if that's such a good idea."

Chantelle spun on their heavy boots and eyed up Madeline. "My dear, every idea I have is good. It's up to people like you to make them feasible. Now, if you will excuse me, I have an interview to get to."

Dumbstruck, Madeline watched them climb into the back of the familiar Tesla and speed off into the city for another wild adventure. Was she supposed to do all that? The only fancy party Madeline had ever attended was her sister's wedding, and they'd had pigs in a blanket as a starter course.

"I have no idea what I'm doing," she muttered under her breath.

A low chuckle rumbled behind her. Everett scrolled through his phone and turned the screen to her. "Welcome to my world," he said, revealing a mess of appointments and checklists they now had to figure out together.

Chapter Fourteen

"You did *what*?"

It was good that Madeline had called Beth instead of explaining in person, otherwise she'd have a ninety-pound woman shaking her by the shoulders. "Chantelle thinks—"

"Mads, he broke your heart. You were…you were a puddle for two weeks because of him. Do you even remember Christmas?"

"Yes." Most of which had been spent ensconced in her duvet, a two-foot-tall tree without any breakables on it her only light source. She couldn't face home, not with her sister once again in the family way. Not with the rest of her relatives eyeing up that lazy Madeline and wondering what her problem was.

"Do you need me to email him for you? Tell him that this deal is off?"

"I don't think—"

"That he'd get the message?" Beth leaped right over Madeline's stalling. She suspected that Everett needed all the help he could get — and her rescue center would benefit from the team-up. But he also wouldn't hold her to it if she wiggled her way free.

Why don't I want my friend to fix this mess?

"I'll deal with it. Look, it's all for charity. We need to support the firefighters, or we'd all burn up like old Chicago and that cow."

God, she had no believable excuse. Madeline pinched at her forehead while staring at the unbreakable cloud line. It wasn't raining, thank goodness, but it kept up the threat the longer she stood to the left of the open garage door.

A long, deep breath rattled over her phone. "Madeline Prix," Beth declared in a slow voice, "you are too nice."

Always be nice, kind, and quiet. That had been practically burned into her hide at age three to whenever death came for her. Be polite. Care for others. Never ever complain.

And deep down inside, you don't want to give this up. You want a second chance.

Against Kathy 'her beauty stops a stampede running down main street' Clark? Right. *And pigs'll get their pilots' licenses.*

"You doing anything Friday?"

The sudden abrupt turn caught Madeline, and she jerked to look as a firetruck rolled up the driveway beside her. A five-alarm fire broke out on her cheeks, and she turned so whoever was inside couldn't see her. "Going over spreadsheets for the budget to see if…"

"So no," Beth finished.

Sorry, I don't have a billionaire boyfriend who thought we needed to enjoy a long weekend in Paris. Madeline snorted at the very idea. What would the French think of her barely passable Creole?

"Because I have recordings from the latest rehearsal, and I thought we could listen to them while dress shopping."

Already? Dread at having to face the torture of shopping at bridal stores reared up at her. *Stick your leg down this tube of tiny satin and pretend it looks good on you. That'll be $500 please.*

"I...I thought that you, you hadn't even picked colors?" That had to give her time to stall or find a lookalike to stand in her place.

The sound of fluttering paper came over the phone. Oh no, Beth was looking in the planner. "All the books say to start looking for the dress as soon as possible."

She meant her dress. Thank the stars. Madeline chuckled to herself when the enormity of the situation hit her. "What about your...your mother?"

Beth went deathly quiet before she whispered, "I'd rather it just be us. Keep it simple, you know."

All the silly worries about how she'd look like a bag of sausages stuffed inside satin vanished. "Sounds wonderful. I can't wait. Maybe we'll even find the one."

Beth snorted. "It took me thirty years to find Tristan. I'm worried it'll take sixty to find the dress. I've gotta go. Interviews to be had. Celebrities to shill for. Bye."

As Madeline slipped her phone back in her pocket, she tried to feel excited for the wedding. She was happy for Beth, honest and true. Tristan was okay once he got used to people. He reminded her of a standoffish cat that hid in the corner until enough time passed. But Beth adored the grouchy, loyal man. She gave off that happy glow whenever talking about him that could turn green inside the eternally single.

"At least she hasn't ditched me for yoga moms in the suburbs," Madeline whispered to herself. She needed the distraction as she faced the first meeting with her new partner. Trying to not scrunch all the way into her jacket, she slipped in under the open garage door and gazed around.

It's business, Madeline kept repeating to herself, even though she couldn't escape the reminder that the last time she'd snuck into the fire station, she thought she was gonna be Ev's girlfriend. What was that thing they said about assumptions?

An older gentleman walked past, glanced to her, but didn't tell her to get out. Madeline took the opportunity. "Excuse me? Could you tell Everett Berry that I'm here?"

"Uh, yeah, sure. Hey, Ber!" he shouted at the top of his lungs.

Madeline full-body winced. Heads prodded from around corners to see what was going on. She almost missed the blond one poking from a door above her head. "What is it, Will?" Ev shouted back, when he gripped to the railing and stared down at her.

Limply, Madeline lifted up the binder she'd started and waved. "Hi."

Holding up a hand, Everett called down, "Wait, I'm coming. Wait right there. I shouldn't be... What time is it?" He stared at the wall where a massive clock hung inside a tire before clattering down the stairs. It sounded like a parade of moose trying to escape down a boardwalk. Still, Madeline kept her smile on even as she went from watching Everett to staring.

Stars above. He had on what'd looked like a simple gray T-shirt from the ground, but as he got closer, she noticed the fire emblem with his station. The shirt was so tight, the Berry tag strained over the sleeve suctioned to his biceps. But what made her squirm were the suspenders dangling off the fireman pants.

The bright yellow strips bounced back and forth as he dashed, smacking into his thighs and back area. He looked like he'd been caught mid-changing, and Madeline's brain skipped straight to Everett Berry peeling off his fireman uniform and dripping water down his smoking hot muscles.

"Hey, are you okay?"

She bit her lip hard to contain the squeal and nodded.

"Just...you look kinda red. Do you need to sit down?" Ev pulled a chair out from under a workbench and guided it closer.

Madeline stepped back. "No, no, I'm fine. I wanted to stop by to touch base. About the ball. I'm trying to figure things out."

"You and me both," he said with a puttering laugh and roughed up the back of his hair. "I swear I don't understand half of what's in here." Ev cracked open the folder he'd been carrying, revealing reams of paper with napkins and receipts stapled to them. "Is this even in English?"

"Let me have a look." Madeline tried to slip in beside him as she opened her binder. It was an awkward fit, Madeline having to crane her neck to read the surprisingly delicate handwriting. She pulled out a pen to jot down some notes, when a hand pressed against her shoulder.

She watched her curls smack Everett's cheek and his green eyes lit up with a laugh. "Thought this might be easier," he said. "Or am I wrong?" His entire arm rested over her, his hand limp and easy to toss off. It wouldn't take her anything more than a shrug of her shoulder.

"No, it's…" *Nice.* So close, she breathed in the smell of coastal waves instead of smoke. He probably wasn't fresh off a job then, so no bathing of the fireman. Shame. Madeline tried to buckle down on her work, but there was no escaping the protective warmth radiating from his body brushing against hers.

"Please tell me you at least have the venue booked?" She caught the mention of a hotel ballroom and her mind blanked. If that thing wasn't secured at least a year in advance, there was no hope of a ball even happening.

"That's not a problem. They have a deal with the station come heck or high water."

"Good, good. 'Cause Beth's been putting feelers out, and if she wanted to get married in the city, she won't be doing it for three years." Madeline spoke without thought, then paled. "Not that…it doesn't matter. Venue secured. Done."

"I was gonna head over there tomorrow to check it out. Would you like to come?"

Go to a fancy hotel with Everett Berry? In any other reality at any other time in her life, Madeline would have squealed a yes so fast it'd have sent him toppling. But Beth's words rang in her ear. *He hurt you. Maybe he didn't mean to, maybe it was all my fault. But that damn hurt doesn't listen to logic.*

"I'm not certain if…"

"Don't we need to see it, for themes or layout or whatever?"

Damn, he was right. Madeline nodded, accepting the cruel twist of fate that wouldn't let her walk away and forget Everett Berry. It wasn't as if things could get more awkward.

"Hello there, lovely!"

She didn't even turn at the voice, despite recognizing Hayden. Madeline dismissed it as meant for someone else despite the man coming toward her. The arm that she'd forgotten was around her retreated, all of Everett fading as Hayden swept up. He reached for her hands but paused before taking them. His smile brightened more as he stared over at Ev a second before fully focusing on her.

"What brings you in? Don't tell me the roof flew away and the walls fell over?"

"No, no." She laughed and tugged on a curl. "You did good work, really. It's still standing solid. The electricians will be by soon and then there will be lights." Why was she babbling?

Hayden focused his gaze behind her as he said, "Wonderful news. Any chance you'll be needing another pair of hands? You had an awful lot of fencing on that lot."

"Oh, goodness no. I can't ask you to help any more than you did."

To her surprise, Hayden's grin dimmed. He looked crestfallen that she wasn't going to take advantage of him. Madeline reached out to cup his arm, terrified she had done something to hurt him. As her fingers touched below his shoulder, the entire length of Hayden's arm flexed tight and bulged. She clung on rather than let go, squeezing into the muscle while he beamed his gaze on her.

Why is it so hot in here? She twisted on her feet, feeling about to collapse to the floor while Hayden's smile pierced through her chest.

"Maddy has a lot of work to be getting to."

The steely gaze broke off her, causing Madeline to pull in a breath. Hayden didn't just glare at Ev overstepping his bounds but snarled. As she turned to stare at Ev, then back, it was gone. Only Hayden's understanding smile remained.

All that overhead fluorescent lighting must have messed with her.

"He's...right. I should be returning to the thing I do." The longer she stood between the two men, the more Madeline's brains boiled over. She had no idea what was going on, but she didn't like being caught in the middle. Releasing her hold on Hayden, Madeline moved to step away, when a warm hand slipped to the small of her back.

Three months of hardening her heart to stone crumbled to dust and a small part of her soul leapt at that familiar touch. It was the same way Ev had led her through his house, a tender and caring hand she'd never gotten from anyone else. Melting, Madeline glanced over her shoulder prepared to offer Everett whatever he wanted, only to find darkness behind. She blinked, the shadows fading to black hair and Hayden's bright eyes.

"Do you like sushi?"

That was not what she expected to hear. Madeline had to blink a few more times to stall as her brain wound back the tape. "Uh, yeah. I think. I mean I've had it before, so yes?"

"Excellent. There's a new sushi restaurant I've been wanting to try."

"Okay?" Why was he telling her?

Hayden clapped his hands like they'd settled everything. "How does tomorrow at seven sound?"

Now she was lost. "I don't know? Maybe a sort of bell clang."

The wide grin faltered, Hayden cricking his head. "What?"

"You asked what seven sounds like, and I was guessing that…" *Holy guacamole, Madeline. That's a date. He asked you out on a date.* A combination of gasp and hiccup burst from her, and Madeline slapped a hand over her mouth.

She had to be wrong. Hayden looked like the kind of guy to have two hot blondes on his arm when he went to the DMV. He couldn't possibly be…

"That won't work," Everett said, turning both Hayden and Madeline to him.

"What, are you her keeper, Berry? I promise I'll have her back before eleven…unless things go *really* well."

How bad would it be if she full-on swooned? Taking into account the cement floor that'd crack her skull, Madeline held onto a desk while Hayden focused on Ev. Pulling in a slow breath, Everett raised his head giving him an inch on Hayden.

"Or do you have some reason why I shouldn't ask an attractive and vivacious woman out?"

There went that swoon urge again. Madeline reached over and pinched her arm, but this couldn't be a dream. She was never so kind to herself in sleep.

Ev's green gaze darted to her, and he held it for a beat before tossing his head and walking back a step. "No. Of course I don't… You can do what you want. Both of you."

Madeline fought to keep her face neutral even as Everett stomped on her heart and kicked it to the curb. Why'd she even think for a second he'd challenge Hayden for her? He had Kathy — his life was perfect.

"I meant that we have a work requirement that day."

"And you think it will run into the night?" Hayden prodded.

"Maybe. I don't know how this works. I don't know how anything works." Everett slumped a shoulder down and stepped further away. He was literally trying to put as much distance between himself and Madeline as possible. Her stomach churned with butterflies made of razorblades.

"Look, I don't want to be a bother. Just…" *Forget it. Forget for even a second you wanted to ask me out. I'm not worth it.*

Hayden snapped his fingers. "Why don't you join us?"

"What?" Ev gasped while Madeline's mind shattered. Both of them?

"Yes, you can bring along that girl of yours. Kat."

"Kathy," Everett mumbled, his gaze trailing to the same patch of cement Madeline's had wound up at.

"Sounds like a perfect solution," Hayden declared as if the entire matter were settled. "I can't wait for tomorrow," he said to her, then cast a look at Ev. "Try to wear an unstained shirt. The place is nice."

With that, Hayden walked to the big red fire truck and began to wash it down with the others. Any other time, Madeline would have sat and watched his T-shirt soak and shrink to his body, but her heart was a seething mess of barbed wire. Judging by Everett's face, he wasn't doing any better.

"You don't have to do it," she whispered.

"What?" Confusion swept across his face, blotting away the look of absolute terror.

"Go on a date with me. I know, it's…" *Your living nightmare.* "You don't have to, I promise."

"Maddy, I..." Ev glanced over his shoulder to Hayden, and his voice hardened. "I'm coming." His death glare didn't shift off the smiling man even as Everett walked away.

All that remained was Madeline twirling in a quagmire she struggled to understand. Hayden had asked her out—that was exciting. A date, the first one since Ev...but that wasn't a date. It was her first in years. She should be dancing in excitement. What girl wouldn't want Hayden to ask her out?

But the entire time she'd fight to make small talk and try to look nice, she'd be sitting next to Kathy Clark. Her stomach braided itself into a Gordian knot. Gathering her things, Madeline eased her way to the door.

"Maddy!" Ev's voice rang out above the rush of water and chatter of coworkers. She glanced over her shoulder to find him. "You ain't a bother."

Chapter Fifteen

All he needed was to change his clothes. Everett held his breath, taking the stairs with his arm flattened against the wall so they wouldn't creak. He was supposed to meet Maddy at the Grand Royal hotel in under an hour and any place with that much gold in its stationery wouldn't let a sweat-drenched fireman near their lobby. They'd probably demand a spritz of cologne even if it were on fire.

Ev reached the landing and moved to turn for the bathroom, when a low groan rumbled through the floorboards. He full-body winced and whipped his head down the construction hell of the second floor. The bedroom door didn't open. Maybe she was out, or taking a nap. *In and out fast before she even notices.*

Once in the safe confines of the bathroom, he hung up his jacket then took to stripping off the layers. It'd started off freezing cold in the morning, and Ev had thought he was being smart breaking out the Henley to go over his tee. It was brilliant right until the sun broke free and beamed heat on every covered inch of his body. He felt like a baked potato wrapped in foil and tossed in the back of the car.

He should take a shower. At least make himself look presentable for...the hotel people. Not like anyone else would care. Staring at the mirror, the whole of his skin red and blotchy, Ev froze. Dark circles hung under his eyes. He'd slept at the station again in the hopes he'd be bushy-tailed for today. That used to work when things got bad, at least until she'd calmed down. But the droop of his brow and hunch to his shoulders seemed to grow worse no matter what he did.

Everett rubbed random patches of stubble across his cheeks. Pockets of it came in long while others seemed to be struggling. It'd be best if he shaved it all off, but every time he picked up a razor and held it to his face, his hand started to shake. All that work hanging over his head, the station, the ball, fixing his house, Maddy...

If he could just get one thing done, then it'd be better. Tomorrow's dawn would be brighter. It had to be.

He didn't realize he'd pushed aside his hair until the bare light struck the spot. It'd looked like a horn when it was first burned, tomato red and damn near glowing under his blond hair. Even though it hurt like hell, he'd worn a hat to hide it. She'd sworn that'd be the last time.

The funny thing was, he didn't blame her for it like the way he didn't blame the wind for knocking over a fence. He blamed himself for being stupid enough to believe her.

"What are you doing home?"

The rickety door almost burst on its hinges from how hard Kathy knocked on it. Ev swiped his hair back in place and gripped the sink. "I have to get ready," he said, his eyes closing tight.

"Ready for what?" She was in a bad mood, her syrupy sorority voice in full manager-wrath mode.

Ev snatched up the shirt he'd left under the sink and tried to button it on. "For my job. I'm meeting with the hotel. I told you about it."

"Are you talking back to me?" Kathy roared. The doorknob shivered in its old fittings, sending Ev scuttling back to the hole where the bathtub used to be.

"No, I just…I thought you might have forgotten."

"Ev-er-ett Ber-ry!" She bashed on the door with every syllable. "Get yer ass out of there right now or so help me."

In a fluster, Ev crammed on his pants and reached for the first pair of shoes he could find. "Look, it's all for work."

"You, going to a hotel in the middle of the day? Do you think I'm an idiot? Who is she?"

"Who?"

The doorjamb splintered, and Kathy forced her way inside. Her face was twisted in rage, her sundress askew as she bunched her fists in his face. "The girl you're fucking. Who is she? Some cheap whore you found online. Give me your phone!"

Rote memory caused him to reach for his back pocket, when he froze. "No," he said, raising his chin higher. The wrath of God shot from Kathy's eyes, but he couldn't stop now. "I ain't cheating on you."

"Is exactly what a fucking liar says. You're nothing but a pathetic, ignorant excuse of a man."

She didn't swing at him. That was all the hope Ev had as he ducked to the side of her and dashed for the exit. "I've got to get to work, okay," he said, clinging with all he had left to his truth. He wasn't cheating on her. He had to go there. He was not a bad person.

"You're fucking worthless. There's Girl Scouts more manly than you." Kathy followed him out of the bathroom. She clung to the banister while Everett shuffled fast down the stairs. "There ain't a woman alive who will put up with your sorry ass and you know it, you cheating bastard!"

For a brief second, he glanced up at the raving woman with her whole waist leaning on the railing as she screamed. It'd take almost nothing for the old fixture to snap, for her body to tumble over the edge and crash to the tiled floor below. *That'll shut her up.*

Pain struck Ev at how quickly that thought came to him. He turned away, certain she could read his cruel thought. "Goodbye," he shouted and waved while walking out the door. "Love you."

At the stoop, Ev fought to pull in a breath that didn't whistle wrong in his nose. He was a horrible person, and nothing would ever change that.

* * * *

"Sorry I'm late. I got held up by..." Everett's mad dash through a lobby with a fancy piano and fountain of tiny Cupids slammed to a halt. He anticipated glowers and mutters of 'hick'. A mountain of springy red curls tumbled to the side as the warmest smile greeted him. His lips responded in kind, the tension from his confrontation with Kathy fading from his veins.

Unaware of how quickly she had calmed him, Maddy's cheeks turned pink. She scrunched the top of her nose and dipped deeper into her coat. "Ev, hi. I was…waiting for you here."

"Long?" he asked, sliding up to the front desk and ringing an old-fashioned bell. No one appeared right away, so he glanced over his shoulder at the woman staring up at the overlapping floors stretching into the sky.

"No, not…very. A few couple dozen minutes."

He couldn't stop the snicker at her careful answer. "Madeline Prix, always so nice."

"I'm not that nice."

Ev smiled wider at her, and an urge rose to sweep her into his arms until her nervous energy calmed. "Yes, you are," he said. *Too nice for someone like me. Kathy got that one right.*

Defeated, he turned away and focused on the desk when a man in a black suit stepped out of a backroom door. "Hello," Ev said.

"Is this your first time in the city?" The man didn't bat an eye. He jumped straight to assuming they were tourists. Everett coughed, realizing he had put the drawl on thick.

"Nah, I mean no. I'm here about the ballroom. I'd booked an appointment to view it this afternoon."

"Of course! So sorry, sir." The stranger snatched up a binder on the wall and dashed through the door to join the pair of them. "This way. I'm Jacques, event coordinator for the east wing. Lovely to see you. This way." He said that all so fast, Ev was left reeling. All he could do was point in the direction for Madeline and toddle along behind.

"Only the east wing? Who runs the west wing?"

Jacques locked in place, his back straight as he thundered, "We don't go into the west wing. But don't concern yourself about that problem. You're going to love having your event at the Presidential Ballroom. All catering is included, of course. Our chef will be more than happy to work with you for taste tests and, should you not have a cake yet..."

Cake? He leaned closer to Madeline to whisper in her ear, "Do I need to get a cake?"

She shrugged and whispered to him, "Maybe one shaped like a fire hydrant?"

"Or get a fireman rescuing a cat out of a tree." He didn't realize how close he'd dipped to her cheek until it drew back for her laugh. If he dipped down not even an inch, he'd almost kiss it.

"Whatever you decide, the Grand Hotel is happy to provide," Jacques declared as he approached two imposing doors. They looked as boring as any conference hall, a single sign hanging beside them declaring it to be Ballroom A. It reminded him of the VFW hall back home, with the pool table and the basketball hoop where they'd had prom.

When Jacques opened the doors, all the air rushed from Ev's lungs. This was no VFW hall. There was a noticeable lack of folding chairs. Instead, there were fancy dining ones covered in their own sheets with bows tied around the back. The tables were decked out in white cloths with gold leaves stitched down the sides. Each place setting had what looked like four forks made out of real silver, and at least three crystal glasses.

But what nearly sent Ev crashing to the ground was the golden chandelier dangling above a dance floor. It had at least twenty candles in tall sconces, though he hoped they were electric. Pearls and crystals hung off the loops of the three-tiered chandelier, reminding him of the ladies of a certain age who ruled over church services.

"Sorry about the mess, we're still setting up for the Greensburg Bat Mitzvah, but I think you get the general idea. The DJ would be placed beside that standing wall. Or…" Jacques pulled open a hidden panel in the wall and pressed a button. Curtains moved on their own from the back of the hall, revealing a small stage. "We have a lovely set-up for a live band."

"I need to get a band?" Ev squeaked. There hadn't been any mention of that in the notes.

He must have looked paler than usual as Madeline reached over and rubbed his shoulder. "You don't have to get anything you don't want," she said as if that were the most obvious thing in the universe.

Right. It was his party. A party to raise enough funds to keep him paid, but his party. No band. Ev cupped her comforting hand with his and caressed his palm over her knuckles. "Thank you," he said, clinging tighter to her. She was too nice.

Maddy's pale cheeks went rosy red again, and she glanced down, but didn't take her hand back. It wasn't until Jacques let out an "Aw," that they both stepped apart.

Their event coordinator turned and touched his ear. He whispered some incoherent code, then put on a fake smile. "I have to attend to a small matter with haste. Why don't you both get a feel for the room? Walk around, test the linens. Here's the book." He passed over his binder which had the heft of a brick. Ev pried it open, and his brain numbed over at the mention of a thread count in tablecloths. Where he came from, tablecloths were plastic.

Jacques dashed for the exit, but before he went, he pressed another button. Soft music one would hear in old romantic movies rose to life around the room. "The surround system in this room is state of the art," he declared before slipping out the door and leaving them alone.

Moving between tables, Madeline clinked some of the silverware together and brushed over the tablecloth. "This place is decadent."

"You mean far too fancy for my backwater ass?" Ev said it with a chuckle, but he feared moving. All the tables were festooned with fancy drippings that probably cost his yearly salary.

Madeline picked up a coffee mug on a porcelain saucer and raised her pinkie. "Are you saying we're not sophisticated enough for New York pomp?"

She was adorable, her smile brightening with every twirl of that extended pinkie. "I would never presume to accuse you of being unsophisticated, Miss Prix," Ev said. He reached around the table and caught the coffee cup. Once it was in his hands, he realized how delicate even that was and very slowly placed it down. "I'd rather have a proper barbecue on some picnic tables behind the church."

"Stucky's wings," she cried out in joy.

"I say go whole hog. Bubba's pulled pork sandwiches and Anne Marie's grits 'n' gravy."

Madeline clasped a hand to her mouth and squealed.

"You ain't heard the best part."

"No." She shook her head and caught his arm as if to stop him from daring such a thought.

Leaning closer, he brushed back a curl of her hair with his nose and whispered, "Gramma Bess' chess pie."

Madeline's groan was near orgasmic, her eyes rolling back at the memory of the best pie in all fifty states. As he watched her shimmy in excitement, a flutter caught in his stomach.

Remember the last time she made that sound because of you? How bad do you want to hear it again?

With everything in my heart.

"Dance with me."

She blinked fast, her big blue eyes softening as she stared up at him. "What? You can't be serious."

"They said we should try everything out. Might as well give the floor a spin." He held out his hand, prepared for her to crush him with a rejection. God knew he deserved worse.

But sweet Maddy delicately dropped her fingers in his palm, and Everett guided her to the dance floor. He placed a hand to the small of her back to help her around the tables and he didn't remove it when they got below the chandelier to face each other.

So your plan was to get her to dance, then what?

Everett extended a hand, and she took it. With care, Madeline slipped her other arm around his shoulders, and she strained to reach. Ev pulled her to him, closing the gap between them until she felt safe in his embrace. Now came the dancing part, the bit that he had never figured out.

Uncertain, Ev began to two-step in a wobbly circle, trying to guide Maddy while figuring out what to do at the same time. She followed at least, her smile not dimming. "This is a good floor. Very sturdy."

"Mmm. I suppose." Should he do a turn? Did he even know how to do turns?

"I haven't had chess pie in years."

"Really? That can't be right."

His arm slipped lower, his forearm caressing the sway of her hips and her hand bunched against the back of his neck. "You need a proper Southern meal. Something that sticks to the bones and isn't just another bagel without the good bits."

"Where exactly would I get a proper Southern meal?" the one who'd been living in New York for years asked him.

From me. You deserve that and so much better. Ev opened his mouth, prepared to tell her such, when Madeline's smile faltered. She winced and tried to shrink back.

"What is it?" he asked in a panic.

"You stepped on my toe is all."

Oh, God. "I'm sorry. I'm so sorry. My stupid feet, they're all…" He dropped his hold on her and scurried away while glaring at his offending appendages. It wasn't just his feet—his body was a walking natural disaster. "I knew I can't dance. I don't know why I…"

"Hey."

He flinched at the hand before realizing it wasn't going to smack him. Instead, it settled on his arm, and Everett risked a glance to find she wasn't gnarled up in rage. If anything, she looked as worried as he felt.

"Toe-trodding happens."

"You're not angry?" he stuttered.

Madeline grew confused. "Why would I be? It's not like you did it on purpose."

"No, I would never," he insisted, when an old favorite twinkled in the speakers. Madeline tapped those toes he had stomped over, and Ev reached a hand out to her. "Do you want to try again?"

She bowed her head and took his hand. As they folded back together, Madeline shifted her feet so there was more distance from his toes. "Just in case," she said.

"Good idea," he agreed even as his skin bristled in shame. Rocking back and forth in his arms, Maddy closed her eyes. Her lips moved to match the lyrics no one sang but she obviously knew by heart.

She put her all into the words that didn't pass her sweet lips. How her nose crunched up when the orchestra reached the accusation part, how her cheeks slackened for the sad refrain. "'Little more than acquaint'," Ev sang, the rush of the past coming for him. Maddy's eyes flew open, and she stared in shock at him.

He risked turning her in a spin while continuing the duet, "'For I am neither man nor god, neither sinner nor saint'."

"'Do I know you?'" she sang back, her feet shuffling to catch up to him. "'Have we met in some prior place? Did I hold your hand, stare in your eyes and memorize your face?'"

The coach had talked him into the musical, all but browbeat him into it with a threat of expulsion if he didn't put on tights and dance on stage. It had been the first most humiliating moment of his life. Ev couldn't sing, moved like a three-legged cow and broke into hives at the idea of memorizing lines. But at that moment he felt like a star working centerstage with Maddy on his arm.

"'Forget me as you all forgot, remember me as I remember you not. Your memories are all a lie,

Edmond Dantes was left to die. Few are worthy of this world's love..."' Pain he couldn't explain stewed inside, rippling through Ev's heart. Not just the past day's problems, but a lifetime of him failing to measure up crashed like thunder. The musical, his marriage, college, a decent job, giving in on thinking he'd ever deserve better than Kathy.

Warmth blossomed over his cheek, and a sob caught inside. There, with her palm pressed to his face so he could look in her eyes, Maddy sang, "'I do know you.'"

Bending his head, Everett leaned to her parted lips holding that focal 'you'. All he'd wanted was someone to know the good in him — all he feared was someone good seeing the worthlessness in him. Maddy curled her fingers behind his ear, and he wanted only her kiss.

"Sorry that took so long. How did you find the room?"

The crisp professionalism of Jacques wrenched Ev away. It wasn't until he stood at his full height that he realized he'd dipped Maddy. She sprung up onto her heels and struggled to right herself. Everett held her hand and caught the small of her back to help.

"It's a lovely ballroom," she said.

"Wonderful." Jacques clapped his hands. "Let me show you what other programs we have." He cycled through a handful of light shows, projections of snowflakes, fireworks and bells orbiting over the floor while the colors changed above.

"I don't know if we'll need all that," Ev said. He tried to ease away from Maddy without making it look like he had. Somehow a gap formed, both folding their hands in front and staring at the event coordinator.

"Details to be decided later." Hustling over to them, Jacques opened yet another folder with serious paperwork inside. He clicked a pen and put it in Everett's fingers before anyone knew what was happening. Jacques smiled. "May I say, I've been doing this a long time, and I think you'll make it."

Ev started to loop around the E in his name, when he paused and stared at the man. "Make it?"

"I know it's not polite to prognosticate on a couple's future, but between you and me, some have it and some don't."

"Couple? Oh stars, we're not..." Maddy gasped, then slapped a hand over her mouth.

"We're just...friends?" Ev asked, uncertain if they had even reached that stage after what he had done. Maddy covered the entire bottom half of her face with her hands, only the peak of her brows giving any hint to how she felt about him. It couldn't be good.

Whipping his head from one half of the not-couple to the other, Jacques asked, "Are you not the Dashwood-Benson wedding?"

"No!" Ev shouted to the glass roof, Kathy's accusations rearing up to sink their fangs. But he also caught Maddy slinking back at his reaction. And the dumb fool had almost kissed her. "I'm with the fire union two-twelve."

"Ah." All that excited courtesy fled, Jacques no doubt realizing he wasn't going to be seeing a fat commission bonus for this tax write-off. "Of course, I see here we'd had you penciled in as well. You've seen the room. It should be acceptable."

"And the food...? I should pick the menu."

"The chef will choose something acceptable enough. If we're quite finished, I need to be returning to the desk." He reached for the binders in Ev's arms.

"Mind if I keep these for a few days? There's a lot to choose."

His grin turned damn near nefarious, but Jacques gave in. "I trust you'll return them to us. They can be quite costly to reproduce."

"Of course. Not a problem." Ev smacked the back of the binder and returned the same tight-lipped smile. With that, Jacques hustled out of the ballroom, flipping off the light-show and music as he went.

In the near dark, Ev muttered, "Why do I think I just got the ball talked down to cold hotdogs over the kitchen sink?"

Maddy chuckled and the two of them began to walk together out of the royal splendor. "Maybe that picnic idea isn't the worst after all."

Out in the hall, Ev paused. He held the binder between them like it was high school and he needed a textbook to hide away his boner. "So, um, you want to help me pick between the tablecloths in unwashed gray or stained red?"

She bounced up on her toes, shaking those curls, and Everett leaned closer. "I can't, sorry. And you can't either, remember."

Right. Hayden's date that he had so *graciously* invited him to. The last thing he wanted to do was watch Hayden charm his way into Maddy's drawers, much less while sitting next to Kathy's murderous glare. He doubted she'd even show. She had barely listened when he'd told her about it.

"Maddy, about the dinner, I..." Ev began, when he caught the screen of her phone damn near exploding with texts from Hayden. "I'll meet you there."

Chapter Sixteen

It looked like a restaurant out of a futuristic utopia. Neon lights danced across the front of the stark-white bricks, playing out scenes of silhouetted fish leaping over ocean waves. Madeline clung tighter to her clutch as she watched a little green fish pursued by a massive blue shark. The neon fish wiggled its tail and the light jumped to the other side of the sign. She was about to breathe a sigh of relief, when jaws opened up around the fish and all went dark.

"Good evening." An excited voice rolled around her, pulling Madeline away from the fish repeating its loop of death.

Bright teal lights beamed over Hayden, who'd styled his hair into tufts of spikes that reminded her of a hedgehog waddling in the garden. *Probably not the right thing to say.*

"Hi." She flung her fingers from her clutch for a wave, only to clasp them back.

Hayden canvassed down her and smiled. "You look nice."

"Thanks." She'd settled on the flowing white top and, still unable to face that black skirt, had dug out the heart-pocket jeans.

"Shall we?" Hayden extended his arm like a true gentleman, and Madeline took it. She'd never had so much fuss given to her—first a man guiding her into a fancy restaurant, then Ev asking her to dance.

Why did she agree to that?

Because his smile makes your heart flip, and his touch melts you to jelly.

Other than that, of course. A part of her had hoped all those stupid butterflies had died over the winter. That once she was back in his arms, she'd feel nothing. Instead, perfect, amazing, wondrous Everett Berry had trodden on her toes and it made her fall even harder. If she didn't get away from him soon, she might never.

"Have you had sushi before?"

Hayden pushed open the door and helped her inside. Ceiling-tall fish tanks lit up in blue, purple and green. The real fish swam in lethargic circles behind a woman at a hostess stand. Madeline couldn't see any of the tables, the dining section hidden behind white room dividers that swayed like waves on the ocean. *Where is Ev? He said he would meet us here.*

Why are you looking for him?

"Hm?" Hayden stepped in front of her, startling Madeline. She'd been up on her tiptoes trying to peer around the frosted glass to find…a man who wasn't her date. *That's rude. And he asked you a question you ignored. Even ruder.*

"Ah, yes," she said.

Hayden mentioned his reservation to the hostess, then swept an arm around Madeline's back. It lingered above where Ev's had touched. "Don't worry. You've got me here to help you."

"Thank you," she said out of knee-jerk politeness. She'd been eating sushi since her college days with Beth. Hayden stared past her down the winding carpet that led to a bar. The bottles on the wall lit up with the same oceanic neon colors.

"Why don't we start in there?" he asked, jerking his head to the stools. "Something easy for the first course."

Madeline wasn't a teetotaler but preferred a peach tea with dinner instead of a cocktail. Still, he seemed insistent, so she smiled and said, "That sounds…"

"You're here." Rushing from around the wave came sandy hair, then the blushing face of Everett Berry. He struggled with an unknotted tie wrapped around his neck. When he started to go under instead of over, Madeline began to reach out to help. Another hand cupped under hers, locking around her fingers and pinning her tight.

Guilty, she glanced at Hayden but the man grinned wider like he didn't mind having to remind her who she was on a date with.

"You could have told me this place required ties," Ev muttered, finally getting the red tie knotted on.

Hayden shrugged. "It slipped my mind. We were going to enjoy drinks at the bar…"

"Don't bother," Everett interrupted. "We got a table already."

We. That meant… Madeline's heart sunk as Hayden pulled her after the retreating Ev. There, haloed by a ring of lights set inside a captain's wheel was a princess. Maybe not by birth or country, but when little girls saw her on the street, they'd run up wanting Sleeping Beauty's or Cinderella's autograph. Kathy Clark's long white-blonde locks glowed gold and showered down her shoulders. She wore a red cocktail dress that accentuated her perky, perfect breasts thanks to a low-cut neckline.

All the momentum Madeline had gained from her cute jeans imploded. Frumpiness rampaged through her system, halting her in her tracks. No matter how strong Hayden was, he couldn't tug her on. When he turned to look at her, all she wanted to do was run. "You...I should put on a dress. They require dresses here."

"Don't be silly. You look fine," Hayden assured her, his mouth tight. Still, he dropped her arm and walked to the table. Kathy rose from her seat like Aphrodite riding the shell and extended her hand to him.

Flee into the night. Join a circus. Never look back.

"I like the jeans."

Madeline swiveled to find Everett Berry staring down at her legs and...the backside. Seeming to realize he was caught, he jerked his shoulders up and he turned red. "It's more practical."

"Every girl wants to be practical."

"And the hearts are..." He swallowed, his voice dropping to a whisper. "...cute."

"Madeline, dear," Hayden called, yanking her away from the flustered Everett to find her date had pulled her chair out.

Ducking her shoulders, she dashed for the seat and sat down. *Please don't try to push me in.* Kathy was staring at Hayden and if he showed any strain, Madeline would die on the spot.

Before he even tried, Madeline hooked a hand under the chair and hunched over while walking it and herself against the table. She landed too close, her boobs nearly spilling out over the place setting, but no way was she moving again. Putting on a smile, she looked up to find instead of the princess, the prince sat across from her.

"Hi," Ev said, waggling his fingers.

"Good to see you again," Madeline responded when the waitress arrived and passed out the menus. She tried to focus on that instead of the piercing green eyes watching her. A shadow loomed over her shoulder, and Hayden's cheek brushed hers.

"Let me help you with that," he said.

Madeline nibbled on her lip, letting Hayden take control. Suddenly, Kathy reached over and ripped the menu from Everett's hand. The movement was so shocking, it stopped the waitress from filling their glasses with water.

She giggled and ran her fingers through Ev's hair. "Don't mind him. My baby doesn't have the head for sophisticated fare. Do you?"

The menu wasn't in Japanese. But Ev dropped his eyes to his hands and muttered, "No, ma'am."

The double date was off to an awkward, painful start. It couldn't get any worse from there.

* * * *

When the dishes arrived, most picked by the sushi expert, Madeline pulled in a sigh of relief. At least now the awkward silence could be replaced by eating. She hadn't been very hungry before, her stomach filled with butterflies, but looking at the tuna rolls, she was tempted to shove them all in and run.

"A toast," Hayden called, lifting his glass of sake. Kathy raised her rosé and tossed a golden curl off her shoulder. Ev fumbled for his beer and Madeline reached for the peach tea they'd been kind enough to mix up for her. It wasn't until she got it shoulder high that Hayden turned to her.

"To Madeline and the success of her kitten rescue center."

Gosh. Her cheeks lit red, and she shrunk deeper into the chair. "Thank you," she mumbled. Her long-dormant senses kicked in, and she felt the glare of the popular girl on her.

Kathy's predator gaze caused Madeline to sink further down. If it weren't for her damn breasts, she'd have slipped under the table. She had braced herself, when Ev spoke up.

"What are ya gonna call it?"

"Huh?"

"You keep saying center, and rescue center and kitty hotel. There's got to be something better."

"I…" Madeline blanked. They'd settled on a color for the logo but not a name? How did that slip through the cracks? "I'm not sure." Maybe Chantelle had something. She should call and check.

"Whatever it is…" Hayden threw an arm around the back of her chair, pulling so hard the far leg rose off the ground. Madeline slapped a second hand to her glass to keep it from spilling. "I'm sure it'll be great."

His all-encompassing smile ordered her to turn to him. Her breath stagnated from the intoxicating confidence in Hayden's face.

"Of course, Maddy's always been creative," Ev spoke up.

Hayden put her back on the ground, jarring Madeline in her chair, and he sat up higher. "You must have had a wonderful time together at the hotel."

She didn't do anything, he didn't do anything, but an insinuation lurking in Hayden's tone set her heart pounding. She looked everywhere but at Ev, while Kathy zeroed in on him. "What?"

"He didn't tell you? They're working together on the ball. It's rather sweet, old friends and all."

Kathy snorted once. "You and Ol' MacDonald?"

A thousand old wounds opened at once. Absently, Madeline bundled up her hair in a hand, trying to hide it and flatten the clown curls. She could smell the hamburger papers they'd stuff in her locker and the ketchup packets they'd put in her shoes. It was a joke, they all remembered it as funny, and Madeline would laugh along because what else could she do?

"What was I worrying about?" Kathy shook her head and sighed as if all her fears were washed away. She pulled in a sip of water and stared dead-eyed at Madeline.

Her legs locked, causing Madeline to stand. It was such a reflex, she forgot to step away, causing her breasts to knock over her tea. "I'm sorry," she sputtered, reaching for a napkin, when she caught the slow, dismissive eye of a girl who knew that Madeline was less than worms below her feet. Locking her jaw to keep the sob in, Madeline broke into a run and dashed straight for the only escape she knew — the bathroom.

"Sorry, sorry," she kept apologizing while dashing past waiters clutching silver platters and menus. With every step, she grew more aware of her body, wishing she could pull and tug it inward until it wouldn't touch anything. There was the ladies' room.

Madeline approached the door, but instead of fleeing inside, she stared up at the sign. The little silhouetted woman who represented all women in distress didn't have an hourglass figure. She wasn't model thin with sticks for legs and arms. No, this woman who welcomed all to the porcelain throne in times of need and distress was wide-bottomed and didn't apologize for it.

"Maddy…"

The tears started, and she turned away from Everett rushing to her.

"I'm sorry about…all of that."

She was gum under the desk, a hard pink blob people dared the other to touch. No one wanted that disgusting gum, but they could use it to torture others for fun.

"Kathy is…frankly, she can be quite cruel."

All her life she'd heard Kathy Clark described as beautiful, vivacious, hot, the girl next door. No one, not the teachers, not the other girls, not even her victims ever called her cruel. The people she went after deserved it, because Kathy was too pretty to be wrong.

Staring at Ev with his head hanging down, his hands cupped to his thighs, a strange kindred feeling passed through her. Madeline reached over to him, to try to console him, when a dark thought clanged in her mind. *He left you for her even knowing how cruel she is.*

Madeline's hand fell.

"I told her not to… It's so fucking childish."

"Forget it." She dabbed at her eyes and put on a smile. "It's…" *Inevitable.* "Not your fault."

To her surprise, Ev didn't grin and skip on back to his date. A shudder passed across his body. "I wish I could think that, just once."

What?

"Anyway, your food is getting…warm. I didn't want you to miss out on all that raw fish because of her. Is it really raw?" He sounded in a near panic at the thought and a strange chuckle broke through Madeline's cloud.

"Ain't I seen you eat frog's legs before?"

"At least they were cooked. What if it's got parasites?"

"Everett Berry." Madeline placed her hands on her hips and stared him down. "Don't you trust me?"

She didn't expect him to shake his head, to take her hand and look her in the eye. "To the ends of the earth."

"We should…go back to the table." Where her date was, where his date was. The woman who had called her a clown. She needed to be anywhere but in this secluded spot of the restaurant staring intently at Everett's lips.

To her relief and regret, he nodded and released her. Madeline took a step to join the two left behind, when Ev leaned in to whisper, "Hayden, do you like him?"

"I…" *Don't have a clue.* He liked her, and for people like her, that was enough. She looked past Ev to spot Hayden sipping his sake and staring into space. Why didn't she ever stare at his lips and ache to kiss them?

"I suppose so," she said, leaving him alone with that question turned into a statement.

Chapter Seventeen

If he didn't think of the fish wiggling down his throat as he swallowed, the sushi was pretty good. Wasn't gonna beat out pork ribs slathered in mustard sauce, but Ev could see himself eating a few rolls in the future. He placed his fork down between the set of chopsticks and reached for his napkin to place on the plate, when he caught Maddy's eye. She worked the chopsticks like a professional, even eating her rice with them.

Extending her roll caught between the chopsticks, Maddy gave a little kick of her wrist and the seaweed-wrapped rice began to sway back and forth. Everett began to reach to give a little tug on the seaweed wrapping, when Hayden leaned over. He draped his whole arm across Madeline's shoulders and pulled himself to her. Dropping his hand under the table, Ev tried to look anywhere but at the man animatedly explaining something. Whatever it was went in one ear and out the other for him, but Maddy seemed enthralled.

She even…nibbled on her lip in response and blushed. An overwhelming urge to send Hayden toppling ass over end until his head struck a fish tank overcame him. A low cough distracted Ev from racking up an assault charge. Kathy glared at him, then darted her eyes to the check that'd been sitting on the table for the past ten minutes.

"Well…" Everett began, shifting in his chair to pull the two lovebirds apart. "It's getting late."

"Nothing saying you have to stay." Hayden dismissed him with a toss of his fingers, then he focused on Madeline. "I was entertaining the idea of a nightcap."

Ev clenched around his fork while Maddy shrugged. "I don't know. I have a lot of work in the morning…"

A beep rose from Hayden's phone, and the impolite bastard raised a finger to shut her up. He dug into his pocket and actually checked the damn thing.

Everett leaned closer to Kathy to whisper loud enough for anyone to hear, "Guess they don't do manners up here on dates."

At that moment, his phone went off too. Without a thought, he reached for it, when Hayden's dark gaze lifted from his screen to catch Ev being as uncouth. Not wanting to let him win, Ev was about to let it go, when another beep rose. He pulled it out, prepared to silence the thing, when a text appeared.

Emergency. All hands on deck.

"I'm sorry, I've got to go. There's a big fire," he said, standing up while staring at his phone. They forwarded the address and it kicked into the back of his brain, but he didn't know why.

Hayden stood too and gathered up his jacket. "This was not how I wanted the date to end. Can you forgive me?"

"Don't be silly. Fires are more important," Maddy said, jerking her hand for the door.

The sly bastard caught her gesture and kissed her knuckles. "Such a caring heart. I hope we can reschedule another."

"Um…" Her entire face turned beet red, and Maddy cast the edge of her vision Ev's way.

"What about the bill?" Kathy punctured through the romance like an icepick to the skull. "Or were you going to run off and leave us to pay?"

As if you ever would.

Ev clenched his teeth and dug for his wallet, needing to get to the station ASAP. It must be huge for them to call in everyone. Maddy cracked open her little purse and fished for a credit card, when Hayden swept up the little plastic tray and dropped three fifty-dollar bills on it.

"It's impolite to expect a lady to pay on the first date," he declared, then stared at Ev. "I guess they do have some manners up here after all."

"You really don't… I can chip in." Maddy tried to add a twenty on top of the pile, but Hayden placed his hand over the tray.

"I won't hear of it," he said and leaned in for a kiss. At the last second, Madeline turned, causing his lips to land beside her mouth instead of on it.

"Are you finished?" Ev pushed, aching to get out there.

Hayden tipped his head in a little bow and strained his arms to put his jacket on. Ev started to undo the borrowed tie around his neck when arms grabbed his shoulder. He didn't realize he was falling, until he felt a hard line press to his slack lips. It wasn't so much a kiss as a marking of territory.

"Good luck, babe," Kathy said, her smile all ice.

Trying to not shake, Ev slicked a hand through his hair, and he stepped away. "Yeah, thanks," he muttered, in too much shock to respond in kind.

With Hayden a step in front of him, the two men left the girls behind. "That went well," Hayden said, strutting like the cock of the coop. "We should double date more often."

Thank God he had a fire to fight instead, or Hayden's perfect smile would be missing a few teeth.

* * * *

Standing beside Kathy outside the restaurant while waiting for her Uber would normally rank as the most awkward time of Madeline's life. But after that dinner, it didn't crack the top ten. Men would ogle Kathy's long legs, which were barely hidden by her high skirt. Then, if their gaze shifted to Madeline beside her, they'd rear back as if they'd been poisoned and were about to scratch their eyes out.

Madeline was aware of it the way she knew the neon fish was being devoured or swimming away. It all fell into the background as she tried to do everything in her power to not think about Everett or Hayden running into danger. A big fire? How big did that mean? Were they at risk of dying? And how was Kathy so calm?

Kathy touched up her lipstick in a compact mirror shaped like a diamond and teased her hair. "You're lucky, you know," she said.

Because she wasn't in a relationship with a man who ran into fires instead of away from them? Because she couldn't be knotting her fingers together at the thought of him not coming back?

Kathy slapped her compact shut and cast a look back. "Curly hair is so popular."

Absently, Madeline patted the curls she'd been ridiculed and attacked about all her life. "What?"

"That whole lazy bedhead, doesn't care what other people think look." Kathy eyed her up and pursed her lips, "It fits you better than me."

She's cruel.

Ev was risking his life to save lives, and all she was worried about was putting down someone as insignificant as Madeline Prix? For the first time, Madeline saw the cracks in perfect and beautiful Kathy Clark. She shrunk before her, a cloak of pettiness struggling to hide away a bitter and shallow personality. Madeline almost felt sorry for her.

A chime rang from her phone, and she checked it. Her driver was coming up. Madeline texted back a reply, but when she looked up to find the blue Hyundai, Kathy was already opening the door and getting in.

"Um, excuse me…" Madeline tried to run after her, but Kathy slammed the door and stared straight ahead. She'd already forgotten Madeline even existed. Madeline's car sped off into the night, leaving her to request another. Above her head, the little green fish was devoured by the blue shark.

It took another fifteen minutes before a second car arrived, a green Civic. She moved to sit in the back, when the driver called out, "Um, would you mind sitting up here?"

Always being polite, Madeline slipped into the front seat as the driver kept talking. "Sorry about that. Usually I don't have, well…" She pointed behind to a mass of pet carriers buckled in to the seats. Madeline's interest piqued.

"Who's in there?"

"Oh, don't worry. They're all empty. I was helping a friend move some cats she found on her property and forgot about the carriers."

"What color?" Madeline asked as the car merged into slow-moving traffic.

"Orange tabbies mostly, though one was gray. You a cat lover?"

She chuckled while finding one of Monte's hairs stuck to her jeans. "You could say that. Actually, I'm running a cat rescue center in the neighborhood."

"No kidding? What's the address? I swear my friend's house is like a doula for cats."

Madeline cracked open her little clutch. The single business card inside was one she got handed for a window place. They should get some printed up…once the center had a name. She wrote out the address and handed the card to the woman.

"Thanks. It's been hell finding places for the older ones."

"Tell me about it. Oh, but the center's not going to be open until May," Madeline added.

The driver smiled and nodded once more. Pleased that she'd made someone's life better, and possibly rescued cats in danger, Madeline leaned back in the seat…for the car to screech forward and slam to a stop.

"For fuck's sake!" the driver shouted. They were trapped in the middle of an intersection from a sudden block of traffic ahead of them. "Move. Your. Ass!" She laid into the horn, and Madeline winced at the force.

"I wonder what's causing this?" They were drawing close to her apartment, in a part of the city she knew by heart. Traffic was a pain but never at a standstill this time of night.

The cars crawled forward enough they were able to get out of the intersection, not that it mattered. A handful of people tried to turn into the blockage, dooming more to the wait. Her driver leaned on the horn and used a full range of curse words.

"This is close to my place. How about I walk the last part?"

"You sure? It's dark out."

It'd take her fifteen minutes at most to get home versus sitting next to the raging volcano for an hour in this jam. "I'll make sure to stick to the streetlights. It's no problem." She opened the door and unhooked her seat belt.

"Okay. Thanks for the card, Cat Lady!"

Madeline stumbled across the road as the traffic surged a few more inches. She stopped to stare at the driver with the backseat crammed full of pet carriers. So it had finally happened. At age twenty-nine, Madeline Prix was the cat lady. No husband, no kids, just the cats to keep her company…and the people who loved cats, too.

Why not be the cat lady? Was it so wrong to live helping homeless animals even if she did it without anyone to go home to? As long as she had her friends and… Crud, she forgot to text Beth. Madeline strode down the sidewalk, turning the corner for her apartment, bent down in her phone telling her friend the date was over and Hayden didn't try to murder her.

Madeline waited a few seconds to see if Beth responded, when she raised her head and hellfire rained from the sky.

* * * *

The air boiled in the freezing April night, flames licking up the side of a building nestled among a full block. Ev stared up the winding side with windows blown out from the heat and crash of burnt floorboards. If they didn't stop this soon, it could take the whole building or worse—jump to another. The one saving grace—the wind was low tonight.

"L.T.!"

Everett dropped from the side of the truck and hustled to the side of Captain Reed. Half of her gear was covered in black ash and tar, only the whites of Jill's teeth evident through the thick mass on her helmet.

"Captain!" he struggled to shout through his mask, the blaring sirens, the screams of people yanked from their homes and the crackle of fire eating a building.

"I've got three on the hose, and Crawford is making a sweep for survivors, but the building's supports are cracking."

"What do you need from me?"

As he asked that, a window blew. On instinct, he turned away, as did Captain Reed. Glass sprinkled across the ground like a jagged rainstorm. Ev pulled in a breath, expecting to feel shards had ripped through his coat and impaled him in the back. But as he looked up, he caught a flash of red curls in the crowd.

It couldn't be—

"Get in there and search for any survivors," Reed shouted next to him. "Third floor."

"Yes, ma'am," Ev said. He jogged to pluck an ax from the truck, when he looked over his shoulder and a billboard for organic toothpaste wrenched him back to November. It'd been advertising a beer back then, which he'd stared at while waiting to make sure Maddy got into her apartment okay. This was her home plunged into fire.

"Berry!"

Ev shook his head. At least he knew Madeline couldn't be in there. The rest of her life, however… Not the time to worry. Nodding to the captain, he fought every instinct in his body and ran headlong into the flames. Smoke choked out the entrance, the mailboxes dripping to the floor like metallic paint. The heat smashed into his lungs like a sledgehammer, but Ev kept his head level and dashed up the stairs. The cement cried out but held better than anything else.

"Fire rescue!" Ev screamed at the top of his lungs. "Is anyone here?" He struggled to listen for meek cries over the grind and pop of five stories of wood cindering to ash. If the floor above him gave out, he didn't stand a chance of surviving. The whole thing would bury him.

Hustling up the second floor, Everett tried again, his voice straining as the smoke's tendrils clawed apart his throat. "Hello? Is anyone trapped here?"

"Berry!"

Hayden's head swung over the banister above. As he did, the old railing warped from the high heat like a piece of licorice. "Help me break down this door!" he shouted.

Hustling up the stairs as fast as he could in full gear, Ev struggled to breathe when he reached the third floor. They were close to the fire itself and the belly of the beast. If this was what hell felt like, the devil had his work cut out for him.

Everett began to jog down the hallway, when the left side started to pitch. His shoulder bounced against the wall, but he kept going, running to catch up to Hayden who was smashing against the door.

"I heard something inside," he said and lashed out with his foot.

Ev hefted the ax over his shoulder and brought it through the door. It cracked where the lock would be, sundering whatever remained, but the door refused to budge.

"Something's blocking it. Shove with me," Hayden ordered. With all his might, Everett slammed against the door. Heat broiled up through his gloves, his palms inflamed like he touched the sidewalk in the middle of summer. *Fight through it!* He shoved harder, hearing the same low whimper that Hayden must have.

"Come on!" Everett cried, pushing with all his might while Hayden smacked his shoulder repeatedly against the door. A loud crash broke from inside and both men were sent tumbling into the apartment. Black smoke and a storm of sparks rushed out at them. To his shock, Hayden caught Ev's arm and kept him from falling into the blast.

"Hello? We're here to save…" Hayden shouted into the smoked-out room when the whimper grew louder. Fifteen pounds of fur leapt into Hayden's arms, and he stared dumbfounded at his rescue. "A fucking dog?"

The poodle lashed out, its whimper growing to an agitated bark. "I risked my life for a goddamn dog,"

Hayden muttered. "That's it. I didn't hear anything else on this floor. Let's get the fuck out of here."

"Wait." Everett stared down the rickety hallway to Madeline's door. "There's a couple cats inside, I know it."

"So what? They're just animals. We need to get out before the whole thing collapses. Berry? Berry!"

Ignoring his superior's orders, Everett hefted up the ax and pushed his way deeper into the mouth of hell. The air thickened to a black fog, clogging the mask strapped to his face. There was Maddy's door. She'd even put a cute daisy outside, the paper already curling from the heat alone. Hefting the ax up, Ev shouted, "Any cats in the way better get back."

With all his force, he swung through the flimsy wood. The lock rocked in its jamb, hot metal searing through the door. Ev could only smell the stench of smoke all around him, but he felt the heat rising from inside. The fire was getting close. He swung twice more, the ax's head bashing through the middle.

Ev lashed out with his foot, hoping to jar open the last bit, but nothing gave. Sweat that didn't evaporate dribbled down the gap of his helmet, the salt dripping into his eyes. He shook it all away and raised the ax up once more. For Maddy.

The door shattered in half, the top falling inward to the black charred apartment. Everett kicked the bottom from the lingering lock and tried to gird himself for the worst. A whirlwind of smoke erupted from the fire as he walked into the kitchen.

"Monte!" Ev shouted like the cat was a dog. As he did, a cough rattled in his throat. An orange light burst from the living room like the couch was made of coals and his heart sank. The chances of either of those tiny bodies surviving was…

Claws sprang from the black air and sank into his arm. Ev fought off his first reaction to fling the attacking creature into the living room. With tears welling, he looked down into the full-on panic of Monte. The cat meowed at him, his cries barely legible over the fire. "I'm here to get you out," Ev told him. He wrapped an arm under the older cat and carried him like a pipe. Monte didn't seem to care, but there was another needing rescue.

"Where's your brother?" Ev asked, getting more terrified meowing from the eldest. "Spark…" He raised a hand to his mouth to aid in his shout, when the far wall collapsed. The entire board of Madeline's rescues erupted into flames, white-hot ashes bursting up off the floor and sticking to Everett. He didn't have much time. This apartment, the entire floor was going to go.

Where would that cat be hiding?

The living room was caved in, her couch and TV tumbling to the floor below while flames crawled down from the ceiling. Smoke gushed from where the bathroom and bedroom were. If the kitten tried to hide in there…

An explosion rocked the floor under him. Everett crumpled over Monte, tucking the cat to his chest as he put his back to the oncoming flame. Just as it was about to hit, the fire danced back to spread over the living room wall. That was pure luck. If he stayed any longer, he was dead.

Ev took a step for the door, the entire exit blinded by smoke, when all of the chaos, the splintering wood, the exploding electronics, the gush of ash, fell away. In that micro-second, he heard a tiny whimper and looked up above the cabinets where a pair of yellow eyes looked back.

"Sparky!" he shouted, reaching for the tiny tuft of black fur hiding in the shadows. The kitten wanted nothing to do with this fire and leapt to his arms. With both cats secure, Ev took a step back, and the floor collapsed under him.

Chapter Eighteen

Everything was up in flames. Madeline's soul watched her building where she'd spent the last ten years of her life fall into the burning inferno climbing up the side. White ash danced like dandelion seeds on the spring wind. Her body numbed over, all emotion frozen from the state of shock at the whole of her future turning to nothing but cinders.

"Get back." A cop tried to push the people gathered outside back. Some of them were neighbors, people she'd see standing by the mailboxes or catching a smoke on the steps. Others were strangers, no doubt *concerned onlookers* who wanted to film the building going up in flames and set it to ironic music for likes.

"Where's Berry?" a voice shouted above the gush of water churning through the hoses trained on the building.

Madeline pushed aside a man filming to stand right before the barricade the cop guarded. Between a stack of cracked wood stood two firefighters, one whose uniform was coated in black soot. "He's supposed to be right behind you."

"Fool went back for something. I don't know if—"

A great crack rattled the building, causing everyone to scamper back. Windows burst, sending glass raining down from above as two floors crashed. Madeline watched it all in a near faint. She recognized the silhouette of the fridge that plunged past the window and down to another apartment. A cute retro one with pink paint and too many cat treats on top.

There were a dozen mice caught behind that fridge thanks to her kittens batting them out of reach. Monte often climbed up there for a nap. Oh God. Tears burst in her eyes, and she clung to the barricade to keep from falling to her knees in despair. Why'd she leave him? Why'd she go on some godforsaken date and leave her poor baby behind? He couldn't even get out to save himself or Sparky. She was the monster who had made sure of it.

Her cruel imagination churned with images of Monte's single blue eye lit orange from the flames chasing him down the hall. She saw Sparky curled up and struggling to breathe, his black fur caked in tar. No.

Ev's in there too. But he's trained for it, he has to be...

The lead firefighter pointed to the floor and shouted, "Jesus Christ. Get out of the way before the whole thing comes down!" She waved her arm, redirecting the men at the hoses to shift sides. They left the hellfire to chew apart where Madeline lived, focusing all their energy on the middle of the building to stop its spread.

The chatter between the firefighters plummeted once they all learned one of their own was inside. Every trained eye turned to the destruction. It looked like a meteor had fallen from the sky and shattered through the side of the building, leaving flaming chunks behind. No one could survive that. No one offered to run in and save one of their own.

Everett Berry, so help me God, if you die in there, I will never speak to you again!

Madeline's tears fell harder than before, and she bit her hand to keep from screaming at him. It didn't matter why he had stayed behind — he shouldn't have done it. *Goddamn fool, you belong here away from the fire.*

"Hold up!" the firefighter called, halting the hard spray of water against the front door.

Two shoulders stepped into Madeline's view. She struggled to rise on her tiptoes, but that wasn't enough. *What is happening?* Forgoing every nice Southern lady manner drilled into her, Madeline shoved the men aside and watched a silhouette stumble down the stairs. The arms were wrapped around something close to the chest.

A heavy boot hit the ground, then another, when he collapsed to his knees and the other firefighters came running. The woman helped to pry the mask off his face, the whole surface black as death. They fought against the buckles, the man tipping back.

Please, for once in your damn existence be merciful, oh Lord...

Everett gasped for air in the smoke-stained night. The other firefighters held his blackened head and pressed an oxygen mask over his nose and lips.

Thank you. Madeline had her hands clasped together in prayer and she raised it to the sky. As she did, she noticed the other fireman — the one who'd mentioned Ev — chase something on the ground. Whatever it was ran farther and farther from the building, giving him quite the challenge until he got both hands around it and popped up in front of her.

A slow meow rolled from the dark shadows in his arms. "Monte?"

Madeline barreled through the barricade, taking it with, as she fought to get to her cat. Something held her arm, but she ignored it while staring at the panicked orange and black face of her spoiled baby.

"Oh goodness, it's him. He's okay. Monte!"

"Madeline?" The fireman holding her kitty tugged down his mask to reveal it was Hayden.

"You saved him," she sputtered, reaching for her cat. "You saved my Count." Her arm stuck, refusing to raise.

"It's okay, officer," Hayden said, his voice steady and commanding. The cop that'd tried to hold her in place shrugged and gave up. She wrapped her arms around her baby.

He stank of acrid smoke, her eyes welling up from it, but Madeline buried her nose against his head and held him tighter. "Thank you," she said, in near hysterics. "Thank you so much. I feared, I didn't even think..." Red-eyed, her lips aching from a cry-smile, Madeline looked up at Hayden. "Thank you."

Hayden reached over with his gloved hand and said, "I'm sorry this is happening, but if saving your cat can bring you some small comfort..." He dropped a finger near Monte's face and the cat swerved his head, fangs trying to sink into the heavy padding.

"Monte!" Madeline chastised him, yanking him away as Hayden did the same with his hand. "I'm sorry, he's...he's a frightful mess and not himself."

A strained smile appeared on Hayden, and he nodded. "Understandable given the circumstances."

"I swear, I'll give you nothing but treats here on out," Madeline promised her cat while rubbing her face over his head. A low purr rolled from him, as if he needed to soothe himself after that trauma. With Monte tucked safely in her arms, she looked up at Hayden. "What about Sparky?"

"Hm?"

"The kitten. I had a…a little black kitten too. He was, he was a rescue I'd…" It didn't matter that she'd known the baby for a few months. She loved him just as much as Monte.

But Hayden's face fell, and he looked away.

No. He was smaller. He was so dark that he'd blend in with the smoke. His tiny body couldn't handle the flames. She clung tighter to Monte, watching Hayden refuse to meet her eye because Sparky…

"Maddy?" a voice croaked in a painful cough. Through her tears, she found Everett sluggishly pulling his body closer.

At least he was okay. That still meant something in this, to know Ev would get to see another day. "Are you…?" she began, when Everett pulled down on the zipper of his coat and a pair of yellow eyes burned from inside.

"Sparky!" she shouted. The kitten didn't leap for her the way Monte did. Everett pulled him free of the safety of his arms.

"He took a lot of smoke." Everett coughed as he handed her the baby. "We all did, but I think…I hope he'll be okay."

Sparky brushed under her chin, his purr engine at maximum. She held both her miracles so tight and stared up at the third. "You didn't have to…"

Ev scratched against Monte's head, her cat rubbing back at the touch. With a slow intake of shallow breath, he looked at her. "Yeah, I did."

Clinging to her cats with the cold hand of April's weather cutting across her bare shoulders, Madeline watched her building turn to ash. It might have taken hours of the men and women bravely fighting the blaze, but it felt both longer and instantaneous when the rush of water stopped, and people raised their hands to clap. It was over.

It'd just begun.

She checked her phone, every text to Beth unread. What was she going to do? Her only home had gone up in flames. With two cats in tow, would a hotel take her? She hadn't even brought her whole purse with her, just a small clutch that carried the basics. Pain pressed on her chest, as Madeline realized she had nowhere to go.

"Berry, what are you doing?" a firefighter shouted, her voice amplifying off the concrete and glass ash where a building used to be.

"Checking the—" Ev said alongside the others who'd been manning the hose.

"No, you inhaled enough smoke to kill an elephant. Get home and clean up. Crawford will take charge of that. If he's gunning so hard for chief, might as well make him earn it."

The firefighter gave one hard pat to Ev's back, almost causing him to crumble, and walked away. As Everett placed the hose on the ground, he turned and glanced at Madeline holding her cats and praying for a miracle. He limped over to her and tugged off his helmet.

All those golden locks were stained a charcoal black. She wanted to reach over to try to shake the soot away, but Ev beat her to it with his hand. "You…you got somewhere to stay?"

"Oh um, well…" Madeline bounced on her knees, fighting to keep the tears out of her voice. "My friend is…I think she's having a date night and she won't pick up, so I don't know. I don't. I am…I'm homeless. I don't have any clothes, or my computer. Or a lamp. I'm lampless!"

"Here." Ev reached over and slipped a warm arm across her shoulders. The heat of the fire clashed with her frozen skin, but Madeline leaned against him, needing any rock in this winding typhoon. He held her close and guided her to the fire truck.

"Chris, we got a passenger, so drive carefully," he called to whoever was up front before saying to her, "I've got to drop my things off, then you can stay at my place until we find you a lamp and everything else. Okay?"

His place with Kathy. No. Madeline didn't belong there. She should refuse. "'Kay," she whispered.

Ev gave Sparky's sooty head another scratch. He checked the buckle across her lap and vanished to the other side of the truck. After they reached the station, it took a while for him to check his coat and other firefighting things, leaving Madeline standing under the fluorescent light while she tried to keep two cats under control. The other men who came back with him kept staring at the stranger without a home, but no one would talk to her.

Only Everett, who wrapped another comforting hand across her shoulder, would give her the time of day. He guided her to his truck and helped her up like a prince would assist a commoner onto a horse. "Sorry I don't have any carriers for these guys," he said.

"Monte'd scratch out your eye before you could get him in one," she said in a monotone. Ev was being so sweet when he didn't need to be, when he shouldn't be. How much had she ruined his life tonight?

They sputtered out into the dark streets two hours after midnight. She glared at the clock on the dashboard, certain it had to be lying.

"Sorry about the breeze," Everett said over the silence. "Or the smell. Usually I try to wash the soot off before going home, but I didn't want to leave you standing there. Should I close it?" He pointed to the window down a crack, but Madeline wasn't paying attention.

"Do you do this a lot?"

"What?"

"Help people who lost everything in a fire?" *Save worthless girls left blubbering before a fire?*

"Back home, worst I dealt with was a grease fire in a garage. So I guess you're my first lost home. Maddy, I am…"

"You have nothing to be sorry about. You and Hayden saved my cats. Everything else was just stuff."

The silence honed to razor wire. All Ev did was wring his hand over the steering wheel and say, "Yeah." They completed the rest of the drive in the awkward noise of a cracked window.

"There's a bed on the ground floor. It ain't much of a bedroom yet, but I hope it'll suit you for the night."

She couldn't argue with him because even if it was a mattress under a leaky roof, it was still a bed and a roof. As she stumbled into Ev's home, Monte had had enough of being treated like a baby. He sunk his claws into Madeline's exposed arm and made a break for it. She hissed in pain, causing Everett to turn around.

"It's fine. I'm used to it." She tried to wave him off, but Everett brushed his fingers near the wound and down Madeline's naked shoulder.

"Are ya bleedin'?" he asked, his accent thickening. Only the streaks of outside headlights across the window illuminated the room. A flicker caught on his smoke-stained hair. Another rolled across his chest barely contained in a fresh white shirt. Madeline struggled to swallow, every breath making her more aware how close Ev came to caressing her bra strap.

How easy it'd be for him to tug it down.

"Where have you been?"

Madeline stepped back as a blinding light appeared on the staircase above. It silhouetted a woman in a tight nightgown, her arms crossed as she glowered from on high. Kathy stomped her foot against the top step, and Everett moved to climb it to her.

"Fighting a damn fire."

"It takes you all night to do that?"

"When it's a big one, yes. That's how that works."

Trying to shrink further into herself, Madeline turtled up as best she could while clinging to Sparky. The kitten wasn't having that. He wanted to join Monte in some late-night mischief. Sparky gave his tiger squeak, and it drew the ire of the woman of the house.

"What the fuck is she doing here?" Kathy shouted.

"Her place caught on fire, and she needs somewhere to stay," Ev said in calm tones. But Kathy was one flame he couldn't fight.

"No. She brought some flea-ridden pests, too. No. I won't hear of it. This isn't some sleazy motel where you can bring over whatever girls you want."

Crap. Madeline stared at the unfinished floor because she couldn't face the wrath raining down from above. She needed to get out of there. Waving her hand, she tried to get Monte to come closer so she could pick him up while inching for the door.

"Not in my house," Kathy said with the confidence of a god.

Damn it. She'd already set her off once tonight, Madeline didn't have the energy to face her again. Calling for her cat, she tried to hustle for the door, only for her hip to catch on a toolbox. It didn't fall, but shifted enough it drew every eye to the dying violet. She had to get out of here.

Everett's voice rumbled deep across the very foundation. "This isn't your house."

"Don't you dare..." Kathy began, but Ev took a step closer, his head raised.

"This is my house." He jerked a thumb to his chest and came eye to eye with Kathy. "And I say who stays." Ev glanced to Madeline and gave a soft smile before turning back to Kathy. "And who goes."

"You... You got less brains than a dead pig!" Kathy shouted.

Ev crossed his arms. "Don't change the fact the deed's in my name."

He looked pleased as punch until Kathy raised her hand. The atmosphere darkened, Ev's head dipping lower the higher she lifted it. *What is she doing?* Madeline risked taking a step closer to see, when the floorboards under her creaked.

Kathy stared down at the third wheel in the middle of their fight, and she dropped her hand. "Don't come crying to me when the fatty breaks your floor," she snarled and spun away in a huff.

"You come back here and..." Ev began, when the sound of a door slamming cut him off. "Gah!" He tugged on his hair, when he jerked and pressed it back down. "Sorry about her, she's…"

Cruel. Not just to her. Madeline was used to people like Kathy Clark picking on her. But she never thought that anyone could be so mean to someone they cared about, someone they loved. It felt worse than all the shit Kathy had dished out in high school. At least Madeline could get away when the bell rang.

"I should go. I don't want to make things worse for you."

"No." Ev jogged down the stairs as fast as possible until he came to a stop before her. His chest heaved, the breaths jagged from his running into a building to save people. The headlights beamed across his piercing green eyes, and Everett said, "Please stay."

She wanted to fall into his arms. To have him cup her cheek, tip her head up to his and swear that all he wanted in the world was for Madeline to be here in his house—in his life. "I mean, it'd drive her crazy if you did."

He didn't want her, not like that. It was doubtful he ever had, and she knew he never would. Her hopes deflated, Madeline jerked her head. "Okay."

With a painful smile, Everett led her to the bedroom under the stairs.

Chapter Nineteen

Black circled his feet, the soot pooling in the cracks between the bricks of the old shower. Everett nudged at a chunk on the drain with his toe. It tumbled in the cleaning water, revealing it to be a piece of melted plastic with a tiny star on the side. How much more of someone else's life did he carry on his body?

The cool water turned icy, and he shut it off. Even wearing it, he knew he stank of smoke. It'd take days for the scent of charcoal and ash to wear off his skin. Pausing by the dirty sink meant for washing equipment, Ev glanced at his hair. The blond was tinged with a muddy black despite him washing it three times.

Fingers dug into the wet locks, shifting and pulling them, until the bald spot shone below his filthy hair. On the periphery, he kept seeing Kathy's raised hand. She had stopped because Maddy was there. She wasn't going to stop being angry about it. It was only a matter of time before the pattern repeated.

How rotten of a person must he be to deserve it?

A knock at the door caused him to flinch. Naked, Everett turned to the door barely hanging to the cheap plaster walls.

"Um, sorry to bother you…"

His stance relaxed. It was Maddy.

"I was wondering if I could maybe get a shirt to sleep in?"

Of course. Ev mentally smacked himself in the forehead. He yanked a towel off the rack by the washing machine and knotted it around his waist. She was stuck in her jeans and top, not exactly a comfortable way to rest…and she didn't have anything else to her name.

"If you don't have anything, that's okay. I understand."

Everett tugged open the door, and yellow eyes caught him. They belonged to the cat perched on her shoulders. Sparky reeked of smoke as bad as him. Madeline's gaze drifted, the full wobbling breadth of her blue eyes staring up at him. Her entire face went pink, and she bit down on her lip.

"It's no problem," Ev said, fidgeting in place. At the restaurant, he hadn't noticed how low her top ran. With Maddy blushing and standing right before him, he couldn't look anywhere else. The towel jerked, and he ducked his hips back, hoping to disguise how interesting he found staring down her shirt.

She looked up at his weird move, Everett trying to pretend he wasn't doing what he was. Her gaze drifted from his face to the top of his head and confusion rose.

Shit! He had left the bald spot exposed. Raking his hand up, he tried to bat his hair back in place. But his anxious dancing sent the towel dipping lower until one end fell off his hip to the thigh. It was Maddy who reached over and lay his hair back the way he kept it.

"Sorry that it stinks," he whispered.

"I don't mind. Reminds me of barbecue."

That had to be a lie, but she said it so earnestly Ev wanted to pull her into his arms. To hoist her up onto his washing machine so she'd be in the perfect range for him to kiss her, to run his hands up her cute little legs and over her tantalizing breasts.

"Do you, um…?" Maddy licked her lips and turned to stare out into the unfinished room. "Have a shirt?"

"Right. Let me get…dressed, and I'll find you something." Ducking his hips back further, Everett backed up until he stopped near the shower. With a little laugh, Maddy closed the door. He slipped on a white tee stained with all manner of paint and a pair of sweatpants. It was the kind of outfit to send any girl running, but it was all he had at easy reach. Luckily, he didn't bump into Kathy when he made a quick stop at the closet. He didn't care where she had gone off to sulk.

The entire top floor was Kathy's domain. He'd once slept up there in the bed he had refurbished special from an old four-poster Victorian one. But Ev found himself sneaking down to the other working room more and more. Sometimes Kathy would kick up a fuss. Other days she didn't even notice.

That was where he led Maddy. A simple cot with a comforter and pillow were set up next to the cabinets for the upstairs bathroom. What a master of his house — he'd risk back trouble over facing Kathy. Ev stopped before the door to the spare room Maddy had closed. Rather than knock, he froze.

What the hell had happened to his life? How did he wind up having to sneak around in his own home like a mouse avoiding traps?

Crumbling, he smacked his forehead against the door.

"It's safe to come in," Maddy called from deep inside.

Ev fought to compose himself, and he said, "I got a shirt for you." Then he realized she'd already told him to come in.

Sheepishly, he inched his way around the small door, careful to watch for any escaping cats. Maddy sat on the cot with Monte curled up in her lap. Ev tried to find Sparky, when a black blur zipped from one side of the room to the other.

"He seems to be feeling good," Everett remarked.

"Thank goodness. I was so worried. Already booked an appointment at the vet's just in case." She held up her phone like caring about others was a horrible trait to have.

"Here." Ev handed over the shirt. "It's from an old chili contest, pretty long, so I thought, hoped, it'd cover you up. All my pants are…"

"This should work great. Thank you." Despite going through hell, Madeline had a smile on. She placed Monte on the cot's pillow and rose to her feet. It wasn't until she reached for the hem of her blouse that Ev's brain pieced together what the shirt was for.

"Oh…jeez. I…" He froze. Full on, limbs-locked, head snared froze. Maddy's little pink fingernails danced in the light as they clenched around the bright white fabric covering her chest. *Get out of the room, you creep.*

Ev took a step back, and his heel to sliced on the door. The pain barely registered as he scrambled. "I should let you, let you rest and all."

"Wait."

Her plea pinned him in place, Everett facing the door as Madeline said. "No, it's silly. You've been so nice already."

"What is it?" He heard fabric hit the floor. The sound of her jeans unzipping caused him to jerk and try to shake away the really dirty thoughts. Still, she wouldn't say what she wanted. "Maddy, come on."

"You had such a hard day. I shouldn't keep you from getting rest."

Ev risked a quick peek over his shoulder. He caught a long line of tan and was assured she'd put the shirt on. Slowly turning, he said, "You can talk to me."

When she didn't shriek at him, he finished the full one-eighty, and his brain short circuited. The ol' Four Oh Five Chili shirt he'd won for eating ten bowls clung to Maddy's chest like shrink-wrap. Seeing the screen print of a redneck with his beard in chili warped around her beautiful tits created a new and confusing kink.

"The shirt looks good…on you, I mean."

"Thanks." She blushed and tucked a curl back behind her ear. "I was worried it wouldn't fit."

While it bagged around her stomach, the sides caught on her jaw-dropping hips. Maddy kept tugging on the hem as if to reposition it, but all it did was make Everett want to rub his palms up the seams to trace her curves. The fanciest couture in the world meant nothing compared to a girl in his old cookout shirt.

A weight dropped on his shoulders. Everett turned to find a smoke-drenched kitten rubbing his face against his scruff. "Hello to you too," he said, giving Sparky a little scratch. The purr sounded like a motorcycle buzzing past his house. With the kitten content, Ev walked to Madeline's side. He took a seat on the cot while Maddy kept folding up her shirt into a smaller and smaller square.

"I'm grateful for everything you've done," she said. "And I shouldn't keep you."

"Maddy, sit down before you fall down." He patted the cot next to him. It took a few more folds before she stumbled beside him. "It's three in the morning. You ain't keeping me from anything."

"What about...?" Her eyes rolled up to the ceiling where no doubt Kathy was puncturing her heels into the floor for fun.

A slow growl rolled through Everett that sent Sparky scampering away. He watched the kitten, who'd almost been crushed by the falling cabinets, chase after a dust bunny without a care. How did Kathy greet him for his rescue? With a threatening slap. "She can be a pill all on her own, believe me."

"Why...?"

Why was she so mean? God knew Kathy could give a thousand different reasons that were never her fault.

Why did he put up with it? God knew he deserved it. If he didn't, why did it keep happening?

"She wouldn't want me up there anyway. I'll stink of smoke for days."

"But you're a hero." Maddy gasped, causing Ev to blush and look away. He wasn't anything of the sort.

Struggling to his feet, he hunted around the mess of the old gear stored in the room. "If you don't mind, could I stay here with you?"

He clutched his old sleeping bag and turned to Maddy. She chewed on her lip with such fervor he knew what she was thinking about. The last night he'd stayed with her, before the damn wheel took to rolling again.

"I'm just—"

"Sure."

"—worried is all. The cats took on a lot of smoke."

"Ev…"

"We were trained, okay, for people, but it's got to work for them too. We all breathe, right?"

Maddy brushed a hand to his arm, stilling his babbling tongue. Sure, he liked the cats—he liked any animal that wasn't actively biting him. But that wasn't why he didn't want to leave her side. He found himself panting the same as when he ran out of the building, his fingers clenched around hers.

"You can stay," she said, her big eyes peering up at him. Assured all was well, Ev started to lean back, when her gaze darted to his hair and the hole.

Instead of the familiar sting of shame, a duller knife stabbed through his heart—exhaustion. Every damn day he folded up that part of his life and stuffed it into a drawer to keep going. Ain't no one going to take a man who was hit by his wife seriously. Ain't no one going to want a man who flinches if a woman raised her voice. Worst of all, he feared if he broke down and told someone, they'd tell him he deserved it.

"I should let you sleep!" he shouted, spinning in place as if he were about to run out of the room when he remembered he was sleeping with her.

Not like that. He had torched that bridge like so many others. Tugging off the straps, Everett unrolled the sleeping bag and laid it on the floor. He felt Maddy watching with a growing concern, when he unzipped the bag and started to fall into it.

"Don't you dare!" she shouted with full Southern indignation.

Ev froze, one leg partially on the bag, the other with his knee bent at an awful angle. Did she want him out after all?

"Everett Berry, you ran into a fire," she said as if he had forgotten. Madeline stood and plucked her cat up. "You are not sleeping on the hard cold ground."

"It's not a problem."

"No, it is. I will not hear of it." After putting Monte on the sleeping bag, Madeline hooked an arm around Ev's and tugged back. He had no choice but to stand up as she pulled with all her strength. It was cute to see the strain in her cheeks as she guided him to the cot.

"You get the bed," she declared, placing him down on the rickety canvas stretched across the aluminum frame. It wasn't much better than the sleeping bag, truthfully. But he stared up at the woman with so much grit in her face he struggled to argue back. Maddy nodded once as if her job were done, and she slipped for the sleeping bag.

"You're the guest," Ev began, getting a foot out, when she looked up at him.

"And you…" Her certainty cracked and tears rose in her eyes. Ev almost leapt to his feet to run to her side, but she focused on her cat. "I was so scared you'd died. The way the others were talking. Don't you ever do that again."

She was worried for him? Warmth rose across his chest, Ev clamping a hand over his heart as if to calm the rampaging beat. "I'll do my best not to."

"Good." She jerked her head once and wiggled to zip the sleeping bag up around her. Monte leapt up onto her stomach and kneaded the rising synthetic cloth to make biscuits.

The burns, the gashes, the stuff his ex had thrown in the lake were bad, but the scar that couldn't heal was when she'd looked him dead in the eye and said, "*I wish you'd died in that fire.*" Kathy would only care because then she'd have to find somewhere else to live. But Maddy, the woman he kept fucking everything up with, worried about him?

"How do I turn the light off?" she asked, shaking Ev from his thoughts.

"I'll get it." He rose. A strange lightness dropped from his head down through his body and he felt like he was floating as he stumbled for the dangling cord. When he tugged it, darkness wiped away the reminder of the strange circumstance.

He could pretend he was alone, spending another night down here rather than facing the monster he had let into his house. As Ev stumbled for the cot, instead of the unforgiving drip of a sink, he heard the slow breath of the woman worried about him.

"It's a scar from where my ex-wife burned me. She came at me with her curling iron and singed off the hair and my scalp. I've never…" He swallowed hard, fighting down the catch in his voice. "I didn't tell anyone what happened. Made up some excuse for the hospital. Disguised it as best I could."

With his tailbone perched on the cot's frame, Everett clung to his knees and tried to stop shaking. "I knew she was bad for me, even before the wedding, but I couldn't… It's like I'm on this hamster wheel and I think if I keep the pace steady then everything will be okay. But then there's rocks, and I stumble, smash my head, break a tooth. So I keep running, harder, faster, hoping that in the end there's a reason for all the running."

The Band-aid ripped free, Everett unable to stop even as Maddy sat in silence listening to him. "I tried to change. Got away from the town where every stop sign reminded me of how I keep fucking it all up. But the second my guard was down, I went right back to the wheel. I'm sorry."

For pulling you into my hell.
For forcing you to sit through my collapse.
For thinking I could ever deserve you.

A slow breath as if she'd been holding it in released. "Ev, you have nothing to be sorry for."

He knew that was a lie. All those times he could have stopped it, gotten away, and he hadn't—he was a coward. The sound of fabric swooshing over the ground cut through the air. He didn't realize Maddy had wriggled the sleeping bag closer until he felt her hand caress his knee.

"You don't deserve that either. Not from a girlfriend, not from a wife, not nobody. No one does."

"It's not a big deal," he said, wishing he could take back everything he said. "Other people got it worse."

"No. If you're in pain, if it hurts, then it's a big deal, and you deserve better."

Tears burst from his dry wells, Everett grateful for the darkness that let him hide. Maddy kept sweeping her palm over his knee to assure him that she was right. He crumpled against her and reached to wrap his hands around her shoulders.

"I'm sorry," was all he could say, an endless repetition of the sins in his heart. Sorry for not seeing how wonderful she was in high school. Sorry for not chasing after her when it could have changed his world. Sorry for not being a better man.

"Ev…" Fingers lifted through his hair, but it caused him to tip his face lower.

Fighting to sponge away the tears on his cheeks, he said, "For the smoke. It's bad. I should…get to sleep. You should get to sleep." Jesus Christ, what was wrong with him? She had just lost her home and there he was bawling on her lap?

Maddy's hand slipped away from him. For a brief moment he wanted to reach out to take it, but his hands felt heavy as if they were coated in pitch. "I'm here if you need to talk," she said.

He couldn't, not again. She'd already have to look at him like the pathetic sot he was. The sleeping bag slipped back to where he'd left it, and Ev tucked his legs up onto the cot. Laid out like those Egyptian pharaohs in their coffins, Everett tried to find sleep.

"You're a good man, Ev."

If only that was true. He closed his eyes, every wrong word and missed step rolling through his mind. Warm fur bounced against his stomach, almost winding him. He gasped, only for four feet to dash up his chest. The purring began in an instant, Sparky curling in on himself as he found comfort. Everett ran his rough and scarred hand over the kitten. The little life that'd trusted him even as they ran out of hellfire nuzzled back.

Chapter Twenty

Let it all have been a nightmare.

Madeline clutched her hands together and tried to will her wish into being. Her cats bounced against paint cans she never kept in her bedroom, and the unforgiving cement pressed into her hips, but it wasn't real. Her apartment hadn't burned down. She wasn't homeless without a stitch of clothing left to her name.

The unforgiving cry of her phone tugged her eyelids open and forced her to face reality. Last night she'd been running on fumes, happy to be alive, to have her kitties alive. Now…she just wanted to go back to sleep.

Groaning, Madeline rolled out of the sleeping bag and reached for the phone in her tiny bag. That had to be her main purse for the time being since everything she owned had gone up in smoke. Waking up her phone, Madeline was bombarded by a hundred texts from Beth. Each one gained another exclamation point and grew larger the more she scrolled. The messages amounted to "What happened?" and "Where are you?"

Madeline texted back to Beth.

My apartment burned down. I'm at Everett's house.

There. One problem solved, only two thousand more to go. A knock at the door startled her from the cliffs of despair. "Maddy, you awake? I got breakfast going."

"Uh, sounds good. Just let me..." She stared at the jeans and top left folded on a plastic shelf next to a toolbox. That blouse had once been white as snow. Now the neckline, shoulders and sleeves were all stained a murky gray.

It's the only thing to your name.

She reached for it, but shuddered as her fingers glanced over the fabric. "I'll be right there," she said.

"Mind if I come in quick?" Everett asked. She couldn't think of a reason to stop him. The door opened a crack and the man who walked in was the day to the one who'd cracked last night. He'd put on a long-sleeved shirt and styled his hair to hide that...horrific truth he'd told her. Ev smiled wide and he held out two bowls.

"I didn't want my guests to go hungry," he said, placing the bowls filled with chopped chicken and beef on the ground.

Sparky caught the fancy food in an instant. He twisted from beside a stack of tools, scattering a screwdriver, and dove for the breakfast. Monte took his time, but his eyes never wavered far from the fancy food.

"Ev, that's...that's too much."

He shrugged. "After the night they had, I thought they could use a treat. It's no problem. Here." Through the thick air between them, Everett extended his hand. Looking up at him, Maddy would swear she had imagined his confession. He was the same happy-go-lucky, all-American sweetheart he'd always been. Not even a trace of trauma could touch him.

But as she locked her fingers around his and the two of them helped her to rise off the floor, Ev's bright demeanor shifted. It didn't dim, but it softened to a tender vulnerability she'd never seen before. All that he said had really happened. *Jesus.*

"I hope you like eggs and bacon."

"I'm amenable to them," Madeline said, turning to follow him. She made sure to close the door but took one last look in on her babies. Thank God they were okay.

"Miss Prix putting on airs," Everett said, and he wiggled his butt like all the girls who worked the pageant circuit.

She laughed at him. "Fine, I'll go whole hog on it. I barely ate anything at dinner."

"I don't blame you," Ev said, causing her to stumble. How did he know she was careful to never be the fat girl who ate all the food on her plate? "It was such a fiasco I couldn't eat either. So, I may have gone a little overboard."

Madeline walked into a full-service breakfast. Fried eggs piled three or four high sat next to a full rasher of bacon and towers of golden pancakes. As if that weren't enough, fresh biscuits rested on the counter and a pan full of sausage gravy bubbled away.

"What, no grits?"

With a smile, Ev walked over to the stove and hefted up a lid on a pot of creamy grits. "What kind of a man would I be without grits?"

"Sweet Betsy." Most of her mornings were made up of the occasional half bagel or, if she wanted to indulge, a cantaloupe fruit salad. She hadn't had a full Southern breakfast in years. Ev scooped up a plate, added a biscuit, dumped a ladle of gravy on and finished with the grits. The whole thing had to weigh five pounds.

He passed it to her for safe-keeping, and she took a step when he placed his hand to the small of her back. "Dining room's through there, and I hope you'll be pleasantly surprised."

With his breakfast in one hand, Everett guided her past the almost finished kitchen and over the threshold. The plastic sheeting had been replaced by a beautiful archway that led into a gorgeous room. All Madeline could stare at was the chandelier. It looked like he had ripped it out of a castle in France. Gilded in an antiqued gold, it held four tall candles in scones that were each embossed with tiny flowers and finished with s-shaped scrolls.

"What do you think?" Ev asked, his chin nearly pressing to her shoulder.

"That's a work of art." She drew away from the flicker of electric light to notice the room. Dark wainscoting circled the bottom half while a light gold Victorian wallpaper finished off the top.

"I think it's coming along nicely. Still need to find the right table though." Ev jerked his head to the same old piece of plywood with a couple of folding chairs beside it.

Madeline chuckled as she hustled over and put her breakfast down beside the silverware. "I like it. The decor makes me feel like I'm in a fairytale castle, while the table tells me I won't lose my head if I spill."

Ev full-on laughed at that. He swung a leg over his chair to straddle it and stretched his back before sitting down. On top of the silverware, he had also set the table with a mug for each of them, a carafe of syrup and a fancy butter dish shaped like a bullfrog. Without any ceremony, Ev dug into his bacon first. He cut off a slab of butter from below the golden frog and dropped it onto his pancakes.

"I am starving," he said, digging a fork into all four pancakes at once. "How'd you sleep?"

Madeline took a much smaller bite with a dab of syrup on the side. "Sweet Lord, these are wonderful," she gasped. "How are they so fluffy?"

Ev's smile grew wider, and he ducked for the coffee to hide the blush. "I used to help out at the pancake breakfasts. Got to make 'em real good, or we're walking to the fire."

Madeline didn't realize how hungry she was until she devoured the entire stack. When the last bite hung on her fork, she paused and glanced at the man still working through his. Everett caught her staring and he said, "I like cooking for you."

"Oh?"

He nudged her in the side with his elbow and gave a conspiratorial wink. "You appreciate the good things. No turning your nose up at grits 'n' gravy."

"Who in their right mind would refuse that?" Madeline asked while filling her spoon with the grits. They tasted as she remembered, though there was a hint of cumin and hot sauce in there. Interesting.

Ev drenched his in syrup, stirring them thoughtfully. "How are you doing? With everything that happened?"

Did he mean her apartment burning down…or that he had admitted he was trapped in an abusive relationship? Madeline didn't know how to answer so she stared into his eyes. The spinning spoon stopped, and the grits oozed over the sides. Ev reached for her hand. The warmth struck her, causing Madeline to realize how cold she was. But he warmed her up while running his fingers over her skin.

"Maddy, whatever you need, I can…I want to help."

"You don't have to…" She tried to turn away, but she was entranced by him.

Ev scooted closer on his chair, his eyes so close she could get lost in the flecks of emeralds among the peridot. "Anything. If you need a place to stay, I'll—"

"Good morning!"

Ev jerked back and slammed his hands to the side of his plate. Madeline's eyes fell as Kathy swept into the room. She was done up to the nines, her makeup flawless, her hair curled into soft waves and her skinny body in a figure-flattering dress. Madeline tugged on the borrowed T-shirt that clung to her.

"Babe." Kathy perched behind Ev's shoulder, then leaned down to kiss his cheek. He tightened in the chair but didn't fight her. She gently patted the lipstick stain she left behind and chuckled. "You need to shave."

"I…I know," Everett muttered, rubbing where she had.

"And take a shower." Her voice was the complete opposite of last night—a soft birdsong to the hellfire that had rained down on him. "We have a guest after all."

"Yes," he mumbled.

Kathy shrugged her shoulder and fell into the last chair at the table. She stared at Madeline. "Men, what can you do with them? They're like children."

No, he's not. He smells like smoke because he was in a fire last night. He's got scruff because he woke up early to make breakfast. Madeline clutched tighter to her fork, wanting to scream at Kathy, but all those years of being the good girl froze her tongue. The clatter of a fork hitting the plate and a chair's legs scraping over the floor caused her to focus on Ev.

He froze midway in scooting back from the table. All Kathy had to do was say jump, and he was halfway in the air before realizing it. Madeline stared at him, trying to will the truth into his brain. *She nearly hit you last night. She's being mean right now. Kick her out.*

"Oh, babe." Like a conman who could sense when the mark was growing wise, Kathy reached over and took Everett's hand. "Don't do it now. Your breakfast will get cold."

"Of course," he muttered and wrapped his fists around his fork and knife without scooting back. It left him leaning to reach, the once generous forkfuls now little more than a bite.

"You look...comfortable." Kathy's venom focused on the last person left, leaving Madeline swallowing. "Must be nice to not care what other people think."

My apartment burned down. Madeline gripped harder to her spoon, her appetite obliterated. Every snide comment disguised as 'I'm just helping dear' from 'Do you need to eat that?' to 'Running is free' rebounded through Madeline and she snapped. Staring Kathy right in her pretty face, she said, "It's hard to worry about such trivial things after losing everything, but I guess you're too hung up on the petty things in life to see that."

Stabbing her fork into her biscuit, Madeline leaned closer and added the nuclear Southern insult. "Bless your heart."

Kathy's scoff shot through the dining room like a cannon roar. She clasped a hand to her chest and started to rise, when an unassailable and unstoppable voice cut through the house. "Mads? Where are you?"

"Beth?"

As Madeline turned around, the full fury of an investigative reporter launched into the dining room. "What have you done to her?" she forced first on Ev, who held his hands up like Beth was the cops.

"Are you okay?" That she turned on Madeline, wrapping a comforting arm around her. "God's sake, why didn't you call me?"

"I...tried?"

"Here, I brought a coat, and we should get you a change of clothes. There is no way you're staying here. Did you have to sleep on the ground?"

How in the hell did Beth know that? Madeline tried to brush down her curls that stood in every direction. It increased the frizz of her clown.

"Who in the nine bells are you?" Kathy thundered, rising to her feet.

Oh dear. Madeline turned away as Beth launched off her feet, accusing finger at the ready. "I am the woman with three lawyer cousins who all owe me a favor. You want to keep getting in my face, we're gonna have a real problem."

They were all Korean lawyers, but technically true.

Kathy, unaware that she was facing off against her first real opponent, laughed. "That so."

Beth folded her arms and stared her down. "Katherine Clark, who in the last three years flunked out of a Metro Modeling School, married, divorced four months later, then joined a sugar daddy site until very recently." She dangled the receipts in front of Kathy who lashed out at the phone.

Wide-eyed, Kathy stared up at Beth from her crumbled pedestal. "How do you know all that?"

"It's what I do. I'm taking Madeline with me and if any of you have a problem with that…" Beth waved her pen around like it was a dagger, first at Kathy whose glare could shatter glass, then at Ev. His head had dropped, leaving his expression unreadable, but Madeline caught his shoulders shaking as if he had failed to suppress a laugh.

"Beth." Madeline tried to get her to stop, but her friend was on a tirade.

"Where are your clothes? Don't tell me they did something to them?"

"It's fine. They're in the room with Monte and Sparky."

"Good, good. I brought a carrier for them. Well, it's for a dog, but I figure they can share for the trip. Are you okay?"

Madeline was getting real tired of hearing that. She had no idea because she didn't have time to see how not okay she was. Instead, she defaulted to an accepting nod and looked down at her breakfast.

"Come on. Let's find your things and get you somewhere safe. I left Tristan in charge of setting up the guest room." Beth marched ahead while talking as if she already knew where to find Madeline's clothing. Maybe she did.

"Isn't that your office?"

"I've contacted your insurance agent. They're aware of the fire. Next stop is…" Her plans for Madeline's life faded to a staccato slap of her heels while Maddy remained in place.

"Sorry about that," she said to Everett, who risked lifting his head to reveal a small smile.

"She's…very thorough."

"It can be a bit much at times." Though if it weren't for Beth, Madeline wouldn't have a clue where to start in trying to rebuild her life. "Thank you for putting me up for the night." She knew she shouldn't leave her friend long, so Madeline walked for the door.

"Maddy?" Ev said, turning her around. In the background she could see Kathy fuming mad, but her focus fell on the shyly smiling man. "It was my pleasure."

Chapter Twenty-One

Sparky and Monte were healthy, and Madeline had two new sets of clothes. Beth was pacing about her living room, a phone glued to her head. Tristan was in the back trying to practice for the musical without either of them hearing. It was pretty easy when Beth contacted an insurance adjustor who wanted to blame the fire on an act of God.

"I'm sorry, did Pele wander into New York?" Beth shouted at the phone. Then she froze and blinked. "Pele, the Hawaiian...never mind. I expect to see that claim honored in full or you will answer to my lawyer."

With that, she dramatically slammed her finger on the phone to end the call and struck a superhero pose. Madeline shifted in the comfy armchair. "You shouldn't keep doing that. One of them might call your bluff."

"About what? Oh, I have a lawyer. Okay, he does business contracts, but I think it'd still work. Let me see." Beth consulted her big chart on what to do after a fire. Madeline hugged tighter to the guitar-shaped pillow and stared at nothing.

The reason she could afford New York was thanks to her eccentric great-aunt who had rent control from the sixties. Finding an available place would be impossible, much less one that wasn't her yearly salary every month. With each breath, a circling dread filled Madeline that she'd have no choice but to return to North Carolina without a job, a home or a husband.

A soft tone bonged from her phone, and she tugged it over to look. That drew Beth's attention as well, the general on high alert. "Is that the building's owner? They have a lot to answer for."

"No." Madeline shut off the reminder even as she read it. "It's for your dress shopping."

Beth paled, her warrior strut thrown off-kilter. "Well…that can wait for another day. We have more important problems to tackle."

"I want to go."

"Mads?"

She closed her eyes tight, fighting over the instinct to give control of her life to Beth. "Everything's a mess. I can't…I need normal. Please?" God, she was begging for her friend to drag her through dress shops. That was how far she'd fallen.

"Okay." Beth nodded while fishing her keys out of her purse. "Whatever you need, Mads. Tris, we're heading out!"

His rich baritone cut through the walls as he sang to her, "Have a nice time. Love you!"

It was so silly Madeline snickered when Beth ducked close to say, "You should see him act."

* * * *

It wasn't one of those fast fashion bridal shops Beth stopped at, but the kind with velvet curtains and glasses of champagne. The store owner greeted Beth with a great smile, and her friend said, "This is my maid of honor. She'll be telling me what looks best or not."

Yeah, sure. The clerk assigned to the future Mrs. Tristan Hardy handed her pre-selected gowns and guided Beth to the dressing room. It left Madeline lost. She sank into a red velvet chair shaped like a throne and tried to not stare at the mirrored wall beside the platform.

It didn't take long for Beth to dash out of the dressing room, stand on the platform, quirk her head and declare she hated it. God, Madeline would kill to have satin look that good on her breasts or hips. Bundling the long skirt up, Beth spun on a dime and marched for the second gown. The clerk barely got out to fluff the train before turning around to chase after Beth.

No one told Beth Cho how to feel. If she liked something, she liked it. If she hated it, she hated it. It wasn't any wonder she and Tristan had gone from despising each other to singing about their love across a condo. If only Madeline could feel a tenth of her certainty.

The curtain drew back, and an angelic choir broke out. Beth stepped out in *the* dress. An ivory satin bodice without any of the frills Beth didn't need nestled above a skirt with cream silk layered beside a red panel at the front and down her train. The overhead lights glinted off diamond beads sewn into the top of the skirt. As they carried around the back, they scattered down the train to create a delicate floral pattern.

Madeline waited for Beth to break into tears and cry out what they both knew, but her friend cocked her head in the mirror and stared harder. "I don't know if I want to go sleeveless."

"We can add some straps," the clerk said, fast. "Let me get you a veil to complete the look."

"No, thank you." Beth stopped her. "Hm..."

"Is there anything about the dress you do like?"

"The red, like we talked about. Though I'll still want a red one for the reception."

"Why don't I go pull some of the lace ones," the clerk said, dashing away in the name of commission.

Madeline walked up to her friend, who was tugging the satin around her waist and frowning. "What are you doing? You love it."

Beth sighed slowly. "I know. It's got the red that'll make my father happy. No damn lace so I won't snag it on anything. And..." She groaned. "I look like a fucking princess."

"What's the problem?"

Her best friend turned to her and stared with bottomless concern. They'd buy the dress, then it was right back to her life being a total mess. At least she got to spend a few minutes adjacent to the fairytale before it went all Grimm.

"I know," Beth said when the clerk arrived with more dresses. "Let's save this one in the maybe pile." She placed her hand to the one. "Would you mind pulling a few for Madeline?"

The circle of terror opened up below her. She was not ready for wearing so much tulle and satin in front of a mirror. "I thought you hadn't picked colors yet," she tried to say to Beth, but her friend put on a big smile and clasped Madeline's shoulders.

"My friend just got engaged. Why not kill two birds and all?"

"Wonderful!" The clerk, sensing two commissions, broke into a smile. But as she was about to leave, she stared harder at Madeline and bit her lip.

"What are you doing?" Madeline asked while Beth inspected her perfect silhouette in the mirror.

"The whole point is to try on pretty dresses, so that's what we're going to do."

She didn't understand. Beth was a size two at most. The entire world wanted to clothe her in their best couture. It never occurred to her that a bridal store wouldn't have anything in Madeline's size, because they didn't think people like her deserved the princess ballgown or the fairytale wedding.

It's Beth's day. Madeline put on a smile even though she'd be forced into an — at most — size fourteen dress that wouldn't even zip before the clerk gave up. *Be there for your friend.* Beth struggled to get across the floor, the massive skirts pooling around her feet. When she reached the chairs, she picked up two of the champagne flutes and passed one to Madeline. After a quick clink, they shared a toast.

"For happier days," Beth said, then she collapsed sideways into the chair, her massive train trailing across the floor.

Madeline whispered, "For any future."

The clerk didn't reappear for another ten minutes, leaving Beth and Madeline to talk about the wedding and the cat rescue. It'd slipped her mind, what with her place burning to the ground. Who would take care of it when…if she had to move back home? Chantelle had to know people.

"I think I've got something for you," the clerk said, a black bag of mystery slung over her arm. Madeline abandoned her half-finished champagne to the table while Beth waved her on.

Before she vanished into the dressing room, the clerk added to Beth, "Would you like to try another dress on yourself?"

"Nah, I'm good," Beth called, damn near giving away her plan. "I have to stress-test it first."

Accepting she was in for a long day, the clerk helped Madeline into the room. All she could stare at was her face in a half mirror. She tugged off her shirt and waited for the inevitable. A shaft of white flew over her head, entrapping her in a tube of darkness. Was this what it felt like being birthed? When she popped out, she took a breath and found her chest could expand.

"Would you mind tugging down your bra strap?" the clerk asked. "Helps with the presentation. Let me see."

Tightness circled around Madeline's waist, forcing her breasts higher than they'd ever been. A family of gnomes could shelter under her bosom for how well the bodice held it. She took another breath, testing the corset ribbons the clerk knotted around her, when the woman stepped back.

"Why don't you take a look?"

So much fabric poofed off her hips, Madeline had to sidle to the side to escape. As she walked, the skirts calmed down, trailing to the floor where they belonged. She kept her eyes down, not wanting to face the mess she looked like.

"Mads…" Beth gasped.

The clerk helped her up to the platform and fluffed back the train.

"You look…"

Taking a risk, Madeline lifted her head. *Beautiful.* The beading on the bodice was for a princess, the corset for a debutante and the skirts… Tulle flowed from her hips like waterfalls, and over those was a layer of silk designed for walking into Prince Charming's castle.

"Oh, God." Tears gushed from her eyes, Madeline having to smack her palm to the glass to keep from crumbling to her feet.

"Mads?" Beth stood up and hustled to her side.

"Don't worry. This happens all the time," the clerk said, sounding pleased with her reaction.

Everything was wrong. She would never wear this dress, never feel as pretty as it made her, never have someone take her hand at the end of an aisle and swear to love her to the end of time. "No." A strangled sob escaped, and Madeline started to fall.

Beth went with, her head on Madeline's shoulders as the two of them hit their knees. "I am so sorry. I thought, I didn't think. Madeline…"

"I'll go get some tissue," the clerk said, dashing away when she realized these weren't happy bride tears.

"Hey, look…look at how beautiful you are," Beth said, causing Madeline to stare at her blotchy face and red eyes. "So that jackass isn't the one. That's okay."

Beth didn't get it. Her heart didn't skip a beat whenever Everett held her hand. She didn't ache for him to smile or toss and turn worrying to death about how he'd get free of his demons.

"Didn't you go on a date last night?"

"Yeah." *Then my house caught on fire.* The two probably weren't related, but it didn't seem like a good correlation to start a relationship with.

"How'd it go?"

Awkward. Weird. I couldn't stop thinking about Everett and Kathy. Now I really *can't stop worrying about him.* "Hayden seemed…nice."

"Hayden...?"

"Crawford," Madeline said before turning to her friend. "You are not doing a check on him."

Beth threw her hands up in feigned surrender, but Madeline knew better. "I'm just looking out for you. I can't believe you don't even Google the guys you date."

Madeline's tears dried as the clerk arrived with a tissue. Still, she took one to avoid making the woman feel bad and dabbed at her eyes. The mascara she'd put on for the awkward double date had run down her cheeks, making her look like a plump banshee.

"How are you finding the dress?" The clerk glanced at Madeline but focused on Beth checking her phone. No doubt she was reminding herself to dig up everything on Hayden Crawford. Aside from an unpaid parking ticket, what could she possibly find on the man who rescued kittens from fires?

Beth's phone rang, one of Tristan's songs repeating on a loop, and she juggled to answer it. The image of a woman in a beautiful wedding dress while wearing her serious business face on the phone almost brought a chuckle to Madeline...until she heard who was on the other end.

"Ah, Chantelle. Hello."

She wasn't ready to tell them that as much as Madeline dreamed of running a rescue center, she couldn't. Madeline tried to slink away, only for Beth to say, "She's right here," and thrust the phone out.

Madeline shook her head, but Beth jabbed her phone harder. "Hi," she said, waiting for Chantelle's lighting words to zap over the line.

"Darling, are you okay?"

Chantelle had heard the news. That cut down on time. "Yes, I'm with Beth. We're dress shopping."

"I heard about the fire during my spin class. It must be awful."

"I'm…I'm okay. I'm staying at Beth's for the time being."

"Nope," Chantelle said with such distinction, Madeline almost nodded in agreement.

"What…do you mean?"

"You trapped in a two-bedroom apartment with those lovebirds? I will not hear of it. You're my star, the cornerstone of my whole neighborhood revival. Without you, everything falls apart."

Madeline's cheeks pinked at both the praise and expectations hefted on her. "That's very kind of you, but I don't—"

"You'll stay at my summer home. The family's summer home, but they're all off in Europe somewhere so it'd be you, me and your adorable babies. What do you say?"

She knew Beth had overheard. Chantelle wasn't what one would call quiet. Her best friend bristled at having her plans shattered, but Madeline wasn't exactly looking forward to sharing a smaller space with Tristan. Even Beth could be a bit much.

At the same time, she didn't want to hurt her friend's feelings. What were a few weeks wearing her earbuds to not hear the two of them in the next room? "I'll—"

"Accept? Wonderful. I'll send a car around to Lord Harty's place for your kitties. Can't wait to get you settled in." With Madeline's life decided, Chantelle hung up, leaving her limply holding Beth's phone.

"What just happened?" Madeline asked. Beth handed her a full flute, and Madeline downed it all in one throw.

Chapter Twenty-Two

After Maddy had been whisked away by her friend, Everett calmly walked away from Kathy. She raged about Beth while he washed his plates, screamed in his ear about Maddy when he dried them. While he was putting the leftovers in the fridge, she was at full frothing. He should be cowering, agreeing with her fervor and hoping to calm her before things got worse, but it felt like the evil witch's curse was cured.

Everett left Kathy snarling, threatening to call the cops on Madeline or her friend, inventing things Madeline must have stolen. It rolled in and out of his ears like the blast of a jackhammer — all noise, no substance. Dressed for work, he jogged down the stairs and stopped to pick his keys and wallet out of his coat. It was too nice of a day for him to need it.

"What are you doing? Where the hell do you think you're going?"

Since junior high she'd used her superiority like a cudgel. Every day she reminded him how much smarter, better connected, richer, kinder and more talented she was. But after Madeline's friend had read out the list of her abject failures, Kathy's lofty airs had become nothing more than hot wind.

In a soft voice, he said, "Move out, now. Collect your things and be gone before I get home, or I'll contact the authorities."

Her jaw dropped, the wicked tongue for once silent as he jaunted to the door.

"Everett Berry, this isn't funny!" Kathy shrieked. "Ev! Get yer ass back here!"

"Seven p.m., sharp," was all he said.

She tossed her head back and screamed to the void, but Ev was already down the porch steps and on to a better life. The station looked the worse for the wear when he arrived. Equipment was piled up, charred from smoke and ash. One of the trucks was parked near the hose ready to be washed down. The other had been left in the back parking lot.

When he walked in, whistling, it drew the ire of several bloodshot eyes, but it was the captain who confronted him first. "What in the hell are you doing here?" she asked.

"I'm on, aren't I?"

Captain Reed slapped a hand to his shoulder and pulled him closer. "Are you on something, Lieutenant? You can tell me. It'll be a…client confidential or whatever lawyers say."

"No." He shook his head, about to laugh at the idea. "Why?"

"Cause you reek of smoke and your face is as red as your last name. Go home."

Ev jerked his head. "No." He had given Kathy a time. And if she wasn't out by then? He hadn't thought that far ahead.

What was he going to do if…when Kathy fought him on it?

To his relief, Captain Reed shrugged. "Very well, you want to work yourself to death, who am I to stop you? That mess needs to be scrubbed down and later we need a crew to inspect the site."

"I can handle that."

Ev tried to not flinch at Hayden sweeping in from the side. His naturally black hair didn't stink of smoke, and his skin didn't have the same rosacea pallor. He looked like a man who'd slept a full eight hours of perfect sleep while Ev had tossed about on the cot.

"If the captain wants to scrub," Ev said, passing over the bucket. Hayden didn't take it, his smile twisting up.

"Funny. I'll handle the inspection. Lot of politicians' eyes are on it, don't want anyone to mess up." He picked the clipboard off the desk before Ev or Reed could get to it.

"If it isn't the big hero!" Chris shouted, walking out of the break room. "Would you sign my helmet?"

Hayden laughed off the attention and returned to the forms. He'd paraded about last night, giving orders like the star of the fire. It had left Captain Reed on the sidelines, Everett watching as he fought to clear his lungs. It wasn't any surprise the whole station would be singing Hayden's praises.

Chris reached them, massive donut in hand. For a brief second Hayden glanced to him. "Should I sign your helmet or your forehead?"

"What? Not you. You." He jabbed his donut at Everett, who blinked in confusion.

"Berry?"

"He's all over the place. Here." Chris crammed the donut in his mouth and booted up his phone. A video of the night played, focusing on Everett stumbling for the crowd. It went out of focus when he opened his coat, then the pair of yellow eyes opened, and he plucked the kitten from the safety of his jacket for Maddy. "Everyone's going gaga over it. Remixes, duets, think it even got some play on *Wake Up, America.*"

Ev's cheeks felt hot, turning redder than ever as Chris held the repeating video up. Captain Reed stared closer, while Hayden grew dangerously quiet. *That can't be good.*

"There he is!" The chief's voice boomed louder than the fire alarm. Everyone snapped to attention. Chris slipped his phone away, but it kept playing, the sounds of the crowd awing and a kitten's meow muffled by his pants.

"Morning, sir," Hayden said, stepping in the way, but Chief Parsons was focused on Everett.

"My boy." He slapped Everett on the shoulder. "You're famous. We've gotten five calls already for the kitten-saving fireman."

"That's...good?"

"It's wonderful. With calls and media come donations. I'm looking into swinging one of the big morning shows. 'Course they'd want to interview the man in charge, too." Parsons laughed like Christmas had come early for him, a hand over his belly. "Quick thinking hiding the kitten in your coat."

"I didn't have much say. He crawled in there, and I thought it was the safest," Ev needlessly explained.

"Keep up the good work, Berry. What do you have for me, Reed?"

With that, his little moment in the sun passed. There was still work, and fifteen minutes of fame wouldn't get it done. Everett picked up the deodorizer spray, when Chris and Will both flashed their phones playing the same video. Funny. That was going to follow him.

Before he could approach the equipment, a hand pinched his shoulder. "You may think you're clever, but you don't fool me." Hayden glared at him before he flicked Everett's hair, exposing the spot.

As Ev rushed to hide it away, Hayden shouted, "I'm off to inspect the building." No one said goodbye. They were too busy scrolling for more embarrassing videos of the kitten rescue. Only Ev watched Hayden walk off like he already owned the place.

* * * *

"Monte, no!" Madeline shouted to her obstinate cat who'd wormed his way up a trophy case. He glared from between a Tony and a Golden Globe, threatening to shove both.

Hustling off the white-on-white couch, Madeline dashed for her cat just as he made a break for it. Monte was the picture of grace, slipping through the narrow slot between wall and award. At the last second, he lashed out with his foot and sent a Grammy tumbling.

Madeline shrieked as she dove for the tumbling award. A nest of low coffee tables stood in the way. She fell to her knees and reached out. The edge of the gramophone caught on her finger and fell to the tiled floor.

"Is everything okay?" Chantelle called from one of the other two dozen rooms in the house.

Scrambling to her feet, Madeline tried to inspect the award. Maybe it was fine. They had to be built to take a beating. The golden phonograph spun in a circle while the base sat alone, both parts forever ripped asunder. Glue. There had to be glue somewhere.

A spring breeze overpowered with lilacs and cherry blossoms blew in, along with a silk curtain. Chantelle leaned in from the porch overlooking the garden. "Problems?"

Hide it. If she was faster, she'd have stuffed the Grammy under a couch, but Madeline limply raised up the award. "I'm so sorry. My cat, Monte, he was…I'll put him in my room."

Chantelle chuckled and swept inside. The zebra prints and neon wigs were gone. Out of the spotlight, they dressed in a gray pair of sweatpants and a long housecoat with light green vertical stripes.

"Let me see." Chantelle picked the broken pieces out of Madeline's guilty hands.

"I'll…get you a new one." *It's a freaking Grammy. How will you do that?* "I'll pay for it?"

"Look." Chantelle turned the base and pointed to a nub of translucent glue already hardened around the edge. "That's where my nephew tried to use it as a can opener. A little superglue should fix it right up."

Thank goodness, it wasn't Madeline's fault. Still, she snatched Monte off his exploration of the mantel. He thrashed his feet in rage, but she employed the towel method to swaddle him and returned to the couch.

After placing both pieces of the Grammy on the shelves and closing the door, Chantelle asked, "How do you find the place?"

"It's so big."

"I once got lost in the lower wing for two days while playing hide and seek. Kidding, though that story goes over well in puff pieces about me." Chantelle curled up in a cozy armchair. The rest of the furniture was a stark white against the off-white walls and flooring. Even the tables were painted bone white. The one piece to stick out was the chair in a muddled gray with thin tan stripes and an orange and yellow afghan tossed over the back.

Madeline was that chair—so clearly out of place, it was a wonder the trash men hadn't already tossed her out. It'd been a whirlwind as she'd settled in, unpacked one pair of pants, then slunk off to the parlor to stare out the windows overlooking an English garden.

"I promise, once I can find a new apartment, I'll get out of your hair."

"Don't stress about it. It's nice to have someone around in the old place that isn't the watchman ghost."

Madeline laughed at the joke, but at Chantelle's slow look, she swallowed hard. "I could, um, earn my keep by making dinner."

Now Chantelle laughed. "Unless your specialty is wheat germ smoothies and a single fillet of white fish, I'm afraid I'm stuck on my prescribed diet."

"I had no idea the theater was so strict."

"Oh, no. They don't care, as long as you drink three gallons of water a day. My agent has me booked for a hosting gig at the beach which requires swimsuits. All part of the brand. But I found this adorable roaring twenties' bathing suit, going to add some ruffles and maybe a few sequins, a strategic rip here and there. It'll be wonderful...once I lose those winter pounds."

Chantelle picked up their giant cup covered in Korean boy-band members and took a swig with the straw. Judging by their face, it probably had the wheat germ smoothie inside.

"Can I ask you something?"

They looked up, cheeks pulled gaunt from the force to suck up the drink, and nodded.

"Why a cat sanctuary? Why me?"

"The first part's easy. I adore cats. Their style, their grace, their ability to give no fucks about what anyone thinks. Since I'm always traveling, I can't have one, but with a sanctuary…"

"You can stop by and play with the cats whenever you want," Madeline said. She'd been thinking the same on and off, excited at the idea of having new babies to play with before they found their forever homes.

"Exactly." Chantelle jabbed a finger at Madeline with their last remaining acrylic nail. The others had been left on a counter. Sparky had turned them into a new toy. She could still hear the skitter of a nail bouncing off the walls.

"So…what about me? I'm, I mean, you have the money to hire anyone who's done this before." *Who didn't have the entire construction company quit on them.*

Chantelle picked up their phone and scrolled through it. "Did I ever tell you how I met Haughty Harty?"

Madeline snickered at the nickname. "No."

"Early in my career, they pulled him out of mothballs for a charity. At the last second, they added me. I was this knock-kneed kid still arguing pronouns with small-town newspapers. And here was Tristan Harty, recluse and all-around grump. Everyone warned me to keep away, but you know what those fools did?"

"No."

"They gave us a duet. I was shaking so hard, I threw my blue raspberry slushy all over him. What does he do? This powerhouse from when I was a babe? This chart-topping heartthrob as gloomy as the sky in winter? He looks down at his chest soaked with blue liquid, says aloud, 'At least it matches my eyes,' and sings."

That sounded like the man Beth was going to marry, but what did it have to do with her?

"So when Tristan Harty tells me about this woman who loves cats so much she keeps them in her bathtub..." Chantelle revealed an old photo of Madeline when a mama had given birth to five kittens in her apartment. "I have to have her on my team."

Madeline's cheeks burned as she digested Tristan telling people about her alongside the reminder that her old tub was nothing more than a memory. She didn't know how to respond to Chantelle's knowing smile. Gratitude? A compliment? Madeline reached for her phone, the surviving tether to her digital world.

"I was wondering, since we have the time, if you'd like to go over some details about the center?"

"Oh, wonderful." Chantelle folded their hands under their chin and smiled. "So you know, I want to have a hand in hiring."

"I've passed along a few resumes from people who'd want to..." Madeline's voice trailed off at Chantelle's stare. "You mean the cats. The city shelter's happy to pass along some of theirs. I've aimed for older and lazier cats along with a rambunctious handful of kittens."

She'd felt adrift the past three months, like a woman shipwrecked and left to paddle on a raft in the middle of a hurricane. But looking at her notes, her contacts, all the things Madeline had turned real, she'd swear someone competent had been behind this. *When did this congeal into a real project?*

Scrolling past the minor quibbles, Madeline landed on the question of branding. They'd need business cards, signs, things for the Firemen's Ball to put up—which meant they needed a name. "I do have a pressing matter," Madeline said, when the doorbell rang.

To her shock, Chantelle slipped out of the chair while inspecting their phone. "What is it?"

"The center. We can't keep calling it the Cat Rescue Center. It needs a good name and soon." She had kept putting it off because she thought Chantelle would just tell her.

"Mm-hm, got that down. Name." Chantelle vanished down the hall, leaving Madeline alone. As she scrolled and made more notes, the scent of smoke filled her nostrils. She turned and tiny razors embedded into her neck and a purr made up for the pain. Sparky curled his tail over her forehead, rubbed against the back of her head and batted at a curl.

She breathed another sigh of relief at the kitten being alive. Any other rescue and Madeline would have turned him over to the service by now. She'd thought that maybe Sparky would be the first in her new center, but now… "Monte, I hope you like this little spitfire, because I think he's going to be permanent."

Her Count meowed from his prison between her thighs. "You're not getting out until I can trust you. So in a hundred years."

"Oh, Madeline, darling!" Chantelle's voice rang from down the long stretch of hallway. "Someone's here to see you."

Who was it? Beth would have been let right in. Tristan, too. Could it be? Madeline leaped to her feet with visions of green eyes and sandy blond hair.

Chapter Twenty-Three

Everett tightened the last screw on the new locks and tested it. Just as he went to close the front door, one of the movers he'd hired walked through. Relief flooded him at more of Kathy's stuff being carted out of his life. "Where do you want this?" the mover asked.

She hadn't listened to him. In truth, he'd been worried she'd have replaced the locks and refused to let him inside. But Kathy wouldn't know the difference between a flat head or a Phillips screwdriver even if one bought her a drink. She'd waited like the viper protecting its stolen nest, first trying the charm defense. When that hadn't worked, she'd gone straight to attack mode only to be met by the uncaring eye of Three Men and a Truck.

The truck didn't enter his living room but sat partially parked on the lawn where all of Kathy's things were piling up. She stood in the middle, huffing and puffing but unable to blow even a feather down. Ev knew if he hadn't brought witnesses, it would have been much worse.

"Well?" he said to the woman being evicted with prejudice.

She crossed her arms over her chest and scowled. "Do I look like I fucking know, you yellow-bellied coward!"

Ev caught the eye of a man with a gruff New York accent and said, "Add it to the pile."

The mover didn't blink as he dropped a trunk full of dresses into the mud. Kathy, however, shrieked, "I'm calling the cops!"

"Please do," he said. "So I can prove the deed is in my name, not yours."

If this were Williamston, where everyone knew everyone's business, he wouldn't be so cocky. But even the movers gave him the onceover then shouted, "Eh, the kitten guy!" before hauling Kathy's stuff out. Those sixty seconds of internet fame gave him a shield he'd never have had otherwise.

"Ugh!" Kathy shrieked, throwing both her hands up before she spun and landed on her trunk.

Ev cracked open the new lock on his front door and was about to step inside. "Are you gonna sit there all night?" he asked, showing the first sign of weakness.

Kathy responded by squaring her shoulders. If she weren't fuming like a lapdog ready to rip out a throat, she'd look pathetic — the petite blonde girl tossed out on her ass. The illusion worked on damn near everyone, but Ev could finally see through it.

He paused, almost inside his house, said, "I heard talk of rain," and closed the door.

For the first time in four months, Everett Berry listened to the baseball game while he made grilled cheese sandwiches for dinner. Even knowing she was locked out, he couldn't stop checking over his shoulder, waiting for a shriek or slap to come for him. But he didn't stop. He had to eat that childish, fattening sandwich over the sink to prove to himself that he wasn't broken.

Round about the fifth inning with no score on either side, the mover's truck started up. With the neck of his beer, he nudged aside the blinds and peered out. Rain drizzled down in a miserable fog. But instead of finding Kathy wet and pathetic, all that remained of her stain on his life was a muddy mess on the front lawn.

He was free.

Jesus Christ, he was really free.

Ev raised his beer, about to down it in a celebratory toast, when he paused. No more falling into the same stupid mistakes again. No more letting another one walk into his life, then walk over him until he jumped at the sound of a high heel.

Slamming down the half-empty bottle, Everett pawed for his keys. He caught the new one for the front door and its spare on a separate ring. He should have put his foot down then, told her she could stay here.

No, that she belonged here.

In a flurry, Ev scooped up his jacket and raced out the front door. The rain dewed up in his hair as he ran for his truck, but he didn't care. Leaping into the cab like he could fly, Ev wanted to sing.

For the first time in his life, he felt good enough for her.

Pulling out onto the road, Everett set his heart's GPS to Maddy.

* * * *

Clutching Monte, Madeline took a quick peek, to find Chantelle blocking the door. Maybe it wasn't him. Maybe Beth had sent pizza. She tried to temper her expectations, when Chantelle looked over and mouthed, "He's cute."

Expectations sky high, Madeline bit her lip and pulled open the door.

A crash of lightning blinded her. "Ev...Hayden?" The blond in her mind shifted to dark hair. "What are...?" She tried to peer past, but could only spot a car in the driveway instead of a beat-up truck. "What are you doing here?"

He took a step closer, and Madeline clung tighter to her cat. "I secured the site where your apartment was."

The bottom fell out of her stomach, an old ache returning as she faced the gaping chasm of her life. To her shock, a warm hand caught her cheek and lifted her up. Hayden smiled. "That was easily in the top ten of the worst ends to a date."

It was silly, but she laughed. "Only in the top ten? What kind of dates have you been on?"

"Let's just say scuba, plus shaving cut, plus shark does not end well. Anyway, I took a hand at digging through the rubble and I found these." From behind his back, he pulled out a shoe box and lifted the lid.

The stench of smoke lingered on the blackened trinkets. Madeline stared at them rattling around, certain nothing could be hers, when a glint caught her eye. The cat in her hands growled in frustration.

"Ah, I see he's still with you," Hayden said and reached a hand out to Monte.

Her cat fought inside the towel as if he wanted to swipe his claws at Hayden. He was still upset from the rescue. Madeline placed him down, where he promptly dashed away with skidding paws. She dug aside the crispy bits of photos and other things she didn't recognize to find an old spoon with a blue crown on top.

"Oh goodness," she gasped, holding it out in her hands. "This was my grandma's. She always told us it was part of a royal wedding set that real princesses used."

"Wow, it must be worth a ton."

Madeline chuckled. "About five bucks at best. Grandma bought it off the TV and handed them out to all of us for Christmas."

It'd meant nothing to her before, a terrible gift in a long line of them that Madeline kept out a sense of duty. But now it was all she had left after the fire, the one piece of her old life that hadn't gone up in smoke.

"I'm sorry about that..." Hayden reached over to take the spoon back, but Madeline stopped him.

"No. Thank you. This..." She twisted the old spoon in her fingers, noting the char worked into the design. "This means the world to me."

"I'm glad I took the time to sift through all that debris for you."

He was so sweet to her even though he didn't have to be. And what was she doing but thanking him by being hung up on a guy who couldn't want her? It wasn't fair, not to Hayden, not to Everett and not to her.

"You know, I'd still like to make it up to you," Hayden whispered, slipping closer.

"To me?"

"The first date. I had so many better plans that I'd love to show you."

He rose above her, causing Madeline's instincts to cry out. She wanted to scamper away, but she froze looking up at the man leering closer and closer. His minty breath crossed her cheek as he whispered, "Or we could skip right to the ending."

"Uh..."

* * * *

After a false stop at her friend's place, where he got an earful and then some, Everett was finally on the way. His phone led him to the kind of neighborhood people'd put on postcards. If it weren't for the crash of lightning, he'd expect to find sailboats cresting over the waves and butterflies flitting through the magnolia trees, or whatever they had up here.

Maddy was moving up in the world. Would she even want to leave this paradise to stay in his fixer upper?

That's Kathy talking. Stay the course.

Clinging to his steering wheel, while the hairs on the back of his neck stood on end, Everett circled around the winding streets of a rich cul-de-sac. When people had lots of money, they'd use hedges and twisting driveways to keep anyone from seeing the house. Even with all that, he spotted the tips of roofs spiraling up from the darkness like wizard towers.

In his ancient truck with the bumper held on by duct tape, he drove up to a castle. Another car sat outside — one he paid no attention to. Light streamed from the open door. Perfect.

Leaping from his seat, he dashed through the rain for the front door. A shadow stood on the steps, eclipsing whoever was inside. Delivery man? Ev shook it off while bundling his coat closer. The rain picked up, drenching him from head to toe during the short jog.

There, even in the darkness of the clouds and the piercing light of the house, Maddy's curls shone bright. She was right there, the princess waiting for the prince. Smiling wide, he prepared what he'd say to her. "The bitch is gone," seemed harsh, but what'd been rattling in his mind since he set off.

Everett reached the porch and was about to take the side step up, when he recognized the sharp cut of black hair on the no-longer stranger. Before confusion could take hold, Hayden Crawford wrapped a hand around Madeline Prix and pulled her into the rain for a kiss.

Lightning clanged down from the heavens, obliterating Everett's hopes in the same millisecond. In shock, he slunk back, watching their kiss end. Madeline blushed and invited Hayden in. Everett was too late.

Numb, Everett fell into his truck, his calf banging into the runner on the way up. Stupid. If he'd stood up to Kathy at breakfast, if he'd told her off that night. If he'd…if he hadn't been a coward and let Maddy slip through his fingers, then he wouldn't be frozen to his marrow.

"Hey!" A fist banged on his windshield, startling Everett. "Are you supposed to be here?" A man in a security uniform beamed his flashlight into Ev's eyes.

"No." He shook his head sadly and glanced back to the front door. "I never was."

Chapter Twenty-Four

The erupted innards of a seven-foot-tall cat tree lay scattered across the whole of her fresh tile. The instructions told her to insert tab A into slot B, but all Madeline could find were wires C through D and a clasp called omega. She'd bent over to read the instructions, when the branch-heavy top half started to shudder. Fearing for her life, Madeline slapped both hands to the bowing tree.

"Hello? Floor man…?" Oh God, what was his name? "Jack?" she tried, but the chances of him hearing her were nonexistent. They were all hard at work finishing the flooring for the kitten areas and testing the drains. It'd been a constant whir of machinery every day from eight until sundown. If the place weren't almost ready for opening, Madeline would feel more cross that everyone was too busy working hard to save her.

Flailing her foot out, she stomped her toe to the edge of the instructions. "Come on." She slipped closer, only for the whole forest to shift. *Nope. Can't move.* Straining while imagining her leg growing longer like a swan ballerina, Madeline whipped her foot back and forth. A breeze caught under the paper, sending it flying away.

"I guess I live here now."

A rainbow scattered across the walls as the front door opened and Beth appeared with her arms bulging with bags. "Mads, you here?"

"I'm trapped inside this tree," she called, hoisting the branches up higher to try to peer between them.

Beth chuckled. "Need some help?"

"The instructions would be great."

After placing the bags down, Beth picked up the sheet and twisted it around. Madeline stared up at the branches threatening to bow. This wouldn't be a problem if she hadn't already anchored them to the ceiling. "What do I do next?"

"Well, this says something about a yellow slot. But based upon my vast knowledge of seeing a tree, I think you need the trunk."

Madeline blew air through her lips, scattering her curls done up in ribbons. "I know that. What makes the trunk?"

Beth cracked her knuckles and squatted down. "Let's find out."

As they worked to get support under the 'fun and playful' cat tree, Madeline asked about the musical. "Way I hear it, Tristan's getting good reviews."

"'Born to play a dimwit fool full of himself.' He had that one framed," Beth said as she snapped the plastic ends together. "I have no idea how Chantelle can be doing ten shows a week and working here."

"Honestly, I don't think they sleep. I swear I can hear pacing and business calls in the middle of the night."

"Sleep scheduling? If upper management could figure out how to make that a job requirement we'd never sleep again." Beth brought the trunk ends up to the waning branches, and plugged them in.

As Madeline dropped her aching arms, she stepped back and stared at the tree. Beth turned her head and declared, "I daresay it looks like you're ready."

"Hardly. It still needs platforms and connecting to the other tree in the back when the cats want to get away."

"Mads, look at this place. Remember what it used to be?"

"A lot of dirt."

"And now it's a rainbow garden for kittens to spend their days reclining and chasing after toys. You're so damn close. Take a second to step back and revel in it."

Close but not done. The soft opening had been pushed back from early May to June, leaving Madeline some time to at least put in a claim on her apartment, fight with the insurance company and buy some new clothing. She was up to four changes of shirts now. It did leave the whole firefighter ball in conjunction with still-unnamed kitten rescue center in the lurch.

"What are you fretting about now?"

"Just thinking…about how Ev's gotten on with the dance." She winced at the words. She hadn't said his name much in the last month and a half, but it'd be a lie to claim she never thought of him.

"Don't worry about…him. Isn't your new beau helping out?"

Madeline stared long at Beth for using beau. She was digging again. "That's what Hayden said," was her only answer.

"Well, you'll find out tomorrow. At least the invitations went out, so someone doesn't have their head up their ass."

Chantelle was excited, to be sure, declaring it a social extravaganza. Hayden had brought Madeline a dozen roses when he asked her to be his date. If not for that, she'd have tried to skip out entirely. Staying home while everyone else stood around in tight dresses was more her lane.

"You look nervous," Beth said, cutting straight through to Madeline's worries.

"I'm thinking that…I'm glad you'll be there."

"Third wheeling it with your little sidepiece." Beth raised an imaginary glass as if in a toast, but all it did was make Madeline sigh.

"There's nothing wrong with Hayden. You haven't found anything."

"That's just it, Mads. There's nothing. No unpaid parking ticket, no overdue library book, no unflattering yearbook photos. It's like the universe said, 'Create a handsome and amenable man in his early thirties,' and it was done."

Beth had been dancing around the lack of any incriminating evidence for weeks. Madeline suspected she was mad she hadn't found anything. "Handsome, you say?"

"What?" The hard-nosed reporter was thrown off the scent, and she blinked fast. "Objectively, he is an attractive man. Anyone would agree."

"Anyone…like, say, Tristan Harty?" Madeline asked, shaking her shoulders back and forth with the taunt.

"Very funny." Beth folded her arms tighter across her chest as if to protect her heart. Madeline teased because she was fairly certain Tristan's response would be none. "I mean, you must agree that he's attractive."

"Yep." She was dating him, so she must. That was how it worked. And he was kind to her, often whisking her off on cute dates when she found the time. It was only…

Beth dug her purse out of the bags she brought in and tucked it to her arm. "At least he got your mind off of Everett, finally."

Five weeks, six days and twenty hours since Madeline had last talked to him, not that she was counting. Staring past the cat tree to the wall Everett had put up, a surge of excitement struck through her. He was going to be there tomorrow night. "I don't think of him at all."

* * * *

It was a disaster!

Everett ran across the ballroom, doing his best to avoid the tablecloths being unfurled like flags at a funeral. There were supposed to be decorations on the stage, and they had forgotten to add the stage. A pile of firefighting equipment, brought so that wealthy donors could wear it for pictures, had been left in the middle of the dance floor. He stared at the mess, scratched his head and tried to not panic.

Where was that Jacques guy? He'd know how to fix the stage.

Get that stuff off the dance floor. They have to put out the buffet!

In a jacketless suit with the tie left dangling, Everett teetered two helmets on his head, slipped one coat on and carted a pair of pants and dangling suspenders out of the ballroom. He knew he looked insane, when he walked straight into the worst person possible.

Hayden held a hand out and cocked his head. "Whoa, where are you going with all of that?"

"I have to find…" Ev swallowed the explanation, doubting the captain wanted to help him. "It's for the ball."

"Sure. I bet you're doing a fantastic job at it, too." The words were genuine, the tone sincere, but Everett could read it as sarcasm and poorly veiled at that. "Where's the chief?"

"Hasn't arrived yet. I thought you were bringing Maddy." A fact Hayden had made certain Ev knew.

"Women." He shrugged off his duties. "I'll pick her up later. I wanted to check in, see how everything's playing out."

"Why?" Everett asked slowly. He struggled to turn to follow Hayden who had a gimlet glow in his eyes.

"It's the kitty guy!" a voice squeaked, catching Ev's attention. He raised a hand and put on a weak smile as he had been for the past month. The kid snapped his picture with a full flash, leaving Everett blinking, when Hayden swung in.

He whispered against Everett's ear, "Way I hear it, there's gonna be a big change coming. Whose side are you on, Berry?"

Not yours.

"Chief Parsons," he said. Hayden snickered at that and adjusted his lapels. No doubt he was about to say something disparaging, but he had the foresight to turn around and spot who Ev already had.

"L.T.," the chief shouted, his hand extended in a happy wave. "You, uh, planning a raid or something?" He looked to the mess of equipment in Ev's arms.

"No, sir. It's part of the entertainment, for the guests. I need to…to talk to hotel management."

"Eh, leave it here for now. We still have…" The chief swung around his gold watch and his eyes bulged. "Well, some time before the party begins. Crawford, where's your date?"

"Awaiting my arrival. I wanted to see if Berry required my assistance." Hayden damn near doffed his invisible hat at the man.

"Uh huh, that's nice. Berry, I've been wanting to talk to you. Haven't seen much of you as of late." The chief wrapped an arm around his shoulders and pulled him deeper into the ballroom.

I've been busy setting all this up. He didn't say anything, only swayed to the side in the hope the chief would catch his meaning. Dances didn't plan themselves, no matter how hard he wished for an elf to do it all.

"Is…is something the matter?" Everett asked cautiously.

"Nah, it's a good thing. Change. That's what they all say. Oak falls, seedling takes its place. I wanted to know if there was a spot in the program where I could do a little announcement."

So the rumors were true. Parsons was retiring, and Hayden thought he had that promotion in the bag. Everything in his gut told him it was a terrible mistake, but the chief wouldn't take that under review. What could he do?

"Berry?"

"Uh, yeah. Before the cake, or you could go after the auction."

"Hm…no one will listen when there's cake. I'll take the auction," the chief said. He adjusted his cuffs then waved to a dowager type in a silver sequined gown.

Chief Crawford...Ev thought he'd finally gotten it right. Kathy was gone, though so was Maddy. He had thrown his all into work, which left him out of the rumor mill loop thanks to this ball. For every step forward, a hurricane blew him back two. He could fight through twelve-hour days, take sitz baths when the pipes broke, but a life with Hayden ordering him around while he toyed with Maddy would be the death of him.

"Mr. Berry, what are you doing?" Jacques appeared as if he had phased through the walls. "We've established a mannequin and backdrop area for the photos, remember?"

After all of this, was he doomed to return home with nothing to his name but a broken truck and an empty heart?

Chapter Twenty-Five

Madeline brushed down the dress and the two pairs of Spanx keeping her inside of it. At least she could breathe, though eating might be a challenge. Who came to a fancy dinner to eat anyway? Blue silk as bright as the Caribbean ocean wrapped around her bosom and hips. Once there, it took a waterfall approach to splashing against the floor, requiring Madeline to hike it up. If there'd been any time she would have debated about hemming it.

Dressed in a run-of-the-mill tux, Hayden dropped her arm and stepped to the side. "I'll go and check our coats. You head on in."

A single sign told guests to go to the left for the Firefighters' and Kitten Center Ball. Well, Ev had done his best. She followed behind a group dressed for the opera. They gossiped about the dance and how the menu was subpar compared to previous years.

Madeline put on a smile as she reached the ticket taker outside the room and was about to hand over the stub, when the doors opened. *Sugar Honey Ice Tea!* The room glittered like the outside of a Fabergé egg. Golden place settings played against the striped linen of the tablecloths. The chandelier flickered as if it held real candles while a fireman's hose hung off the arms. Below that was the dance floor, where people ready for fancy proms mingled. She spotted Chantelle in more feathers than Big Bird lifting a firefighter helmet off a mannequin to try on.

"Name?"

"Madeline Prix," she said, sending them hunting through a handwritten list.

The person in front of her stopped to gawk at the decorations that must have left Ev in a tizzy. One woman snorted. "I swear, it gets more white trash every year. Is that plastic?" She picked up a fork on the closer table and tried to bend it.

"At least the view's nice," another said in a tone that sent Madeline swiveling around. Standing on the stage was the beach god himself. The stage light caught on his blond hair, turning it pure gold. He'd left the jacket on his suit open, revealing how well he filled out a white dress shirt. The two older ladies were damn near fanning themselves as Everett hefted up a smaller amp and passed it to a stagehand behind.

"I'm sorry, ma'am, what was your name?"

"Prix, P-R-I-X. That always throws people off."

The host frowned and flipped through the pages again. "Are you certain?"

Of my own name? Madeline could fret herself into a thousand tiny knots but that was one thing she was certain of. Unless she wasn't supposed to be here. No. Chantelle was right there, and Hayden had brought her. She belonged, damn it.

"Perhaps it's—"

A low whistle from an errant kettle caught over her voice. She shook it off, until the kettle whispered, "Maddy?"

Ev stared like his jaw hit the floor, and he was about to trip over it. She shuffled her feet, causing her toes to slip off the thin soles. "You look…" He took a step closer, and Madeline looked up, not at him, but the two older ladies dripping in diamonds. If looks could kill, Madeline would be a stain on the floor. Instead of scampering, she raised her head and tossed her shoulders back.

"Like I can put a dress on?"

"That…" Ev tugged on his collar, dislodging his slipping tie. "That wasn't quite what went through my mind."

Without a second thought, she reached over and adjusted his tie. It wasn't until she was sliding the slipped knot up near his throat that Madeline realized how close she stood. Near enough to smell his oceanic cologne, to see the hint of stubble prodding from above his top lip from an earlier shave, to feel the warmth of his chest almost touching her hand. Biting her lip, she stared into his green eyes and found herself falling. "Well, you look…"

Kathy.

He broke your heart.

Hayden.

This is a job.

Her brain screamed every good reason to walk away, but all her heart remembered was that same man with hair of summer gold who'd smelled of the ocean and rescued her. It was the slow tap of an annoyed employee's pen that punctured through her schoolgirl drooling. "I'm sorry, ma'am, but you're not on the list."

"What?" Ev spoke up for her. "This is Madeline Prix. Ms. Prix."

"Oh, one of the cat ladies. Got it."

So she was just a crazy cat lady. The older women, growing aware they wouldn't be able to steal away Everett's attention so easily, turned in a huff. But they did take a moment to snicker at Madeline. She was working her fingers to the bone to save cats. What was so wrong about that?

When the host handed over her table number, Madeline stared around the room with a jaded eye. "Where's...?" The K stuck in her throat and as she met Ev's eye, she switched to, "Your date?"

"Ah, well, I don't have one," fumbled from his lips. He shrugged his shoulders with his hands extended. "Going stag for now."

Ask about Kathy.

Don't you dare ask about Kathy.

It doesn't matter, remember. You've moved on. You're a strong, independent woman.

"I'm surprised"—Madeline found herself babbling, needing to fill the void while her brain shouted at her— "that no one's swept in to claim you."

Ev frowned. "I'd rather be the one doing the claiming now."

Did she shiver? That was a definite quiver, even a tremble down the whole of her body. "I guess that leaves you free to get up to bachelor things at night." In bed, alone, under the covers. Though he'd have to be an over-the-covers kind of guy.

Oh my stars, why did I think of Everett with his water hose in hand? It was the heat of the room, too many people. Or maybe the musk in his cologne was messing with her inhibitions. It couldn't be the sparkle in his eye as he less and less sneakily looked down her dress.

Everett leaned closer and put a hand on her arm. "Maddy, I've wanted to—"

"My dear, so nice to see you waited for me." Hayden's voice bulldozed between them. He wrapped his whole hand around Madeline's arm and tugged her away. Everett stood up taller, staring dead-eyed at the man kissing Maddy on the cheek. "I like what you've done with the place, Berry. Very retro eighties wedding look."

"Hayden."

The bright smile shifted to a glint, and Hayden said, "That's captain to you. Though, way I hear it, that might not be true much longer."

Ev's whole face flashed with panic before he fought it back to neutral. It seemed to pass Hayden by, who slapped him on the back and laughed. "Just kidding. We're all off the clock tonight. Hopefully the city doesn't burn down."

Madeline's heart rate kicked into flight mode. She stared around the place, noting the exits and trying to etch them into her mind. She couldn't stop doing it, needing to know where the extinguishers were in every place she visited. Hayden didn't catch on, but Ev stared at her with concern. He stepped closer, when Hayden spun her in a circle.

Pain radiated up her arm from where his fingers pinched, but he let go. "We should snag our table before someone tries to take it. Have fun working the crowd, Berry."

"There's a seating arrangement. No one will..." Madeline tried to explain, but Hayden was already escorting her deeper into the room. Instead of laying his hand against the small of her back, he gripped her wrist and tugged. She took one quick look back at Ev before steeling her shoulders.

* * * *

Ev's fingers lingered on his tie as he watched Maddy sashay around the circle of the elite. He could watch her all damn night, especially the way that blue dress cupped under there and curved out there. Or how a single red curl kept gracing against her cheek. It had to be even softer than it looked.

An arm slipped across the back of her waist, disguising the swoop where Everett imagined resting his hand. As Hayden tugged Madeline tighter to him, Ev's smile darkened. She'd moved on. And he was fine with it. Happy for her. Really.

"Hey, Ber!" Will shouted from the other side of the room. He'd dressed the way a thirteen-year-old at his first dance would, the pants stopping at his calves in the event of high tide.

He hadn't seen much of the rest of his coworkers. Everett was stuck rushing from one small fire to the next. But he waited for the same mediocre compliments the chief and Captain Reed gave him. Will slapped him on the back, roughed a hand over his neck and pulled him close. "Where's that hot blonde of yours?"

His hackles shot out like a porcupine spines. "She's..." Long gone. "She's not coming."

"Aw," Will said patronizingly. He slapped him harder on the chest, as if to prove he could sling the younger, stronger, wider man over his shoulders. Ev raised up a hand, excuses forming of the myriad of problems that needed him, when Will's head swiveled.

"Are ya sure about that?" he asked, confounding Everett who turned to look where Will was...and his heart stopped. Kathy, dolled up within an inch of her life in a slinky dress for lounge singers, flirted with the ticket taker. The man was blushing bright red, and kept pawing at the back of his neck, but he wasn't reaching for a table number.

What was she doing here? He had told her to stay away. How could she do this now? "She's not supposed to be here," Everett thundered, an anger he'd held in check sparking awake. He pushed Will to the side, prepared to throw Kathy out on her ass if she wouldn't listen to reason. Even in front of his boss.

He got one step closer, his mind churning with a thousand different answers for her excuses, when the lights in the whole room dimmed. What now? Ev snapped his gaze around, as if he could find the source of an electrical failure with his eyes, and a spotlight rose on the stage.

Was the chief already going to give his speech? Kathy wasn't forgotten, but the problem of his past was replaced by the question of his future. Yanking his itinerary clipboard off the table, Ev was about to hunt for it, when a pile of feathers walked onto the stage.

* * * *

Never had Madeline stood in a ring of such esteemed voices with the deputy mayor on one side, a producer for Chantelle's musical on the other and the fire chief in the middle. Nor did she expect for their main topic of conversation to be, well...

"We got Buttercup on this new food, and it was like Hershey squirts for three days."

The producer laughed hard. "That's what happens when Bow digs into the trash. Gives the dog walkers fits, but what can you do? Dogs are natural scavengers."

"What do you think?"

It took Madeline a second to realize the question was aimed at her unimportant face and that it came from Everett's boss. She blinked in shock that anyone was talking to her, when he explained, "She's an animal expert. Saves cats and the like."

"Oh, I'm not...I never studied professionally." Madeline raced to demure away from the unexpected spotlight, when she paused. "But I've fostered over twenty kittens and cats in my apartment."

"A hands-on kind of woman. We need more of those," the deputy mayor said like he was still campaigning. He paused in taking a drink of his wine to eye her up. "What would you do about Buttercup's problem?"

"Well..." Her cheeks flushed as every eye on her turned into a laser beam. *Take a breath. You can do this.* "When I'm trying to switch a cat off of kitten food to adult, I like to mix a little of the new into the old to get them used to it. Helps their tiny digestive systems adapt."

The fire chief smiled and lifted his beer to her. "Excellent advice. I did that with all three of my Staffies when they were pups. You've got a good one there, Crawford."

The hand that'd been loosely draped across her back tightened, pulling Madeline's shoulder against his chest. "Don't I know it," he crowed before putting her back down on her feet.

Everyone with access to glasses took a drink after that outburst while Madeline haplessly fiddled with her curls. As the awkwardness grew, she risked turning away and spotted a familiar sight working through the tables. "Beth!" Madeline shouted like pleading for a life line.

Her friend, dressed to kill in a cream pantsuit, gave a wave. Tristan wasn't at her side. Strange. A lot of the other cast of the musical had arrived, sensing free food and a night off at Chantelle's request. Had he fallen ill?

The worry grew when she spotted the pursed lips and worried brow on her friend. That was an 'I'm sitting on a powder keg about to blow' face, and it was aimed at her. "Mads, I need to talk to…"

At that moment, the lights dropped to near zero, only a hazy glow under the chafing dishes cutting through the room. Madeline's heart knotted, her mind leaping to demonic hellcats invading the hotel, when a spotlight rose on the stage and Chantelle sashayed into the middle. They bumped an elbow into a giant sign hidden under a sheet and smiled. Madeline had no idea what it was. Maybe the firehouse needed a new one.

"Good evening, friends and neighbors alike. You may recognize me as Chantelle, award-winning singer, actor and latest member of the musical *Pride and Prejudice*. *The New York Cellar* said it'd be a sin to miss. But I come to you today as an advocate for the helpless."

The blank wall behind Chantelle lit up with a picture of a black kitten. It took Madeline a moment to realize that kitten was Sparky sitting on Chantelle's counter after he had tried to knock over a house plant and lost.

"These poor babies run rampant through the city, often tossed out by callous souls who treat them as little more than garbage. But thanks to an angel among us..."

The slide changed to the artistic rendition of the rescue center, complete with happy families petting cats while swinging on the porch. "I am pleased to announce a new cat sanctuary opening this June. Families can stop by, play with the kittens, get to know the cats." The images switched to stock photos of pretty people holding various felines as Chantelle talked.

"Most of all, find love and give these lost souls a proper forever home. Tonight we shall be hosting an auction where the proceeds will be split between our cat haven and the fire department."

"What will we be bidding on?" someone shouted from the crowd. Madeline tried to find who it was, but they vanished back into darkness.

Given how quickly Chantelle smiled, she suspected it was a plant. "How does this sound?" They changed the slide, and the whole room sucked in a gasp at the picture of Everett rescuing Sparky from the fire. A cascade of awes erupted, sweeping through the crowd while Madeline stared at the ten-foot-tall image. His hands were cupped so tenderly around the tiny kitten, his eyes soft with worry as he gazed at the woman just out of frame.

"Do we get to take home the cat or the fireman?"

Chantelle chuckled slowly, telling Madeline that one wasn't planned. Pulling the mike closer, Chantelle said, "Depends on the fireman. Kidding. You'll be bidding on naming these adorable bundles of fluff, who will be shown off by the brave men and women that keep us safe every day."

What Madeline thought was a wall pulled aside to reveal a stand of crates, each holding a cat destined for the center. Chantelle placed the mike on the stand then opened one of the cages. They pulled out the laziest and fattest cat Maddy could find in the shelter system. She'd hoped for him to be their sort of greeter, lazing about in the sun or on the porch. Chantelle raised him up and the cat stared with classic feline disinterest.

"Chief Parsons, would you be willing to start the show?"

The man chuckled and leaped onto the stage. "Glad to." He picked up the cat and tucked it under his arm like a gas canister. Luckily, the cat was so laid-back it yawned in response. Raising a hand, the chief walked back and forth across the stage with a wave.

"Bidding starts at one hundred," Chantelle called.

"One hundred!" a man Madeline recognized from the firehouse called out.

"No, two hundred!" another shouted from beside him.

"That's not how this works," the chief said, pausing in the middle of the stage. He drew his fingertips back across the cat's head like a villain launching into his monologue. The cat meowed in response, as if he were chastising the eager underlings instead.

A flurry of phones and hands lifted, one taking video of the 'talking' cat, the other offering money to name him. Madeline laughed at how well this was going and turned to whisper to Hayden. "When are you going to…?" As she turned her head, she realized the space beside her was empty. *Where did he go?*

* * * *

It wasn't time for the cat auction. Everett groaned internally while watching the rescue person take command of the stage…and the entire ball. Pressure built at the base of his spine that'd either end in a headache or an aneurism.

"Sir?" One of the hotel staff tugged on the shoulder of Ev's suit as if picking off lint.

He glanced behind, barely catching their face as they whispered, "There is a small issue with the live animals."

"We already discussed this with upper management," he tried to whisper back to the person while everyone tossed out bids for his boss and the cat on his shoulder.

"I don't know anything about that. Sir."

Definitely an aneurism, maybe even a stroke. Rubbing his temples, Everett said, "Take me to Jacques." His senses snapped from the shift out of the dark, music-pulsing ballroom into the glaring light and soft piano of the hotel foyer. The underling led him to the front desk where, sure enough, Jacques stood with an old phone shoved against his ear. Far as Ev knew, that thing wasn't even plugged in, and the host would slap it to his head when he wanted to ignore people.

"Ah, Mr. Berry," he said in a clipped tone. "With the firefighter union."

"What seems to be the problem?" Ev shook off the rising exhaustion to stare him dead in the eye.

Jacques twisted his head and clucked his tongue. "The arrival of the felines in our Presidential ballroom."

"Was already…we hashed this out weeks ago. I signed a damn paper about it."

"Hm." Jacques pursed his lips as if Everett stank of shit. "Animals require an extra fee…"

"Which was what I signed about. That cat lady was going to handle it all. It's all there in the damn file."

Jacques opened the mega file it had taken Everett over a half hour to finish signing. Slowly, Jacques flipped each paper, most of which were old records from previous balls. Ev reached over to help, which caused the entire manilla folder and a book's worth of papers to go careening over the desk.

"Damn it," Everett cursed, dropping to his knees and hunting for the paper spread all over at his feet.

"It's always a delight working with you," Jacques said. "You're so professional. Ah! Mrs. Taylor, how delightful to see you again."

Whoever caught Jacques' attention led him away from Everett, who tried to stuff all the papers back inside while hunting for the one about the cats at the same time. He hunched over like a goblin under a bridge, the suit straining at the seams, his back turned to the rest of the lobby. In that position, obscured to anyone who wasn't looking for him, he heard a familiar voice.

"You won't believe the one I got on the line now." It was Hayden, no doubt, but his accent was sharper, like a lackey who'd beat up shopkeepers for the mob. The voice moved around the lobby behind Everett, until it came to a stop near the plants beside a bench. "She's a big one all right…in every sense of the word."

Was he talking about Maddy? Ev froze and risked staring to the side. Sure enough, there was Hayden with a phone pressed to his ear. As he watched, Hayden reached into his jacket pocket and pulled out a…

No.

"Gonna pop the question later tonight before the big announcement." He tugged open the box and slipped the small diamond ring onto his pinkie. Then he barked a laugh. "Oh yeah, I'll be sure to get down on one knee. But don't expect me to carry the bride across the threshold."

Everett folded his hand into a fist, taking a paper with. Hayden couldn't hear the crinkling over his cruel laughter. "I need you to have the papers finished. Tonight. I want this done ASAP so I can stop having to give a shit about her cats."

"Mr. Berry, have you finished your cleaning yet?" Jacques' voice peeled off the foyer's columns, startling Everett. Hayden suddenly went quiet.

After a beat, he shouted into his phone, "Talk to you later, Nana," and walked away.

Everett would bet his eye teeth that wasn't Hayden's grandma on the phone. Papers? Proposing? What was he up to? He stood up and dropped the folder on the desk, leaving Jacques to it while Ev watched Hayden's shadow vanish into the ballroom.

Maddy. He was gonna hurt Maddy. Ev curled his hands up, his shoulders shaking in a rising anger. He was not gonna hurt Maddy.

"Ah, yes, there it is. Seems everything is…" Jacques glanced up just in time to watch Everett stalking back into the ballroom. "…in order after all." The host's voice faded to nothing but the washing of waves across the beach. All Everett could hear was the rising timpani of his heart as he stalked after Hayden.

He didn't know how he'd stop him, but he would. As long as Everett had a breath in his body, he wouldn't let anyone hurt Maddy again. Shaking, he reached for the door handle, when a hand caught his wrist.

Ev let go and turned to find blonde hair and a cruel red smile. "Kathy…?"

Chapter Twenty-Six

"Pst, Madeline." Chantelle waved her over with both a jerk of the head and the microphone.

Madeline dashed closer while trying to stay ducked out of the spotlight. "Yes?"

"Where's that fireman boyfriend of yours? He's up next."

"Um...?" Madeline dug into the napkin she'd snatched up, then couldn't put down while staring around the room. People were having a wonderful time, bids rising higher with each cat, and the men and women of the station giving more elaborate dances with their feline friends. It'd be a roaring success if she knew where he was.

Madeline caught a hand waving at her and spotted Beth. When the lights rose a touch to let the crowd find their wallets and purses, she expected Beth to come racing over. Instead, Beth clasped a phone to her head and stared through space. It was either a big divorce scandal or a celebrity caught on camera doing something naughty. No reason to get concerned.

"Did you miss me?" Her ears heard the sentence the second cold lips touched her cheek. Madeline turned to a lightly panting Hayden wearing a smile.

"You. Get up here!" Chantelle ordered, yanking him away before Madeline could answer. They dropped an orange tabby into Hayden's hands. Madeline had been calling her Creamsicle for how fluffy her fur was. Hayden stared at the cat, when a low warning started.

"Um…Hayden." She tried to reach out to stop him, her ears ringing with the sound of a feline about to use those claws.

But Hayden raised his head high and marched across the stage.

"Our next helpful fireman is walking with an orange tabby known for her gentle demeanor and love of catnip."

Oh no. Creamsicle's tail was whipping about against Hayden's jacket. The warning had become a threat.

No one else seemed to be aware of what was about to happen. Chantelle held the mike close to their lips to say, "Quite adorable, eh? The fireman's nice too." A few in the audience laughed, while Hayden slapped a hand to Creamsicle's head and pulled back. Madeline full-body winced.

"You can look, but no touching. This one's already spoken for."

Creamsicle started to spin, the claws flying out and ready to dice up anything in the way. Madeline lunged for her, prepared to take the brunt, when Hayden shifted. It threw off the cat, who sliced through thin air when he took the microphone. Holding it close to his mouth, he tucked the cat deeper into his arm and faced the crowd.

"Would you mind lowering the music please? There's something I must do."

A spattering of whispers broke out, everyone curious. Madeline and Chantelle looked at each other in confusion. She hadn't been told anything.

"Babe." Hayden extended a hand to her, and the whispers cracked into full-on voices. Goosebumps rose across her whole body as she struggled to get up onto the stage in the full view of everyone. It was far from graceful, Madeline racing to check her dress at every angle to make certain nothing rode up. *Please don't let there be pictures.*

"See this…cute lady here?" Hayden said. He dropped her hand and filled it with the mike instead. "Well, there's something I've been wanting to ask her for a while now."

There is?

Hayden's arm opened, causing Creamsicle to plummet to the ground. The cat landed perfectly, but the second she was free, she bolted. Madeline raced to catch the kitty, fearful of the trouble she could get in, only for Hayden to catch her instead. He wrapped his hand so tight around hers she couldn't break free and raised her up.

"Madeline Prix?" He fumbled with both the mike and something in his pocket. Madeline kept swiveling her head around, trying to find Creamsicle, when Hayden yanked her hand down.

She stared at him, and the small black box opened on a gold ring. That was a strange thing to have. Hayden held it out to her and, even more strangely, "Will you marry me?"

Why is he…?

All the blood drained from her face and Madeline's knees started to buckle. *He didn't. He couldn't… That isn't a…*

"Well?" Hayden pulled the ring out of the box and shoved it onto her finger where it jammed at the knuckle joint. "You look stunned."

All she could get out was a meager yelp, her brain dying. The room pressed in tighter, heat sweltering under her arms and breasts. Madeline couldn't breathe. With every rattling attempt, her Spanx cut tighter to her body. This was it — the handsome prince finally asking for her hand in marriage. A month of occasional dates and nothing more than a kiss or two was a damn near lifetime compared to ten seconds in the forest when one of you was technically dead. A real fairytale proposal.

"Maddy!"

The crowd gasped as the ballroom door blew open and Everett ran forward. "Get away from him!" he shouted, leaping onto the stage like a swashbuckling pirate.

Hayden pulled her back, leaving Madeline standing next to a sign with the sheet over it while he confronted Everett. Rolling his eyes, he said with a weary sigh, "What are you doing, Berry?"

"I'm protecting her from you."

What?

Hayden looked back at Madeline with a confused shrug as if he had no idea what this was all about. Then he turned to Everett and tried to whisper, "Seems to me you want to have your cake and eat it too." It carried across the stage designed for that, leaving Madeline privy to everything they said.

"I heard you out there. I don't know what you have planned, but you ain't hurting her," Everett said. His face bulged in repressed anger, and he couldn't cease clenching and unclenching his fists.

Hayden's chuckle could freeze the blood of polar bears. He leaned closer to Everett and whispered, "You expect me to believe you can care about someone like her?" He laughed once more and said, "Get —" only for a fist to shut him up. Dead silence sundered the ballroom when Everett punched Hayden square in the jaw. Everyone watched Hayden spin away but not fall. He shook his head as if that could wipe away the pain that knocked his head back.

Laughing, he touched where his chin had split open and smeared the blood over his thumb. Madeline jerked at the sight, but he seemed unmoved. "Ya done fucked up now, Berry." Hayden launched himself at Everett.

Hands wailed against ribs, legs flailed at shins and thighs. The two men dressed in similar suits became a whirling black and white mass. Madeline couldn't keep up with who was winning, only the incoherent screams as they attacked without end.

"Stop this!" the chief shouted, trying to run up to the stage. He reached out to pull the two apart when a knee struck and sent him flying away. Chief Parsons collapsed to the ground. Luckily, Chantelle was there to check on him, just as Hayden and Everett locked onto each other.

Hayden clung tight to the back of Everett's neck while Everett slammed his hands onto his forearms. The entire time, they spun in some demented dance, snarling and cursing at each other like two toms around a cat in heat. Madeline needed a spray bottle to end this.

"You never deserved her!" Everett shouted.

"What are you gonna do about it? Let another woman beat you up?"

Everett slammed his hands hard down on Hayden, breaking his hold. Before Hayden could get his balance, Everett hurled him off his feet straight into the sign. Hayden smashed into it with his shoulder, both crumpling to the ground and sending the sheet flying. As it settled in a heap on the floor, only the sound of Everett panting and wiping off his blood and the groans of Hayden cut through the ballroom.

Madeline stared from her would-be fiancé to the man that had broken her heart. She missed the shriek from Chantelle, who ran for Hayden. The sign was now in two pieces. "You brutes ruined the surprise!" they shouted, causing Madeline to turn around and find her name in four-foot-tall letters.

The cracking sound of Hayden struggling to rise, then breaking the sign more, caused Madeline to reach over to help him. "Are you okay?"

While wrapping an arm around her shoulder, he focused on Everett. "What do you have to say for yourself, Berry? You just ruined your life and for what?"

Why did he do that? She knew he didn't like Hayden, but he couldn't be so full of hate to act that recklessly.

"Maddy," Everett croaked, a hand extended for her. He didn't even glance at Hayden. "Please. Please don't marry him."

"Why?" she begged, not just needing a reason but wanting one. *Give me a reason, Everett, and I'll do whatever you say.* But his head dropped, and he coughed while holding in his rib.

Hayden rose higher and fumed. "Call the police. This man needs to be arrested for assault. Now!"

"Are you sure you want to contact the authorities, Henry?"

The spotlight swiveled to Beth, who stepped forward with her phone extended like a shield. While everyone stared at her friend, Madeline caught Hayden snarling before he wiped the look away. "What are you talking about? Who's Henry?"

"You are. At least you were when you defrauded that car lot. Or would you prefer Hank? That seemed to be your name across most of the Southwest." Beth strode up to the stage, the tiny woman meeting Hayden eye to eye. While Beth glared him down, a hand took Madeline out from under him.

When it grazed against the small of her back, Madeline knew who it was, and she leaned against Everett.

"This lady is out of her mind," Hayden shouted to be heard through the room. It wasn't to his future fiancée he turned, but his boss. "She's insane. You can't believe a word of this."

"Mugshots don't lie," Beth declared, handing her phone to Chief Parsons whose eyes bugged out as he scrolled through her research. "Mads, are you okay?"

She nodded numbly, having been yanked from one high to a new low and back again. If it weren't for Everett's support, she'd be a puddle on the ground.

"Madeline, love. This is all a misunderstanding," Hayden whinged. He reached for her.

It was Beth who stepped in the way, her eyes flaming. "Is it also a misunderstanding to Barbara Crawford in Tennessee or Nancy Jones-Clark in Utah?"

"What?"

"When he's not defrauding his employer, Mr. Hank Henry Hayden Crawford quite enjoys marrying well-off women, then draining their bank accounts and skipping town. There are warrants for him all across the country."

Hayden, or whoever he really was, looked about to spring forward and attack Beth. But as he stared at Madeline, a smile rolled across his face. He fought to put his hair up. "She's lying, dear. I swear."

"Well…" Chief Parsons smashed a hand to Hayden's shoulder. "We'll let the police decide." The other firemen who'd paraded around the cats all stood close to Hayden, pinning him in as the chief hustled him off the stage. "The rest of you, please keep partying while we tend to this little matter."

Numb, Madeline stared at her finger and the gold band cutting off blood. It was kinda ugly, really. She laughed at the thought. *And I bet the diamond's glass.* Yanking the ring off her finger, she pulled in a breath that filled her lungs and tossed the cheap jewelry to the ground.

The ball was a disaster, her boss was struggling to get anything back in order and the audience was far more interested in the conman she could have married. "He'd have felt so foolish if he married me," she whispered to herself, tears beading up in her words. "I'm not worth anything."

"That is not true." Everett slipped his hand off her shoulder as if he would want to tuck her into a hug. She wanted to fall into it. To feel his lips press against her hair, to lay against his chest until their hearts beat in time. But as she stared across the room, she spotted the blonde beauty moving through the crowd, and Madeline cracked.

The fat friend didn't get the hero.

She got a room full of cats and carton of ice cream to cry into.

A sob caught in her throat and a thousand shards of invisible glass sliced across her soul. Each was a piece of the life she'd dared to dream of now shattered into the false mockery. A man only dated her because he wanted to steal her money.

Gulping in air, Madeline ran through the audience flocking to laugh at her, past Kathy standing for the princess' kiss she deserved, and out of Everett's life for the last time.

Over the jackhammer of her heart, all she could hear was the soft whisper. "Maddy?"

Chapter Twenty-Seven

Madeline burst out of a side door into the hotel parking lot and nearly collapsed to the ground. Chilled rain slapped against her face and drenched her hair, twisting those soft curls she had spent hours on into a frizzy mess. The makeup designed to contour her face into a skinny oval dripped down her cheeks. All the pretend washed away, leaving her as the same round-faced, double-chinned, clown-haired lump she'd always been.

Her teeth chattered as she stumbled away from the hotel where everything had fallen to pieces. Where was she going? Away. What would she do? Get away.

Who could ever want her?

"Maddy!"

The lightning rolled, sparking through the dangerous clouds above, as she turned back to the man standing in the doorway. Everett held it open like he expected her to come running back. "It's raining," he said.

She froze and threw her hands to the sides. *So what? So maybe I like the freezing cold rain that's turning my feet to icicles. Did you think of that?*

Everett glanced up at the sky gushing buckets and did the stupidest thing possible—he ran out to her. With his jacket held out like a peace offering, he said, "You're going to freeze to death." He almost had it wrapped around Madeline's shoulders, the warmth of where his body had been calling to her, but she stepped away.

"No. I can't do this… Hayden, you…you hit him. A lot!"

Sheepishly, he raised up his knuckles which radiated a painful red even in the dark night. "I couldn't let him hurt you."

"Not like you…" *Did.* She was so tired of it, going round and round fighting the same fight over and over. It didn't matter how hard she clung to the razor wire that he'd stretched across her heart. It still beat for him.

"Kathy," Madeline whispered. She couldn't keep doing this. She wasn't the girl sitting by the phone waiting for a booty text when he was bored. Not anymore.

"Is out of my life," Everett said, causing Madeline to glare at him. She'd seen her with her own eyes. *Stop lying.* "I swear, Maddy, she is not supposed to be here. I kicked her out of my house, changed the locks. Everything."

A teeny cynical voice in her brain said that he could be lying. But he gulped at the end and stared her dead in the eye as if he needed someone to believe this truth. The rain bunched through his hair, exposing the scar where nothing would ever grow again. He needed to be free, or the Everett she knew…that she loved, would dissolve away. But nothing in those rules said it'd be her.

"You...you don't want me," she said, shaking her head as the rain drenched her cheekbones. "You can't want me."

"Why not?" Everett sputtered.

Raising her chin, Madeline put all her force into the next two words. "I'm fat."

"Well, I'm stupid." He ran a hand through his hair and shrugged, tugging on his white shirt turned transparent.

"I don't even have a place to live," Madeline retorted even as she took a step closer.

"I just punched a coworker, so pretty sure I'm out of a job." He held his knuckles out for proof and as if in shock that he had done it. Tenderly, Madeline caressed her fingertip below the damage.

All her life, if she'd needed defending, it had had to come from herself or her friend. Even then, it had come with caveats. *"Don't pick on her because it's not worth it,"* never because she was good enough to be worth saving.

"You're too kind," Madeline sputtered, tears catching in her voice. "Too handsome, too sweet, too adorable, too loving..."

Everett brushed his cheek closer. Her chilled breasts nearly pressed to his wet chest as he drew a hand across her wide hips to the small of her back. "I know," he whispered, glancing his forehead against hers. "I'll never be able to deserve you."

As drops of rain tumbled from heaven, Everett pulled Madeline off her feet for a kiss. When his lips as tender as the petals of a tulip brushed against hers, she opened up to him. Everett crushed his hands tighter, lifting Madeline even higher as he deepened the kiss. His warmth swam through her, chasing away the final chill of winter, leaving her skin tingling like the summer sun kissed it.

They breathed together, cutting apart the kiss, but not ending it. In her heart, she knew there'd be another, then another, and it made her want to sing.

"Maddy, I..." Everett swept a hand across her cheeks, knocking away both the rain and tears. "I want to deserve you with everything inside of me."

"Ev." A laugh bubbled inside, and she caught his hand. It was her turn to wipe away his tears, the both of them barefaced with nothing left to hide. "You already do."

His smile chased away the clouds and Everett leaned closer to kiss her.

"You cheating bastard!" Shrieking at the top of her lungs, Kathy lunged out of the hotel.

"Shit, she's got a knife!" Everett shouted. The streetlamp shone against a silver edge in Kathy's raised hand. He pushed Madeline out of her path and lifted his arms up. "Kathy, stop. Put that down."

"You're a worthless piece of shit, Everett Berry! You don't deserve anyone, not even MacDonald. How dare you get rid of me!" Screaming in the yelping dog range, Kathy lunged with her knife extended for Everett. He threw his forearms up to shield his face.

Launching from the shadows, Madeline wrapped a hand around all that long blonde hair and yanked...hard. Kathy shrieked, but Madeline cut it off with a quick elbow to her throat that sent the woman crashing to the cement. When she hit, Kathy's hands opened up, and Everett kicked the steak knife out of the way while Madeline panted over top of her.

"How did you...?" he sputtered.

"Took some self-defense classes when I got here. Thought they might come in handy." Her heart raced at how fast she had dropped the woman that'd rotted through her psyche like cancer. Now she was a mewling, bleeding mess in the gutter.

Everett reached for her, and Madeline caught his hands, expecting a hug. But he kept going until he could swing her up into his arms and brush the tips of their noses together. "You saved my life...again."

What are fat sidekicks...no, fat princesses, for?

Running her fingers through his hair, Madeline whispered, "You deserved it."

They kissed as the sound of sirens broke through the thunderous applause in the clouds above.

Epilogue

After sliding out of his truck, Everett checked the cuffs on his suit. It was a good thing the guys from the station couldn't see him in it or the taunts would never stop. And they had just stopped calling him 'Right Hook Hero'. Before taking off, he looked twice across the street. The love ballad from *Pride and Prejudice* played in twinkle bells from an ice cream cart. He recognized the song in an instant, having heard it so often from the kitchen, laundry room, bathroom and bedroom he could sing the entire musical by heart. Not that he would...if anyone could hear. The ice cream man, in a paper hat and fluffy mustache, handed a cone to two children then waved at Everett.

He gave a tip of his fingers back, then took off for his destination. Morning glory vines had already covered the fence, obscuring his view until he slipped inside the gate and an orange body curled around his leg. In zero-point-two-seconds, his black trousers were coated in orange hair, then the rest of the suit as he picked up the cat.

Tang gave a mewl, more to remind Everett who the king of the jungle was, then curled up in his arms for a nap. As he walked down the front path lined with rainbow mosaics containing the names of beloved cats, a handful of the patrons looked up. Most were too enthralled with the new litter of kittens enjoying free time in the grass.

At the front porch, where an elderly couple sat sipping 'organic' lemonade, Everett placed Tang on the swing. The couple greeted him and took over petting the cat. "I assume...?"

"Inside," the older man, who was less an employee and more dedicated customer, said with a laugh.

Everett shook his head. "Does she ever take a break?"

Before he pushed open the glass door covered in hand-painted pawprints, he adjusted his loosened tie. He flung open the shop door and a rush of familiar sounds came to him. Tiny jangles of collar bells from cats leaping across the tree branches straining above his head, the quiet meow of other cats slipping into the back when they grew exhausted, ecstatic people dangling string and toys. In the middle of it all was the woman who made it work.

"Ah, yes, I think there's a chance Chantelle might be stopping by." All her hair was tugged back in a messy bun, but a single red curl had slipped free and kept brushing against her cheek. Everett watched from a distance as she smiled so bright while helping a customer buy treats for the kittens and balancing a phone against her ear.

"If by stopping by you mean kicking it up in Barbados…" one of the ladies who worked at the bookstore said while stirring a cup of proper sweet tea.

Those sweet cheeks pinked at being caught in a little fib, and Madeline shook her shoulders. "You never know, they've surprised us before." She glanced up and her big blue eyes somehow became brighter than before. "Ev!"

"Here I hoped I could sneak you away for a late lunch," he said.

"Things are so crazy right now. But, I mean, count my blessings and all. It's a good crazy, when I can get a second to myself." Even as she talked to him, she dashed around checking on the cats, and looked behind to the viewing window over the fenced-in back park.

Taking care where he stepped, Everett walked closer to her. She nibbled on her strawberry lip and looked over at him. "How'd court go?"

"About as the lawyer said it would."

Her stormy brow didn't lighten, and she pulled the cat-toy ribbons through her fingers in rapid succession. "I should have been there. I mean, I was there. It involved me."

"Maddy." He caught her worrying hand, then threaded their fingers together until she looked up. "Don't worry. They granted a five-year restraining order against her. She's never coming anywhere near us."

She caught his cheek and pulled Ev closer until their noses touched. "I will not stop worrying about you. You're gonna have to accept that. I'm a fretter. I fret."

Even as she tied herself into a knot over him, Everett couldn't help but smile. To know that she'd be there, ready to throat-chop any armed attackers should the situation arise, that she'd sit up all night until he came home from a fire, filled a hole he hadn't noticed. It was as if his whole life he'd walked around with a chunk of his soul missing and no one had told him. Then, there was Maddy, teaching him what love — real love without the fear and anger — could be.

Madeline glanced to the adorable cat clock on the wall, then over to him. "I don't think I can get away for lunch, but what about a walk?"

"Sounds perfect." Everett crooked out his arm and, after she slipped off her apron, she took it. He'd been so damn certain when he woke up this morning, but when she curled around his body and he smelled her strawberry shampoo, Everett's spine began to melt.

It's not the right time. You're not going to do it right. You're going to mess it all up!

Maddy rested her head on his shoulder a minute and he dropped her arm to hold the small of her back. That caused her to sigh in contentment, and Everett breathed. *It can wait. There is no reason to force this.*

Together, they pushed open the cat sanctuary's door and walked out into the sunshine. Happy cats rescued from dumpsters and gutters all purred and meowed in their exclusive sunbeam from heaven. "This is" — Maddy smiled, and it sent his heart reeling — "perfect." Her eyes opened, and she rolled them up to stare deep into his.

Before he could think, Everett's lips parted. "Marry me?"

Oh, gosh. He froze on her cute, white porch and spun in place. Dropping so fast to a knee that he heard a pop, Everett fished through his pocket.

"Madeline...Maddy, you are everything I never thought I could have. You're adorable, singing every morning even before coffee. You're kind, giving everything of yourself to people and animals who ask nothing back. You're…"

His finger finally clenched around the damn band, and Everett picked it out. "You're beautiful. There are times I walk through a room and stop and look at you in shock. The good kind where I can't believe that an angel is missing."

The script slipped from his mind, so he held out his hand, revealing a tiny white gold band with four pink diamonds in a setting that mimicked a cat's paw. "Will you — ?"

"Yes!" she shouted, then slapped a hand to her mouth and squeaked.

God, she was too cute. Everett pulled her hand away, wanting to hear every word as he guided the ring up her finger until it rested safely in place. He expected her to admire it, but she wrapped a hand around his and helped him to his feet.

"I love you," she sputtered, pulling him in for a kiss. "And I love that you make me feel like I deserve to be loved."

"Maddy, I am…" He wanted to tell her that she made him feel safe, whole, himself. That there was no one in the world more deserving of love than her. But as he leaned closer, a roar of applause broke around them.

The world clapped and meowed for the two fools newly engaged on the porch of Madeline's Park.

Want to see more from this author? Here's a taster for you to enjoy!

Coven of Desire: Badge
Ellen Mint

Excerpt

Ink

A hand pierced the grave, shattering the witch's pentagram as it strained for the sky. Lightning crackled through the dark clouds above, the fully emerged arm somehow perfectly lit despite the night around it. While the sorceress cackled in glee, the dirt fell away, revealing a face of ashen pallor with minor skin inflammation and a withered nose.

"Ah, he suffers from the great pox," I said aloud, and a shushing broke from the blubbery lips beside me. There was no doubt a person was attached to said flopping skin bags, but I could not discern them in the darkness. The air bulged with barely coherent desires, the shadow in the chair beside me wishing only for my death.

A shame, for after two thousand years I had yet to ascertain any way to cause such an end. I began to lean over the divider keeping us separate, when a palm graced my knee.

The chasteness of the touch nearly caused me to chuckle, when my bond whispered, "Watch the movie."

I folded my arms. Having already dispatched the box of chocolate balls, I had grown bored of this display of flickering images ten minutes in. I tipped my head to her, spotting the blond locks of the wolf to her other side. He seemed to be enraptured with the tinny trite, a full fist of popcorn raised to his mouth. I intended to tell her I'd had my fill, when her eyes darted to me.

Please let me enjoy this.

Her desires did not require my talent of reading through the colored fogs surrounding the gray mass of humanity. I felt her request singing through every nerve and a smile replaced my smirk. Taking her hand, I raised it to my lips and whispered against her knuckles, "As you wish."

She rubbed my knee once more and left her palm upon my thigh. The greens and purples of the giant screen reflected off her fingers, each digit delicate and also hard as stone. She'd chipped a nail recently, no doubt the damn specter's doing. I clasped my hand over the back of hers and held tight when a finger jabbed into my shoulder.

The wolf had raised his hand from Layla's shoulders in order to prod me. "This is the best part," he said in a harried but exuberant voice.

I jerked my gaze to the grumbling guardian of silence beside me, but it remained resolutely still. *I see, so Calvin can speak whenever he wishes, but I must be held to a higher standard.* Humans never could wrap their minds around the concept of justice.

Rather than pick a fight, I turned my gaze to the screen. The syphilitic man was moaning, no doubt from the pain he now found in urinating. Around him circled the sorceress, her silver cloak flapping in a wind that did not move the trees in the background. She spoke gibberish Latin and lightning lit up the white sky. In an instant, all of the graves cracked open like elevator doors and people climbed out.

"Is she attempting to build an army of undead?" I scoffed. "No villain worth their salt would waste time with such a foolish plan. You have, at most, three days before rot causes your army to bloat, then explode. Even less in the summer."

"Will you shut the hell up?" My neighbor greatly disapproved of my logic, even if it was sound. Humans were basically walking candles — one light and the whole of the army would go up in smoke, leaving the sorceress alone and awkward on the battlefield.

"Ink…" Layla leaned closer to me when the man with the pox leaped forward and bit off the sorceress' nose. As I said, a very foolish endeavor. My smug righteousness only lasted a moment when Layla gasped and clung tight to my leg.

My heartbeat increased with hers, a flush of those endorphins she devoted her study to rushing from her to me. While the undead man crunched on the offscreen sorceress' body, my bond turned to look at me. Pink tinged the soft tan of her cheeks, the dark depths of her eyes wide in shock.

She glanced to where her nails tried to dig through my flesh and blanched. "Sorry," Layla said, but before she could retract her hand, I pressed it tighter.

"You need never apologize for that," I said, catching her chin. I pulled her closer and whispered against her lips, "I am built for your punishment."

The kiss sent a wave of spicy pink desire through me. It radiated down my tongue, encouraging said nimble organ to toy with Layla's lip. As I plunged deeper and tasted of her mouth, the desire pulsing from her transformed to a sultry fuchsia. I let my touch land on her shoulder, all manner of horrific undead attacks forgotten. Each traipse of my fingers winding down the ribbons on her blouse toward her breast sent a touch of satiety through me. It was little more than a bite, a nibble really, but the fuel fed my fire.

Layla's wily hand had found itself trailing up my thigh then retreating. She fought the internal war far too many of my prey carried the mantle for. *What I desire versus what society deems proper. Ever at odds, never satisfactory.* The whole concept of morality had been invented to keep people anxious, unsatisfied and in search of a cold bath. But within my bond, the electric desire was winning out.

I took her breast in my hand and Layla bit down to silence her moan. That seemed to shatter the mood and she froze, causing my elaborate dance to pause as well. "Ink, we should…"

"Take advantage of the flickering ambience of mutilated corpses in this foreboding dungeon?" I whispered, tucking back her hair and tracing around her ear. She closed her eyes, lost in the simple pleasure of my touch.

Alas, it was my neighbor who once again could not cease to thrust himself into my affairs. "Will you shut your fucking mouth already?"

I scoffed and shook my head. "No. I do not believe I shall, and you are the better for it."

The man, for his visage grew more evident in the rising light of the screen, folded his hand into a fist. He popped it up as if he intended to knock my teeth out, which only caused me to smile. Whatever nerve he thought to have had fled, and the man rose and abandoned his seat in the back of this darkened theater.

As he stomped his feet and cursed under his breath, his shadow cast over the screen, hiding away the funeral march.

"Down in front," I called to his retreating form.

"Now you've done it." The cursed specter slipped into the vacated seat, proving I was never afforded a moment of peace in this world. He managed to look smug despite being without a body and forced to stand in the aisle.

"What? You think he will challenge me to a duel? Even with two of his sturdiest gentlemen at his side, it will be nothing more than a jumping behind the pub."

The ghost only stared ahead, not saying a word to me, but his eyes flickered to Layla who was quickly losing the thread of desire. That would not do. I had seen little of her in the past week, though I'd had more than my share of the vagrant ghost we'd acquired. Whenever I would reach for her, either the wolf or the dead man would be there first. Typically, I could work with such a scenario, but the ghost was without form and the wolf…

I sighed, staring askance at the man doing his best to ignore his own animalistic urges and the tenting in his trousers. What everyone needed was to break this tension with a day-long celebration of the joy only three bodies could bring. The ghost could sit and watch for all I cared.

"My bond." I pulled aside her spirals and breathed heavily in her ear. That sent the heat rolling once more and she clenched her fingers tighter to my thigh. "Why hesitate?"

Her deep eyes opened wide and she stared as if in shock that I could yet read her mind. "I know…" Gently, I dropped my finger to the top of her cleavage.

"What you truly…" I swept it down between her breasts and over her belly.

Where her thighs split, I clutched onto her skirt, and began to raise it. "Desire."

Layla squirmed in her seat, her eyelids heavy as she succumbed to my logical charisma. I abandoned any prelude of remaining in my seat and turned to press my cock against her thigh. She struggled to fight a gasp and I drew my touch up the hot spread of her underthings. I never needed to test if she was wet, but I quite liked the glide of the proof of my pull and how she flexed to let me in.

As I tugged aside the edge of her panties, I leaned into her ear. "Go on," I whispered, toying with the succulent lady lip at my finger. "Tug on him."

The wolf turned, his eyes blazing with a hunger I knew he too was fighting and failing to ignore. For him, it ran either burning red or muted yellow. Tonight, it burned hotter than the flames of Hades. Cal took Layla's cheek and pulled her in for a kiss just as she reached for the waistband of his jeans…and slipped under. His groan trembled through my hunger, smelling of a feast but failing to satisfy. I paid it barely any heed, Layla's response to him far more delectable.

Her body burned with a rising tide of desire, and my innocent little flick of the bean wouldn't do. I abandoned the seats entirely and took a knee to the floor. The wolf was trying to not thrust his hips in his seat even as he rolled a hand over Layla's breast and panted. Their deep kiss broke and she looked at me in shock.

"What are you doing?"

"I'd think it'd be rather obvious," I answered. Her heart thundered like a rain of timpani. I wrapped my hands under her thighs, clenched her hips and pulled her to my mouth. The underthings meant nothing to the slip of my tongue or the press of my lips. I licked and sucked around, under and over them, soaking her already drenched panties to total saturation. Layla raised her leg and placed it on my shoulder. As she did, Cal reached over to run his hand over her thigh and lift it higher.

Her hand worked fast under his jeans, bringing the unresolved tension to a proper crescendo. I too felt the swell inside, the only way I knew sex to feel. The slumbering hunger sharpened its fangs, my metaphorical mouth drooling while my literal one supped upon the beautiful woman's clit. She arched her back, pressing more of herself to me and pulling her head down the chair.

I glanced up a moment, delighted by the response, when I spotted the ghost standing behind watching. No, he was whispering words to her, no doubt ones stolen from better men. But they seemed to be working to bring Layla to a frenzy. I dipped deeper, every pulse of my tongue filling my body with the strength of a dozen men.

When she began to clench, nearing her climax, my first instinct was to stop. Not in pleasuring her — that I could do for days without end. No, I nearly paused in pulling her energy lest I take too much. But that was the joy of taking a witch to bed — there was never an end. Her magic fed me, letting me feast without risking her loss.

"Ink…" Layla whimpered. With one hand, she clung to the wolf's impressive John Thomas. With the other, she wrenched on my hair, ordering me to finish her off. Gladly.

I dipped back for the last taste that'd fill me to bursting when a bright light blinded me. Blinking against the harsh rays that highlighted the nearly empty theater seats ahead of us, I turned to find a man not yet old enough for a hair on his chin dressed in a crimson uniform with his arms crossed and a glower on.

"Hello, my good man," I said, rising to my feet. He flinched as I held my hand out to him. "Would you care to join us?"

About the Author

Ellen Mint adores the adorkable heroes who charm with their shy smiles and heroines that pack a punch. She has a needy black lab named after Granny Weatherwax from Discworld. Sadly, her dog is more of a Magrat.

When she's not writing imposing incubi or saucy aliens, she does silly things like make a tiny library full of her books. Her background is in genetics and she married a food scientist so the two of them nerd out over things like gut bacteria. She also loves gaming, particularly some of the bigger RPG titles. If you want to get her talking for hours, just bring up Dragon Age.

Ellen loves to hear from readers. You can find her contact information, website details and author profile page at https://www.totallybound.com

Home of Erotic Romance

Sign up for our newsletter and find out about all our romance book releases, eBook sales and promotions, sneak peeks and FREE romance books!